The Galaxy Game

THE GALAXY GAME

Phil Janes

MILLENNIUM
An Orion Book
LONDON

Copyright © Phil Janes 1993

All rights reserved

The right of Phil Janes to be identified as the author of
this work has been asserted by him in accordance with the
Copyright, Designs and Patents Act 1988.

This edition first published
in Great Britain in 1993 by
Millennium
An imprint of Orion Books Ltd
Orion House, 5 Upper St Martin's Lane
London WC2H 9EA

A CIP catalogue record for this book is available
from the British Library

ISBN: (Csd) 1 85798 116 2
(Ppr) 1 85798 058 1

Millennium
Book Fourteen

Phototypeset by Deltatype Ltd, Ellesmere Port
Printed in England by Clays Ltd, St Ives plc

Dedication

This is for
Richard Lunn, who bears a lot of the blame
and of course for Julia, who bears me

PROLOGUE

Human beings, by and large, are made of water, with various other chemicals arranged in such a way that they do not just soak into the carpet, but tend to hang together in a sort of fleshy mound.

Richard Curtis had a problem with this, because if you put the fleshy mounds into a space-ship and then accelerate the space-ship very quickly indeed, then they are apt, almost immediately, to become messy pink smudges on the rear wall of the control room. More than apt, in fact; they really have no choice in the matter at all. And if you open your mouth to complain, the 'G' force will ensure that you'll never be able to close it again. It's the perfect example of an open-ended argument, because that is just what you'll end up being.

Now, if humans had the good grace to be made of oak, for example, then the problem would not arise. There would be other problems to take its place no doubt, like woodworm, squirrels and cock-legged dogs, but Curtis would at least have been free to accelerate people as fast as he liked.

Curtis needed to do this in order to reach the stars, like a latter-day pilgrim, which was his first avowed intent. If a ship travels the sort of distance required to reach the stars at a reasonable speed, then by the time it arrives the fleshy mounds which started off will be far too old to be alive, which, for them, really takes all the fun out of it.

It's all because stars are such an inconsiderately long distance away. You can walk sufficient miles to qualify for dozens of mammy's smiles and still not be within spitting distance of a star unless you happen to be someone who can bull's-eye a spittoon from a range of several trillion kilometres.

A ship travelling at a reasonable speed is therefore not really viable. Curtis proposed to build a ship which would travel at a quite unreasonable speed, which was quite feasible; but it was reaching that speed which required the acceleration, and thereby provided the current and seemingly insurmountable problem, which went under the name of inertia.

Inertia was a law, and not one of those, apparently, that was made to be broken. Marching down the high street carrying a large placard bearing the legend 'Down With Inertia' was not going to help, although if it would have done, Curtis would certainly have tried it. He marched around his bachelor flat instead, bending his impressive mind to the seeming impossibility, and ending up with a grey-matter pretzel.

He did not know, as he paced up and down, that he was being watched through the ether by a being who knew the answer to his problem, and was just about to share it.

As flies to wanton boys are we to the gods.

Well, not quite.

Gods don't wave at us and yell 'Bugger off!' as we salivate over their slice of pizza, and wanton boys don't destroy a whole race of flies by smashing a meteorite into their planet, though they probably would if they could.

One thing we have in common, though: as flies to wanton boys we do occasionally irritate the hell out of the gods.

'Humanity!' The thought, accompanied by a brief flash of ultraviolet, pulsed through the Champion's being, but was not allowed beyond. 'I've drawn humanity!'

It adopted a grim mien, which was all it was able to do because the Champion and its kind had long since forgone the requirement of a physical body, evolving from silicon-based substance to an hermaphroditic energy form which simply occupied space – and on a no-rent basis as, to all intents and purposes, they owned it.

Its thought continued, behind a shield more impenetrable than US Immigration.

It had to play the Final of the Game, it had to stake its position as First Elder, as Supreme Being, using a team made up from the ranks of humanity! A carbon-based catastrophe if ever it had clapped sensors on one!

This was not a happy Supreme Being.

'You have played with Humanity before, Exalted One?' the Challenger asked, guessing its rival's thought, and allowing its energy to shimmer comfortably, almost visibly. It expressed the word 'exalted' in the same tone of thought you might use for, say, 'fetid'.

The Champion regarded it: the seventh Challenger in seven eons of successful title defence, one Game per eon. It sensed its adversary's satisfaction, and allowed resignation tinged with content acceptance to escape into the ether, the wavelength in the infrared frequencies. To go further than contentment, to approach microwaves, would have been too much, and even this reaction would fool almost none of the beings practically none of the time.

'No, *Second* Elder,' it replied, with hardly any derision. 'Not in the Final.'

'But in earlier contests, when you were rising through the Elderhood.' The Challenger was looking for a psychological advantage, obviously; 'obviously' because when you haven't got a body it's about the only advantage you can get. The Champion allowed a mental shrug to answer in the affirmative, suggesting that it didn't really matter, but the Challenger was not about to let it go at that.

'The *Marie Celeste* episode was one of yours, I recall.'

Shrug.

'And the Bermuda Triangle.'

Shrug.

'Dan Quayle.'

Wince.

'And you have drawn the trands?' The Champion diverted the subject. The Challenger had indeed drawn the trands, still carbon-based bipedals, but a more than competent bunch, albeit about as interesting as a current account.

'Indeed. They should have little trouble in the first round' . . . which demanded that the team travel from their home planet to one orbiting another star more than four hundred light years distant. This would pose no problem for the trands.

'Especially as I may not interfere with your team,' commented the Champion. The Challenger, however, *could* interfere with the Champion's. It was bad enough having to compete using humanity without that added complication. Damned silly rules.

The task was not impossible, but then neither was counting all the individual molecules in the Zenglon Nebula; they were both just bloody difficult and a pain in the arse, or they would be if it had one.

And if it were to lose, then it must fade, dissipating its energy into the ether and existing no more, for there was nowhere for a Supreme Being to go but tautologically downwards.

But it had to face the possibility, or rather, frontal aspect the possibility. This Challenger was one of the best it had met, while its own team was almost bound to be one of the worst.

And then, in the depths of its depression, the Champion had come across one Richard Curtis, already half-way towards designing a craft capable of performing the required first-round feat, and needing only a little help in the area of inertia, a law which the Champion and its kind had repealed long since. Things began to look a little better.

Curtis's pacing had used enough available energy to put him in need of some more, and he wandered into his kitchen and opened the cupboard. There, on a shelf, minding their own business for want of the ability to do anything else, were three boxes, cuboid in shape, each with a wire and a plug sticking out of the back and each with the words 'Inertialess Device' neatly printed on the top.

That's handy, thought Curtis, and he was not wrong. The Champion made sure that he did not think any more than that at the time, and the alien mien lightened a little.

Curtis turned one of the boxes over in his hands by way of inspection, and dropped it, seemingly to no effect. The Champion hardly noticed the display of dexterity, which, looking back, was a pity.

The first member of the team had been chosen, and the Champion was still well pleased that it had been fortunate enough to come across one Richard Curtis. What the Champion did not know, but was shortly to find out, was that one Richard Curtis was most definitely a one, if ever there was one.

I

The committee room of the Arnold Curtis Space Research Centre contained all the members of the management committee save Richard himself. Curtis had, rather flatteringly, he thought, been elected Chairman by his doting staff. Admittedly, he did not get a vote that way, but it was nice to be held in such high regard. The reason for his absence was that he had been given a time of commencement some half an hour after everyone else. For the first half-hour, apparently, Curtis was to be the subject under discussion.

The Director, Big Bill Bowen, so called because he resembled that vegetable from which Cinderella's fairy godmother had conjured a stage-coach, and because 'Tiny' was already a cliché fifty years before he was born, was looking, aghast, at another member of the committee.

'I do not believe that you can sit there and seriously suggest that we murder our own Chairman, the President and benefactor of this establishment!'

The disbelief at such a suggestion showed clearly in Big Bill's wide eyes. The moral outrage was graphically stated by the darkening of the face and neck, and the tenseness of the muscles therein. The hands gripped the edge of the table, and the knuckles showed white, straining to prevent the pent-up horror from expressing itself in physical, and perhaps violent, form.

'We'd lose all the money, you moron!'

'Well, it was only a thought,' countered the now firmly in her place recipient of Bowen's reservations. She shifted her arm carefully, and the sling with it.

('Here, let me help you,' Curtis had said on entering her laboratory.

'Hold this phial very carefully, and for God's sake don't drop it,' she had replied after a few moments while common sense and politeness had a quick row inside her head.

'Okay, oops,' he had said with hardly a pause.

'Bang,' said the phial.

'Hello,' said the wall.)

'Maybe murder *is* going a little far, but we've got to do something to stop him, or get rid of him. And preferably both. While he's here we get the biggest staff turnover since the court of Caligula. And if Curtis goes

1

on the trip, then all the work we've put in on *Pioneer* will be totally wasted.'

The jerky head movements and frowns of a couple of committee members who had recently added to the statistics which apparently pushed Caligula's court into second place gave away the fact that they were struggling to keep up with this conversation. Bowen sighed, and turned to the Head of Research.

'Vyland, give us a quick rundown on what this is all about, will you.'

This was not a question. Big Bill Bowen did not ask questions like that.

Professor Paul Vyland gave Bowen a look normally associated with someone who's just got 'turn off power' and 'remove wires' the wrong way round. Vyland was not used to taking orders like that, and especially from the likes of Bowen, whose struggle up the evolutionary ladder Vyland clearly considered to have faltered on a fairly lowly rung.

If Bowen had run to fat – sprinted to fat by the look of him – Vyland had been left on the blocks of that particular track. He had an aquiline nose that was just perfect for looking down, and a goodly part of his hair had been pushed out by his expanding brain (in Vyland's ever humble opinion). His eyes were somewhat sunken points of dark brown, and his cheeks looked like they were trying not to be outdone by the eyes. He looked as though he'd been dead for a couple of days and no-one had quite had the nerve to tell him yet.

'Phillips?' invited Vyland, without looking to the assistant who sat on his right, but causing that individual to jump with such a start that it was a wonder he didn't dislocate something. Which was odd, since Phillips was very used indeed to taking orders, and especially from the eminent Professor Vyland. He swallowed a couple of times to try to get his heart back into his chest – where there was sufficient room for it to pump as fast as it obviously wanted to – and spoke to the table top, which was the only thing not staring at him.

Given that the man doubled as Vyland's press officer and was used to explaining things to the common man with the confidence of one who knows, the reaction only served to confirm gratifyingly in Vyland's mind how far he was from being common.

'We officially announced the *Pioneer* project to the press last week, as most of you will have noticed even if you were not directly involved. *Pioneer* is the space-ship which will take men to the stars for the first time.' He enthused this line right into the plastic of the table top – plastic designed to look like the wood which their grandparents used for furniture in those good old profligate days when Brazil was more than just a big field.

'The ship resembles a long thin silver dart, and is powered by a combination of photon drive and controlled atomic drive – that is,

2

nuclear explosions contained in a powerful magnetic field. This method of propulsion has not been used before, but our tests and calculations confirm that it will be capable of propelling the *Pioneer* at close to the speed of light.'

'Which is bloody fast, right?' Bowen confirmed, raising Phillips's head from the table top with the sort of question the common man was wont to ask.

'It's, er, very bloody fast sir, yes.' Phillips answered the question in a manner the common man would understand. Vyland glanced at him as one would at a worm who had burped at dinner.

'And we know it'll work, huh?' Bowen pressed. Phillips paused momentarily. Vyland didn't, and spoke in a tone that could lubricate an earthquake.

'If we push that much out of the back of the thing, no less an authority than Sir Isaac Newton decreed in 1687 that it must go forwards at the required speed, and I don't envisage the *Pioneer* presuming to argue with Sir Isaac and three hundred and sixty years of scientific establishment.' Bowen nodded shortly, taking that as a 'yes', and a brief look from Vyland kick-started his assistant once again.

'Now, according to Einstein's theory of relativity, anything going' – he paused and glanced momentarily to his left, where Vyland was doodling with a stylus on the screen in front of him, but looked to be listening, so – 'that fast is going to get to wherever it's going much quicker than it should.' Vyland twitched, and removed the doodle from his terminal with a two-fingered touch of the screen, just so. Phillips rushed on.

'What I mean is that it is subject to something called time dilation – the stretching of the passage of time for the space-ship and everything in it, so that a second takes more than a second to pass if you watch it from the outside, and takes longer the faster it is moving.' Another brief pause, while he looked at Bowen's face for a sign of understanding, then round some of the others when that particular search proved fruitless.

'Basically, what it means for the expedition is that when the *Pioneer* leaves for Alcyone – that's one of the stars in the Pleiades cluster, which the IRAS III space telescope has suggested might be orbited by a habitable planet – it will cover the four hundred or so light years to its destination in just about two weeks, according to the astronauts.'

'Time dilation has of course been proven empirically,' Vyland threw in.

'Of course,' Bowen threw back.

'It won't occur to the people inside the space-ship that their time is passing any slower than it always does,' continued Phillips, and decided to use one of his favourite ad-libs, 'especially on wet Sunday afternoons.' He laughed, which was just as well, since no-one else did.

3

'But they will get to Alcyone much quicker than you might expect.

'It won't seem that way for the people left on Earth, though. As far as they are concerned, it will take the craft over four hundred years to reach Alcyone, and well over eight hundred to do the round trip.'

'So when they wave their families goodbye, that'll be it?' asked Bowen, with a strange look in his eyes. He did not have to understand it to believe it, and the belief appeared to trouble him. Phillips nodded.

'They won't wave them hello when they get back,' he confirmed. 'At least,' one last try, 'not unless animated exhumations have become fashionable by then.' His speech ended with the chuckles of his listeners ringing only in his imagination.

'Everyone happy with that, then?' asked Bowen, after a short pause, suggesting that his questions had merely been for the clarification of others. Since most of the others were scientists, while his education in the field had ended at the stage of setting fire to things with a Bunsen burner, this was perhaps less than likely. Everyone was apparently happy.

Explanations and attempted witticisms over, Phillips subsided back into his seat like an air cushion with a slow puncture, and this acted as an invitation to rejoin the discussion which had dragged him to centre stage.

'Aren't we over-reacting a little?' asked a woman whose name tag announced her as Pamela. 'Just because Curtis is on board, you don't *know* the *Pioneer* will be a failure.' She used the same tone as one would use to say, 'You don't *know* the sun's going to rise tomorrow.'

'I'd bet you Curtis's money it would be,' someone else said, and a number of nods left Pamela lonely.

'How did he get all this money, anyway?' she asked, by way of changing the subject.

'He inherited it,' Bowen informed her shortly, 'after he killed his father.' A small but quite heavy silence fell on top of this unsettling piece of information. Apparently it did not completely bury it, however.

'He what?'

'It was an accident,' explained Bowen with a dismissive wave of his hand. 'Arnold was hanging some curtains in their penthouse and Richard managed to trip over the pattern in the carpet and sent him through the window.'

'How awful!' Bowen shrugged.

'I don't think Arnold was too surprised. His last words, apparently, were "You prat, I knew you'd . . ." He shouldn't have turned his back. You've got to keep your eyes on Richard; that's mainly why Arnold put me in charge here.' He paused a moment in quiet recollection . . .

'You've met my son, haven't you, Bill?' Arnold had said one day after calling Bowen into his office. Bowen was on shore leave from one of old

4

man Curtis's oil rigs, which he managed. At the question, he looked around in the nearest he got to alarm – he *had* met Richard, and did not particularly want to meet him again. Curtis spotted the signs; he'd had a lot of practice.

'Don't worry, he's not here.' Arnold paused and toyed with a pen for a moment before looking up to Bill's face once more. 'You obviously share my opinion of Richard.'

Tricky one. With the end-of-year bonus about to be assessed, 'Yes, sir, he's a complete prat' would perhaps be overly brave. Arnold saved him the trouble.

'We both know he's a disaster. But,' he sighed and wiped a hand down his face, 'he is all the family I have, since my dear wife died during his birth.'

'I'm very sorry, sir,' muttered Bowen, and Arnold shook his head apparently in sad reminiscence.

'Amazing foresight, that woman.' Maybe admiration. 'Anyway, I've found him something to do. He's good at numbers, if nothing else, so I'm setting up a research centre into space flight.'

And then he dropped his bombshell on Bill's comfortable two months on, two weeks off life by putting him in charge of the centre, where his main task would be to stop Richard destroying it.

'I'm counting on you, Bill. I'll make a success of that boy if it kills me,' Arnold had finished, prophetically . . .

'Are you all right, Mr Bowen?' Pamela was asking as the reminiscence faded.

'Fine.' Bowen cleared his throat, where the thought of Curtis seemed to have lodged. 'None of you were worried about Curtis going when I mentioned it before last month's meeting.' It sounded like an accusation.

'We didn't know the ship worked last month,' returned the defence. 'It *didn't* work last month.'

And now it did. The ship had been tested, and proved; or rather, one of its twins had. Three ships had been built and one of them had taken a chimpanzee called Tonto into the void beyond the solar system. The chimp had a supply of bananas to keep it happy for a few hours, after which it had been trained to hit a button to bring it back to Earth.

A suitably tumultuous reception greeted Tonto's ship as it landed gently, a reception which would have grown when the chimp appeared in the doorway, had it been given the chance. Unfortunately, it was Curtis, in the control centre, who pressed the button to open the door, and you know how one button looks much like another, apart from size, colour and the words written underneath. As the cameras waited for the door to swing back, Curtis cleverly launched the ship again. Tonto, although slightly confused, had assumed that it was just another test,

5

since he did not know Curtis very well, and he floated off to look for some more bananas.

But they did not need another test. The *Pioneer* worked.

The bit that surprised them most about that was Curtis's one undeniable contribution to scientific advance, and the thing which had made the difference to the *Pioneer*'s inoperability the previous month – the inertialess device. Curtis had apparently come up with a device which cancelled inertia. Simple as that. No-one knew how he had done it – indeed, they had not even known that he had been working on it – but one day he produced a little metal box with 'Inertialess Device' neatly printed on the top of it and a wire with a plug sticking out of the back. It did not open, and Curtis would tell nobody what was inside. But despite initial scepticism – which is rather too small a word for the complete lack of belief experienced by everyone bar none – it worked.

'Ladies and gentlemen.' The voice was now smooth, suave, un-hurried and unworried, sarcasm banished, an oasis of calm in their desert of indecision, probably an indication of the relatively short period of time that Vyland had been at his post. 'As I understand it, you perceive two problems facing you now. Firstly, that Curtis himself wishes to go on the trip,' he paused for effect, 'as Captain.' Vyland allowed the right half of his top lip to crawl upwards by way of comment. 'And, secondly, he wants the ship to be run by his own computer.'

The various members of the committee nodded their confirmation of his understanding.

'You seem to feel that either of these possibilities would seriously jeopardize the chances of the project's success, and that both together is a cast-iron recipe for disaster, although I confess I am at a loss to understand how your fear can have grown into such a frenzy.'

Bowen opened his mouth to answer, but Vyland's raised hand stopped him.

The loose sleeve of his jump suit fell to the elbow to reveal several bones with some skin stretched over them. You could almost hear the Creator muttering, 'Flesh! Bugger it! I knew I'd forgotten something!'

Bowen stopped, more in surprise than response – at the audacity, not the arm.

'No matter,' Vyland continued. 'I called this meeting because I think I may be able to provide a solution which will solve all your problems at a stroke.'

'We've just turned down murder,' someone warned.

Vyland turned his head slowly and smiled superciliously at the speaker. It was a smile which he had mastered as a youth, having worked on it since infancy, the sort of smile which immediately made one's fist clench and twitch expectantly. Bowen's fist clenched and twitched expectantly, but he kept it hidden under the table. As far as he was concerned, Vyland was one of those who would consider himself in need of a bushel the size of a marquee if he were to hide his light under it. Bowen would probably have put it more pithily. Vyland allowed the smile to fade and continued.

'I propose that we accede to both of the Chairman's requests.' Stunned silence poured scorn on his sanity, but met a particularly non-stick duck's back.

'The time-dilation effect of this trip will mean, as we have just been reminded' – time for another glance at Phillips, carrying the approval one would give to a dog who had fouled your best shoe – 'that not one of us will be alive by the time he returns. We would be quite rid of him for the rest of our lives.'

'We would also' – Big Bill got his breath back first – 'be consigning the whole bloody project to the scrap heap. Can you honestly imagine what the results of letting him loose on a highly advanced space-ship would be? You don't realize yet just what sort of man we are dealing with here. He may have an exceptional brain, but someone forgot to attach it to the rest of his body. He is to co-ordination what a politician is to the whole truth. He is to common sense what the Boston strangler was to ballet. Once a year someone tells the lemmings he's coming to visit them. He – '

'If you would allow me to finish?' Vyland's skin-flaying look did battle with Bowen's thick hide for a moment, and won. 'My research has led me to believe that long before the *Pioneer* reaches Alcyone, this particular concept of space travel will be quite obsolete.

'As some of you know, I have been working in secret for some years on a matter transference device, which reduces matter to its component tachyons, moves them at speeds above that of light, and re-forms them again when they reach their destination. I have recently made a significant breakthrough in my experiments, and will be pleased to give you all a demonstration immediately after this meeting.

'If I am right – which of course I am – then we can wave goodbye to both Curtis and the *Pioneer* with a clear conscience, knowing that it is already out of date. I believe that we could have interstellar travel at the touch of a button within twenty years, if our resources are diverted to that research.'

A reverent silence settled across the board like a gossamer shawl. The thought of a whole lifetime without Curtis was wonderful, and, if Vyland was right, then the consequences of letting him go would not matter. And they would get to keep the money as well.

'It is fifteen hundred hours,' said the clock in the middle of the table, while its holographic design showed a face proving just that to each attendee simultaneously. Having pronounced, and held its new facets

7

for a few seconds, it reverted to an ornament displaying a calming pyramidal waterfall. Fifteen hundred hours presaged Curtis's arrival. He was ten seconds late.

II

The door rattled, but did not open. It was being pushed with considerable effort from the outside. There were two loud thumps as a shoulder was applied. Then a pause. Then Curtis's secretary pulled the door open quietly, and stood aside to let the Chairman enter. He did this with dignity, aware of the awe in which his committee held him, and then paused to survey the scene before him.

The metallic walls gleamed brightly, but non-reflectively so as to avoid the impression during a meeting that seven people were simultaneously, and in perfect unison, addressing an audience of hundreds. It was pretty much standard decor for a meeting room in a city office, but there were differences which marked out the Space Research Centre's purpose. Here and there a picture broke the silver monotony – a close-up of the incredible surface of Saturn sent back some twenty years before by the Cronus probe, and a wide-angle shot of Pluto's moon, Charon, taken with its mother planet and the stars of the cosmos in the background, both overlooking the room with a splendour apparent only to those of an astronautical bent. To Bowen they looked like a close-up of a shiny rock and a picture of a couple of dull rocks. Imagination was not something by which Bill Bowen was frequently troubled.

The table supported a few ornaments, glasses, a couple of water jugs and the odd piece of paper, but it was the computer screens set flush with its top like so many place mats which acted as agenda, minutes, library and doodle pad for the attendees. The keyboards, likewise set into the table, were activated by the styli which were also used directly on the screens.

The table was not quite round, and it was the seat at its head which awaited Curtis. The other members of the committee were already there, he noted, his mind like quicksilver, all smartly attired in pastel jump suits. They too awaited him, like the chair. Eagerly awaited, probably, he thought, as he crossed the unpatterned carpet quite smoothly. Until he reached the waste-paper basket. He took his seat while his secretary cleared it up with a swiftness and efficiency born of much practice.

Curtis picked up the pitcher of water from the table, and began to

9

pour himself a glass. The rest of the committee looked on in silent expectation, and those closest to him edged backwards slightly, looking like a set move in a seated barn dance. But he accomplished the task with comparative ease, probably because he had nothing else on which to concentrate at the same time.

'Good afternoon, ladies and gentlemen.' Grudging whispers of response implied that it used to be. 'You will be pleased to hear that I have improved the Arnold computer.'

Oddly, they did not look pleased. A number of them wanted to point out that to alter its capabilities in the other direction would have been an achievement worthy of note.

'Arnold will now respond to voice commands. With its ability to think for itself, I can now hold a conversation with Arnold, just as I can with any one of you.' Bowen wondered if the computer would now avoid him like everyone else did.

'Gloria.' Curtis turned to his secretary. 'Would you bring Arnold in here, please?' Gloria flashed an adoring smile at him, and left.

Bowen looked at Gloria and sighed again, but inwardly this time. Gloria Parkson had been Curtis's secretary for a number of years, and Bowen thought it said a lot for Curtis's complete lack of nous that he still did not realize that she considered him about three down from God and still rising. He also thought it said quite a bit about Gloria Parkson, for that matter; he reckoned if she had any more brains she would almost have been half-witted.

Any reasonable defence, though, would rightly argue that Bowen was hardly one to look below the surface to the inner man, and especially not to the inner woman, where for Big Bill the surface was all he wanted. And especially so with such as Gloria, whose surface was so pleasant to look upon that it had stopped short better men than Bowen.

Bowen ogled the outer in happy ignorance, and when Gloria left the room, his thoughts – rather smutty ones – followed her.

Gloria put an end to said thoughts by returning promptly with a machine which reclined gruesomely on a trolley.

As a concept, it was quite brilliant, but in appearance it did lack something.

Like, taste.

Curtis's filial devotion had not been lessened by the passing comment of his passing father, and Arnold, the computer, was built as a replica of the head of Arnold, the father. Before the latter hit the ground, thankfully.

Before he made his final impact on the world, if the computer was anything to go by, he was a man in his fifties who wore his light brown hair in a crew cut, because that was the best way to hide any hint of grey. The blue eyes looked vibrant, and the rounded face was flatteringly unmarked by the lines of age. It was probably what Arnold Curtis would have looked like had the top of his head reached its mid-fifties while everything below it was still twenty.

Curtis was proud of Arnold; you could tell from the look in his eyes. He wished for the umpteenth time that robotics had come far enough for him to have created a complete android.

Robotics had actually come far enough, but Curtis had not, and it was easier to blame the science. Deep down he knew that he was not sufficiently experienced in advanced positronic mechanics to attempt the feat. No matter; Arnold was still a great achievement, and all his own.

'Arnold!' announced Curtis, with a grand sweep of his hand in the direction of his creation. Gloria left Arnold for a few moments to re-vase the flowers now strewn over the table.

The main difference in appearance between the computer and the father was a long wire sticking out of the former, and this Gloria lovingly installed into a socket on the wall.

'Good afternoon, Arnold,' said Curtis.

'Sorry?' said the computer.

'I said, "Good afternoon, Arnold." '

'Nope, still didn't catch it!'

'GOOD . . . AFTERNOON . . . ARNOLD.'

'Good afternoon, Dick.'

'It's Richard.'

'Where?'

'Here. I'm Richard, not Dick.'

'You look like a Dick to me.'

While several committee members suddenly felt the need to wipe their noses or scratch their upper lips, Bowen's eyes wandered heavenward, in search either of his former employer, or the Almighty. 'You programmed this, did you?' he asked, more by way of insult than question.

'As far as I could,' said Curtis with a perplexed look passing across his features like a cloud across the sun. 'Arnold didn't seem to like too much programming.' Not as daft as it looks, thought Bowen.

'Would you like to be installed into the *Pioneer* space-ship, Arnold?' Curtis asked.

'Sorry?' Curtis repeated the question. Arnold's eyes took on a quality of child-like excitement, such as that when its parent suggests an early bed-time.

'Ooh *can* I? Can I *really*?'

'Of course you can, Arnold!' The sun came out again, and Curtis beamed as his creation. 'He can express simple emotions such as enthusiasm,' he explained to the committee. None of them explained to

11

him. Arnold's expression moved in the direction of despair, but never reached it as Curtis continued. 'I made him as human as I could.' The expression defined loathing. Half a lip moved upwards like an arching caterpillar.

'Gloria, would you unplug Arnold, please?' Gloria complied. 'Arnold still needs a bit of work, but, as you can see, it is a significant advance in computer technology. I have only been working on it for one hundred and seventeen hours, and another thirty-four should see it fully operational. I propose that it be installed into the *Pioneer* as soon as it is ready.'

The thought was not a pleasant one. A two-week space flight with that gargoyle spouting fluent gibberish all the time would be enough to send most astronauts mad. Mind you, with Curtis on board, they would not be very sane for too long anyway.

Curtis toyed thoughtfully with one of those executive stress reduction things, which in this case was a gyroscope travelling down a length of wire and throwing out interesting flashes of green and red laser light as it spun. The committee watched and waited for the results of his toying and his thinking, both of which were surely going to produce something.

After a moment or two, the gyroscope duly lost its balance and fell off the wire, so Curtis pushed it from his vicinity and his thoughts. Gloria retrieved and began to reassemble it as the Chairman revealed his thoughts. They were not welcome ones.

'With my expertise in the field of computing,' said Curtis, with suitable self-deprecation, 'it has occurred to me that my depriving the world of my presence for more than eight hundred years, by embarking on this mission, would be less than fair.' It wasn't that he was scared at all. 'I think it might be better to allow Arnold to represent me, as it were, and stay here to carry on with my work.'

There was a ghastly aghast hush around the table. The scientists had only just found a possible way out of their problems, and now he was threatening not to go. Something had to be done, quickly, and Vyland did it.

'I think that might be a good idea.' Faces were turned towards him carrying various expressions, all of which suggested that he had turned into something rather unpleasant. What the hell was he playing at? 'There are considerable moral drawbacks to your going,' he continued, ignoring all but Curtis. 'People might think that you had undertaken this epic adventure merely to gain the adulation of the whole world on your return. They might think that you did it solely to go down in history as the greatest scientist that ever lived. They would not think of it as purely a scientific expedition of hypothesis testing, and I am sure you would not want that.'

There was a short pause, during which various words and phrases impinged themselves on what Curtis was pleased to call his mind. Like 'adulation', and 'greatest scientist that ever lived'. What Curtis was pleased to call his mind appreciated the sensation. His features gave no indication of his thoughts, in much the same way as the Empire State Building gave no impression of being quite tall.

'Do you really think they would think that?' he asked.

'They might.' Vyland's tone suggested that he only wished it could be otherwise. 'Unless we can persuade them that you were going against your own desires, but on the recommendation of this committee.'

'But would they believe that I could be swayed by the committee?' Curtis's eyes searched widely for a positive response.

'I think we might be able to convince them of such a possibility, yes.'

Curtis's eyes shone like a couple of OBEs; rather appropriately.

They were still shining when the meeting quickly drew to a close with a promise from Curtis to consider the matter. He was left alone with Gloria, whose eyes shone even brighter, while the rest followed Vyland from the room and towards his laboratory, floating on a flood tide of relief.

In Vyland's laboratory stood two machines, side by side, looking rather like microwave ovens. The glass fronts allowed a view of the contents, and currently one held a wooden ash tray, while the other was empty. The members of the committee, Curtis excluded, crowded round to watch what happened when Vyland threw the switch. He duly did so, and the ash tray disappeared from the container which held it, and something like an ash tray immediately appeared in the other. Not very like an ash tray, admittedly, but the demonstration of matter transference was good enough to raise a small ripple of applause from the suitably impressed scientists.

But only the scientists. Bowen was rather less impressed. Not being a scientist, he was concerned only with the results of the experiment, and not the theory behind it.

'You try putting a person through that thing, and it would come out looking like my wife.'

Vyland glanced at him, realizing, perhaps, why he now spent so much time at the Research Centre despite his obvious lack of knowledge and interest in its workings.

'It clearly needs considerable work,' he said icily, adding, 'The device, not your wife,' before turning his attention back to his fellow scientists. 'I have been working on this with my younger twin Mycroft – some of you may have heard of him. The theory is all but complete now. If we are allowed to work unhindered, then we should be able to perfect the technique before long. I would estimate that . . .'

13

Bowen was no longer listening. The terrible thought which had first occurred to him when Phillips was addressing the committee had re-entered his head. He should not have mentioned his wife. He should definitely not have mentioned his wife. Ethel had been quite pleasant to look at when he had married her – at least in the distance, in the dusk, with the light behind her. But now! Now she looked like Doctor Jekyll after a couple of green and smoking drinks. She treated Big Bill Bowen like he was Very Little Bill Bowen, and there was nothing he could do about it, partly because she had progressed from the sylph-like figure of her youth to being Bloody Enormous Ethel Bowen.

His thought had linked Ethel not with the matter transference device – you would surely need a medium-sized power station to supply enough energy to transfer *her* matter – but with the trip itself. He would only be gone for a month, but the scientists had told him repeatedly that much more time would have passed on Earth by the time he got back. He had to admit that he still did not understand it, but he was sensible enough to believe it. If he were to go, then Ethel would be no more on his return.

There was only one drawback to the idea. He would have to share a delicate and highly dangerous space-ship for a whole month with someone who, when on form, could destroy a dozen of them in a week. No, he couldn't do it! Could he?

What of his son? What of Edmund, the little boy who had perfectly rounded off his life when he was born seventeen years before, and who had then provided a buffer between the growing conflict in the personalities of his parents? Edmund, who still relied on Big Bill for so much – so much pocket money, so much food, so much outsized clothing, so many interactive bloody virtual reality adventure toys.

Edmund, the little boy who had now grown up to be so much like his mother that he was only useful as a buffer these days because that was the way he was bloody well built!

No! It was completely unthinkable!

Spending the rest of his life with that enormous prize turd as well as his heavyweight harridan mother was completely unthinkable!

He was in his early forties, and still had most of his life ahead of him, therefore. The pay that was being offered for this trip was good, and, by investing it, he would collect eight hundred years' worth of interest when he returned. He would be enormously rich. He could live in the lap of luxury for the rest of his days. Also in the lap of someone other than Ethel. Like June Patterson. No, he couldn't do that, of course, because June would be dead as well when he got back. Well, June's great-great-great-granddaughter, or whatever. Or anyone! He would be stinking rich.

A month with Curtis. He might not get back at all.

'. . . that we should go ahead with the project,' said Vyland. A reverent murmur of approval meandered through the congregation as Bowen's mind rejoined them. 'I think Curtis will go to Alcyone – we should have convinced him by now, and if we haven't, it shouldn't be too difficult to work on him a bit more. But we must not let him know what is going on here. If he were to discover that his precious space-ship was going to be obsolete before he was a tenth of the way there, then he certainly wouldn't go. Our main problem now is to find some lunatics to go with him.'

'At least if they were lunatics they'd feel well at home with him as Captain,' Phillips chipped in, spotting a route back into his boss's good books. Bowen winced.

The door opened, and Curtis stood framed in the resultant hole. Bowen was quite impressed that he had managed the feat at his first attempt this time. Must have been practising. Curtis was surprised that there were twelve people in the laboratory. He had expected only Vyland, of whom he was going to ask help with Arnold. Twelve people. That left, taking into account the amount of furniture and equipment scattered around, an average of roughly two point eight square feet per person.

Crowded.

Something must be of interest.

They were huddled round what appeared to be two microwave ovens, and huddled round in such a way that it was very difficult to see the ovens, especially as the scientists kept moving every time Curtis tried to get a better look. He inquired as to the nature of the instruments. A number of the huddle moved their mouths in various directions, but did not manage to accompany the movement with any audible product. Vyland moved forward.

'It's just my hobby, sir,' he said, in a voice which would have made Uriah Heep sound like Rambo after an intense self-assertiveness course. 'I have been working on a method of heating food in microwaves instantaneously. It helps when I work too late on your trip to be able to get a meal elsewhere, sir.'

Curtis beamed. His trip. Yes, it was going to be his trip, he had decided. He announced his decision to the current population of the laboratory. Had they all expelled their sighs of relief at the same time, they would have crushed him against the corridor wall.

The Champion knew better than to allow any hint of disappointment to escape into the ether where this upstart Challenger would certainly find it and take heart, so it merely watched proceedings dispassionately, keeping the x-rays deep within its being while not appearing to do so. It had made its bed and would lie on it. (In actuality it would have floated existentially a couple of feet above it.) What it needed was an outstanding team to counter its leader.

The Challenger had no such worries. Not only were the Champion's chances severely damaged by the old fool's extraordinary choice of a pillock as team leader, but there was also this Vyland character . . .

If the Champion was going to bed, the Challenger was getting ready to dance the night away. As it were.

III

Bowen stood back from the notice board on which he had just affixed the vacancy notice for crew members. His first effort at composition – 'A number of intelligent and highly qualified space engineers required. Must have astero . . . astrern . . . astronortick . . . space experience, education to degree level in mathematics, physics or space science. Death wish or terminal illness a definite advantage' – had been modified and spell-checked, and the result now adorned not only this particular vacancy board and the electronic mail system at the Arnold Curtis Space Research Centre but also most of the national daily newstexts and scientific magazines. Bowen frowned at the board and its new addition, and in his mind's eye Ethel frowned back, impressively. He turned away, a much troubled man, en route to the building's other board with another notice.

And nearly bumped into what might have been a small weasel in a suit except that it wore a name badge which identified it as a Thomas Wilverton. Both men changed direction suddenly, and Bowen steadied himself against the wall with one hand, having to let go of the notice in order to do so. The piece of paper immediately took the opportunity for which all inanimate objects wait with complete vigilance, and leaped to that point in space from which it would be most difficult to retrieve, in this case straight through the open window.

'Excuse me,' said Wilverton, being one of those people who automatically apologizes for everything whether it is their fault or not.

'Grunt,' grunted Bowen in an angry rumble, being one of those people who don't, and carried on down the corridor to 'request' – no doubt in his own inimitable way – another notice from his secretary, oblivious to the fact that the little man had now stopped and was looking intently up at the newly arrived opportunity.

'Up' not because the notice was a particularly long way off the ground, but because Wilverton's eyes were a particularly short way off the ground. He looked unimpressive from the outside, with neat short hair and a neat short parting, slightly pinched features topping off a well-pressed light blue jump suit. Appearances can admittedly sometimes be deceptive, but Wilverton looked pretty boring.

He read the job description and immediately smiled to himself. And that set him thinking.

He was the only person at whom he did smile as a rule, he thought, not through a curdled milk of human kindness, but simply through lack of opportunity. Wilverton knew he was described as a loner by anyone who bothered, and recalled someone telling him that he would make a librarian whose hobbies were accountancy and watching goldfish seem fascinating in comparison, but that did seem to him a little unfair. The recollection caused the smile to fade somewhat. Many things interested him; it was just that they seemed to be exactly those things which signally failed to interest anyone else.

This was peculiar, he considered, since everyone liked reading, and if there was one thing he was good at it was reading – and talking about what he had read. He could discourse on almost anything ever written; if anyone ever gave him the chance, he thought, ruefully.

He read the job notice once again and the smile returned.

A month on a space-ship would not be a lot different from his usual home life as long as he had his books with him, except for the view out of the window, which he did study from time to time if his gaze found itself pointing in that direction. And the view wasn't much to talk about, he considered, although he did every now and then. He had talked about it the other night to that girl in the pub, but she had rapidly gone off to powder her nose, and then, when he tried to re-engage her in conversation on her return, she had gone off to powder someone else's.

He sighed, then stood a little straighter, squaring what passed for shoulders on his body. King Lear was right, he thought – as one does – while the words of the notice applied themselves ever more to him especially. Nothing *would* come of nothing. He had to do something to make his life the exciting series of events which he knew should be his lot, so that he could emulate his heroes.

And now he had the chance. He would be Flash Gordon, Scott of the Antarctic – or, more optimistically, Amundsen of the Antarctic – Christopher Columbus and Rip Van Winkle.

Wilverton was, he knew, an excellent engineer, and an expert on all matters pertaining to space-ships, which was why he had been employed at the Space Centre in the first place, so he reckoned he had a chance of the First Officer position. That would suit him down to the ground, or down to the floor of the space-ship anyway, because in all the Alistair MacLean books he had ever read, the first officer was always the hero.

And Wilverton wanted to be the hero. There was no reason why a minuscule body and the muscles of a mouse should stop you if you had the heart of a lion, except that it might be rather uncomfortable. He *would* go, and he would come back in triumph.

He nodded, decision made, and walked away from the board, smiling in expectation of adventure, noticing as he did so that while he had been standing there thinking all those typically Wilvertonian thoughts, his foot had gone to sleep. He wasn't a bit surprised.

The Champion smiled inwardly, since it did not actually possess an outward, by means of a few long microwaves. This one's mind, at least, was regimented, logical – a good sign in lower life-forms; which didn't generally mean those under five foot eight, but might have done in Wilverton's case. This mind would prove a good foil for the strange conglomeration of notional activity inside the Curtis creature. The Champion had already seen enough of its unfortunate first choice to realize that he needed some considerable foiling.

Its next choice was marching along the road just outside the Space Centre, oblivious to the fact that a job was beckoning from the ether, and also approaching him from above, as a piece of paper fluttered from a window and headed for his head. Captain Marcus Watmore had recently left the air force, where he had been employed not as a fighter but as an astronaut, easily the most accomplished pilot in the country and with a string of medals for various acts of bravery that would make a man of less physical strength topple to his left. He was currently on his way to a meeting of the Mensa top ten when a small voice in his head made him look upwards at the approaching leaflet, and he wondered what it might be.

Before the paper reached him, his attention was taken by the sound, and sight as he adjusted to look, of a man climbing swiftly from a ground floor window about twenty yards ahead of him, and apparently getting dressed at the same time. The paper was forgotten as this more intriguing event took over, the character casting a worried glance back through the window before setting off down the street towards Watmore at a run while disconcertingly doing up the fly of his jump suit. As he passed, so his chest managed to collect a piece of paper which had fluttered down from the window above, and he carried it with him round the corner, unaware of its presence until he stopped to catch his breath and gravity was given the chance to complete what it had started.

Captain Marcus Watmore shook his head in disbelief as he turned to watch the fleeing figure. Thieves generally undertook their malfeasances with secured flies, did they not?

Watmore had a limited knowledge of low-life.

He was *quite* sure that climbing through windows was not the action of a regular chap; more that of a cad.

And he was sure he had seen that face before.

Extraordinary behaviour! he thought to himself. Should probably be birched. Then he continued on his way, shaking his head one last time.

Strangely, to Watmore if not to the Challenger, he never happened to read or hear about the *Pioneer*'s trip to the stars until he saw mention of its launch some time later.

Many eons ago, on the planet which the Champion and its Challenger used to inhabit when they were built for it, there lived an herbivorous creature called a smug, whose wool was used to make the finest garments for those who could afford them, due to its soft texture and tensile strength. The young of the smug wore similar coats to those of their parents, except that the strength of the fabric was not yet apparent and the texture made the mature version seem coarse. The wool of the young was such as the deities themselves might have chosen to wear, so warm and downy was it, and so enchanting to the touch. When the Challenger's ancestors were children, a good deed or a task successfully completed was rewarded by being allowed to stroke the young creatures, a tactile reward more eagerly sought than any other treat. The expression stayed with them while their bodies did not, so that, as it watched Captain Marcus Watmore preparing to take no more part in the Game, the Challenger felt a little smug.

It allowed the extended radio waves of satisfaction to leak from its being, almost regretting its lack of physical aspect, where a gloating smile would currently be well placed. The Champion steadfastly refused to let its thoughts demean themselves, but instead studied the new recipient of the invitation.

Peter Carlton heaved in a chestful of air and let it out, mixed well with relief. That, as they say, was close, he thought. Watmore was correct in his conclusion that Carlton was not involved in underworld activities; he was no criminal. He did sort of steal other men's partners occasionally, but he would swear to a court that it was not intentional.

It certainly wasn't in the case of the woman whose flat he had just unconventionally vacated on hearing that the husband which two hours before she had sworn not to possess was approaching the front door. Said husband was unlikely to be on his side of the argument.

He sighed, and shook his head. How did he get himself into these scrapes? he wondered. It just happened; it wasn't his fault. It was just that when some women saw his dark brown, almost black, blemishless skin, his deep brown eyes, his white smile, the graceful movement characteristic of his great-grandparents' native Caribbean, and the outline of a body well trained in gyms for most of his twenty-six years, they seemed to forget themselves.

He smiled his white smile to himself. Well, they were only human, he thought, and he *did* like it when they forgot themselves!

Watmore had indeed recognized Carlton's face, although he had not remembered, from earlier days in the spatial arm of the forces, where Carlton had risen to the rank of Private and stayed there until he was relieved of his position after being found in another one.

Carlton, like Watmore, was a pilot.

The piece of paper which Carlton retrieved from the ground at his feet promised a two-week outward trip on the *Pioneer* space-ship, plus the same coming back, making eight hundred odd years when the time dilation was added. That sounded reasonable. Eight hundred years in the future was a destination to which he couldn't be followed, and there would be so many women just dying to meet the heroes when they returned.

Carlton was suddenly looking forward to a new career, and on looking around for the Arnold Curtis Space Research Centre, on the headed note paper of which the advertisement was printed, he found it right behind him. Fate was smiling. Not knowing that the Captain – or pillock – of the *Pioneer* was very close to anti-matter in human form, Carlton did not recognize that smile as one produced by a crocodile.

He decided that he would not go for the drink in that pub over there which he had been contemplating as good medicine for his pounding heart after his extra-fenestral activity, but instead brushed the creases from his jump suit and entered the Research Centre, the smile for the receptionist already settling itself into its accustomed winning position.

In that pub over there, Danny Thompson brought two pints – it was one of the few places which still had not succumbed to the litre – of lager back from the bar and placed them on the table which he and his colleague, Pete Watts, had chosen for a lunch-time drink. Said colleague was leafing through his newly arrived copy of some computer magazine, and reading the article which advertised the latest ninth-generation language, already apparently pregnant with the tenth. He pointed it out to Thompson as the latter regained his seat.

Thompson shrugged. 'Computers don't mean that much to me, Pete. I'm just a simple engineer.'

'So am I,' replied Watts, managing to convey outrageous modesty in three syllables. Thompson knew this was rubbish and that Watts recognized the fact, but he let it pass.

Watts turned another page. 'Look at the salary they're offering for that!' He bent the sheet so that Thompson could see the advertisement.

'Well, why don't you go for it? With your qualifications you'd stand a good chance.' Since Watt's qualifications left his headed note paper with room for no more than a brief memo, no-one else need turn up, Thompson thought quietly.

Watts shook his head and his expression reflected distaste. 'I don't want to work for a company; there's not enough freedom. I need to be able to research, to do something at the frontier of science.'

The Champion swelled a bit in the ether, making room for the longer wavelengths of satisfaction. This one's mind almost reached third level. Not much, admittedly, but good for a human.

Watts began to turn another page, pausing only to sip his pint. Completion of the act would reveal a small advert inviting applicants for the *Pioneer* project, promising research like there had never been before at frontiers unsullied by man's footprint, or rocket exhaust.

Thompson reached out for his own pint, and the word '*Pioneer*' caught his attention as he did so, the vertical page visible out of the corner of his eye. The next thing to which his attention was drawn was the glancing blow he managed to impart to the side of his beer glass, sending it toppling and depositing a pint of Australia's best into Watt's lap.

'Bother,' said Watts, or something which meant much the same thing.

'Er,' said Thompson after the initial and heartfelt 'Sorry'. It was difficult to know how to help. Watts saved him the trouble, saying gruffly that he had sufficient time to go home and change before the end of the lunch hour, and stalking huffily from the pub with the assertion that 'It doesn't matter.'

Thompson was left with a feeling of helpless guilt, a near full pint of lager which Watts no longer felt like consuming, and an interesting advert inviting applicants for the *Pioneer*.

A month in space, returning to a world over eight hundred years older and wiser. What a fascinating thought, he thought. He had always wanted to know what the future would hold, and whether mankind would get itself out of the mess that it had been so adept at getting itself into.

A very serious-minded young man was Daniel Thompson.

And he could do some experiments. He could grow some pure crystals, or do some protein analysis . . . and he could take some bees. Now there was another interesting thought. Since bees weren't supposed to be able to fly on Earth but did so anyway because no-one had thought to explain aerodynamics to them, or at least had not managed to convince them of the various laws involved, there had been a number of experiments over the years to see how they got on in zero gravity. Would they be able to fly there? He might be able to add something to the data already gathered.

He looked back to the advertisement. Perhaps knocking that pint over was not so unfortunate after all! Perhaps it was fated! He tore the advert carefully from the paper and slipped it into his pocket.

The Challenger swelled a bit in the ether. Damage limitation – it was an upper second, but better this mind than the one targeted.

IV

Gloria was distraught, but did not show it. Mr Curtis had explained that he was going on the trip, and had told her that she would never see him again. She did not understand the explanation, but like Bowen – who would have resented the comparison, much as he did everything else – she had no reason not to believe it. And she still had not told Curtis of her love for him.

She sat and gazed into his eyes.

He sat and gazed into Arnold's eyes.

Arnold just sort of squatted on his neck.

Curtis was further improving Arnold's capabilities, believe it or not. That involved staying rather longer at the Centre than he normally would. Gloria stayed with him because she adored him, and because all she had to go back to was a small flat, the only other occupant of which was Fred, an old and dilapidated teddy bear, so called because, yes, he was fred bear. It was a joke which her mother had told her, before death robbed Gloria of her only living relative, and the world of a good and simple woman, if not one of the truly great wits. Gloria still thought it was funny. There was a lot of her mother in Gloria, and for all the 'thick as a docker's sandwich' opinions, there were many who would be better for that.

'We'll be staying rather late tonight, Gloria.' Curtis looked up to find his secretary's dinner plate eyes trained directly on him.

Why did she look at him like that? he wondered briefly. Perhaps there was something slightly wrong with her eyesight. Best not to pry, she might think he was being forward, and he knew there was no point in that. He had as much chance with a woman like Gloria as he did of reaching Alcyone without a rocket.

'I want to make sure that Arnold's co-ordination recognition is correct.'

Gloria gave the impression of rapt attention and complete incomprehension. A very good impression, actually. Curtis tried to make it clearer for her, and when Curtis tried to do something . . .

'Obviously, three-dimensional spatial co-ordinates are rather more problematical to assimilate than purely two-dimensional Earth-bound ones, and a slight enhancement to the computer's deductive capacity is required.'

. . . he usually failed.

The look of complete incomprehension on Gloria's face became even more complete. Curtis wisely gave up. 'I've got a couple of Cornish pasties, if you feel like having something to eat.'

A meal invitation!

'I'd love to, Mr Curtis.' She dropped her eyes and blushed. Perhaps she doesn't like Cornish pasties, thought Curtis, but he rummaged around in the bottom of his briefcase all the same, and eventually produced two of the local café's best. 'Best' is rather a misleading word here. The *Good Food Guide* was never likely to devote more than a four-letter word to them, and it would rhyme with 'trap'. They were largely potato and fat, surrounded by the same stuff they make paving stones out of, and, if one were especially fortunate, one might encounter a small piece of gristle as a sort of meat substitute. And they were, appropriately, stone cold.

An idea unusually found its way into Curtis's head, and, finding that there was no competition whatsoever, imposed itself on his brain.

'Vyland's got a couple of microwaves in his lab. We could heat these up.'

Vyland's lab was next door, and Curtis managed the journey with no mishaps, and with Gloria at his heels. The things did not look like microwaves to Gloria – there were no knobs or dials or anything; just a switch. Curtis, without such reasoning, tried to put both the pasties into one of the ovens, and found that they would not fit very comfortably, so he put one in each. He looked round for some knobs or dials or something, and, finding none, he shrugged and threw the switch.

It did not occur to either of the watchers that the pasties had changed places. All they could see was that they had been reduced to something slightly like two cornish pasties. Not very like two Cornish pasties. More like ash trays fashioned by the third grade remedial art class.

Gloria reached into one of the ovens, and withdrew its contents. The pasty was still cold. But Gloria did not care – it was her first meal with the object of her passion, and she was not going to let anything spoil it. She flashed him a smile, using all her perfect teeth, and took a bite. Or, to be exact, she tried to take a bite. The paving stone mixture had set, and Gloria knew very well which of the pasty or her teeth would win any battle. Short of throwing the whole thing down her throat and hoping that her stomach acids were strong enough, there was no way she was going to join the boss for dinner that night.

'It appears that these ovens are as yet inoperative,' said Curtis, carefully trying to wobble one of his front teeth between finger and thumb, and succeeding. Gloria had to agree with him. I don't think she likes Cornish pasties anyway, thought Curtis. They dropped their pasties into Vyland's waste bin, and dented it.

The next day was interview day, and Curtis, Vyland and Bowen were to make up the board. Before setting off for the appointment, Vyland discovered the pasties in his bin and, since only Curtis thought that the matter transference devices were microwaves, a simple analytical exercise told him what had happened. He trusted that Curtis was too stupid to have performed a similar analysis.

Thomas Wilverton was the first name on their short list – a very short list, which Bowen told Vyland had been ruthlessly pruned to three hopefuls from an original application totalling three hopefuls.

As the board took their seats and waited for the applicant to enter, Curtis leaned over and told Vyland that his microwaves did not appear to work properly. Vyland smiled.

'Thank you, sir, I'll work on them as soon as we have finished our business here,' said his mouth. 'Cretin,' said his smile. Curtis nodded happily – Vyland was a good man – and smiled in turn to welcome Wilverton, who entered the room after Bowen had grunted a response to his tentative knock.

'Well, your qualifications are not in doubt,' said Vyland to the little man sitting opposite him, a couple of minutes later. 'Exactly why do you want to be a member of the crew of *Pioneer*?'

'Well.' Wilverton adjusted his seating position to one of more comfort, as if preparatory to a long explanation. 'Obviously, the idea of travelling to another star is one which has fascinated mankind ever since the earliest days when they came to understand that such a thing was possible. I don't mean possible in the sense of having a craft capable of completing or indeed even attempting the trip, but possible in as much as they realized that stars were celestial bodies which were capable of actually being visited, and not merely points of light in the sky, or fixed gleams on the inside of a solid spherical surface. "Possible" in terms of contemplation, therefore, if you like.'

Bowen already didn't like.

What a boring little man, thought Vyland.

'Then, of course, with the advent in the popular fictional books – although I suppose one would have referred to them at the time as possibly pulp fiction, since they only became popular quite some time later; not that the term "pulp fiction" would have been in use then, but you know what I mean I'm sure – anyway . . .'

What's he talking about, thought Curtis, while a smile froze on his face. Bowen tried to stifle an expansive yawn behind a hand, and behind lips which were stretching in an attempt to stay together, while his nostrils flared like magnesium. Vyland started reading the notes on the hand-held word processor in front of him, then he read the manufacturer's name, and counted the number of 'e's. In the good old days, when paper was all they had, he could have filled them in. There's progress for you.

'. . . Pioneering, if you like, which I think is a very apt word for it when you consider that the space-ship in which I hope I will be travelling and furthering that exploratory yearning is in fact known by the name of *Pioneer*.

'Of course I never really thought that I would actually get the chance to make my dreams come true, because so few people do and the dreams rather by definition were things that were very unlikely; however, I did hope that one day . . .'

'The job's yours!' cried Bowen, then heaved a sigh of relief into the ensuing silence.

'Oh,' said Wilverton after a moment. 'Thank you very much.' And he left.

'That was a bit quick, wasn't it?' asked Curtis, trying not to let his gratitude show. 'There may be better people than him to come.'

'I wouldn't bet on it,' said Bowen, checking the list of applicants in front of him.

'Why?'

'Because there are only two left, and we need four.'

'You mean we've only had three applications?' Curtis looked puzzled. As ever. 'How could that possibly have happened?' Bowen shook his head. 'So if we take them all, we'll still be one short.'

Bowen looked at him with a strange expression on his face, and it was not put there by the amazing feat of mathematics which Curtis had just displayed. It was an expression of massive indecision.

'The Great Adventurers' was how the papers described the crew of the star-ship *Pioneer*, when it was announced. There was Richard Curtis, Captain; Thomas Wilverton, First Officer and engineer; Peter Carlton, pilot; Danny Thompson, engineer; and . . .

Apollo 11 could quite happily have landed on the moon with a cargo of nuts, bolts and stuff, arranged such that it could manoeuvre itself to gather rocks and take pictures and sample the moon dust and even hit a golf shot to see how far the ball went. It did not actually need Neil Armstrong or Buzz Aldrin. 'Strolling on the Moon One Day' could have been rendered by a tape deck should this have been considered absolutely necessary. If it hadn't been for JFK, it would have been one small step for a little machine with a spoon in its claw.

However, once you have taken the decision that fleshy mounds must accompany the nuts and bolts and stuff, then other decisions are pretty much made for you. Firstly, you need people who can run all the things on the ship in case the computer which is supposed to run them breaks down, so you need an engineer. If you are going to be in space for a long period, you are better off with two. Secondly, you need a pilot, again in case the computer breaks down, but also so that you can decide on the fine details of your destination when you are in its vicinity.

If you own the space-ship in the first place and you want to be famous, then you need a Captain, which will be you, though it is an added bonus if you are a computer expert as well.

And finally, though optionally, you need someone to look after all the little day-to-day non-scientific things which might be required, like providing muscle while the engineers do the fiddly bits. You need a dogsbody.

. . . and Big Bill Bowen, dogsbody, spelt 'crew member'.

Bowen could still not quite believe that he had actually taken the plunge even when he read his name in the paper. He had put the idea to his nearest and dearest – a phrase he always delivered with an animal snarl – during their daily pre-bedtime row. The thought of her husband – the word passed through her mind like fingernails down a blackboard – leaving for a whole month had been enough to reduce Ethel to tears of mirth. Since he had come back from the oil rig on which old man Curtis used to employ him before the Research Centre was built, she saw the last surviving Cro-Magnon every ruddy day.

Bowen had not seen her laugh like that since he had caught something vital in his trouser zip one morning, and, as she rose to a crescendo of delight, so his resolve to teach the old hag a lesson also rose.

He would definitely go.

When the cacophony died down sufficiently for him to make himself heard, he pointed out that it would only be a month as far as *he* was concerned.

'This Einstein,' he started, trying to remember what the scientists had told him, 'proved that if you travel at some big fraction of the speed of light, then time will pass a lot slower for you. We will be going very close to the speed of light. It will only be a month for us, but it will be over eight hundred years for you. I don't expect you to understand it, but by the time we get back, you will be dead and buried. Once I step onto that space-ship, you will never see me again. Ever!'

Ethel stopped laughing. Her eyes widened.

'You're joking!'

'I am not joking.'

'It can't be true!'

'It *is* true.'

'No!'

'Yes.'

'Really?'

'Really. Look, you dim trout, it has been proven time and time again.

It is a scientific fact. As far as you are concerned, I will not be coming back.'

Ethel stared. Then she rose and walked to the window, looking out and showing Bowen her back; something she had long wished to do.

She shook a little with emotion.

A twinge of guilt passed through Bowen – which he barely recognized as such, it had been so long – but then the shake was joined by a chortle, and the chortle blossomed, threatening to approach hysteria, before Ethel checked herself by an enormous effort of will. She spun to face the bane of her life, and through the tears streaming down her cheeks, Bowen could see the glint of sharpened steel in her eyes.

'If you are lying to me, William Balfour Bowen, I will make sure that you regret it for the rest of your life. And it won't be long!'

Bowen shrugged. He didn't plan to be around for the rest of his life. Ethel beamed once more.

'Wait till I tell the bridge club' – where Bowen had made a guest appearance, once, bidding '*Eight* sodding diamonds, then, you fat cretin!' before being escorted out – 'they'll be so happy for me.' And that started her off again.

Bowen took a moment to hate the memory, then asked, 'Who's going to break it to Edmund?'

'I will.' Ethel dried her eyes with her sleeve. 'He's been a bit upset lately since his girlfriend broke it off.' She did well to find it in the first place, Bowen thought. 'It'll be nice to see him cheerful again.'

After that, for Bowen, it was just a question of ensuring that he was one of those chosen for the crew. Given that he was qualified for space travel in much the same way as a fish is qualified to climb Everest whilst blind-folded and wearing jodhpurs, this posed a problem. He could either exert his authority over Curtis by way of shouting very loudly, or he could ensure, by abusing his position as recipient of the applications, that there were sufficiently few to make the acceptance of his own application a *fait accompli* – he didn't put it to himself in quite those words.

He was good at shouting, was Big Bill. But he was good at abusing as well. And although he would not have admitted it to anyone, he thought there was a chance that, if there were a choice, Curtis would have put his foot down and refused to have Bill aboard if only for the flimsy reason that he could be of no possible use unless they needed ballast, which they didn't.

The latter course was therefore chosen, as were the applications, quite at random as far as Bowen was concerned – planet-bound mortal as he was – from the hundred or so which had arrived on his desk. He simply picked the three which happened to be nearest.

To answer Curtis's question, *that* was how that could possibly have happened.

Bowen's picking of the applicants might have been pre-ordained – 'might have been' meaning 'was', since the three nearest him were those agreed by Champion and Challenger after their initial skirmish – but the name of the Player was not. The Challenger pulsed the question, while the Lessers listened eagerly beneath them.

'Which is the Player to be?'

Carlton of the physical strength maybe? although surely not a match for the trands should they meet. Thompson, the one with more strength of mind than the others?

'Wilverton,' came the answer.

The Challenger tried not to let any surprise escape the vicinity of its being, but the Champion recognized a flash of violet in the visible spectrum.

Wilverton? The small one?

The Player was a crucial member of the team, upon whose shoulders whole rounds of the Game might depend – although not necessarily the first one. And the Champion had picked Wilverton – on whose shoulders even heavy dandruff looked like it might prove too much.

It had to be a sacrifice move.

But the Challenger wasn't complaining, the violet subsiding to infrared as it thought of special treatments for the chosen Player.

V

The vast crowds which turned up on the day of the launch to wish those intrepid explorers bon voyage made the occasion one to remember, even if the amount of alcohol consumed by the scientists at the party afterwards made it one that very few of them could.

Around the perimeter fence and the podium where a Cabinet Minister and her entourage were assembling, people were packed five and six deep, with small children hoisted onto daddy's shoulders looking bored stiff and not understanding that they had to come along and look so that they could tell their own children one day that they had been there, which they could quite happily have done without actually having to attend.

Curtis had looked through the window of the last building he would occupy on Earth for hundreds of years at the thousands of people and felt an enormous pride, but also some puzzlement. If there were this number of people interested in seeing them off, how come they only got a couple of applications asking to take part? He shrugged. It was just one of those things, he supposed. They probably considered the trip too dangerous to risk.

'Will you tell us the secret of the Inertialess Device, Professor Curtis?' asked a member of the press, before apparently trying to thrust a pencil microphone up his nose.

Not bloody likely, thought Curtis. He smiled in what he hoped would not be a nervous manner. Why does he look nervous? thought the reporter.

'The secret is in a vault at my bank, to be opened after a specified period,' Curtis told him. He'd been practising this answer for weeks, ever since he had found the Devices on the shelf next to his cheesy biscuits. It almost sounded convincing. 'I aim to be the first to the stars, and I don't want to give anyone the chance of beating me.' Now the other smile, the one that was supposed to look a little self-conscious in a brainy scientific sort of way. He's going to throw up, thought the reporter. 'You have to allow us professor types our little eccentricities,' Curtis finished. The reporter smiled back, with his 'what a moron' smile. He believes me, thought Curtis.

A couple of reporters bravely approached Ethel Bowen and her pile of

31

son, who were apparently controlling the grief they must be feeling by cramming enough free vol-au-vents and sweetmeats down their throats to sink the Sixth Fleet, and washing it down with champagne to the approximate volume of Lake Windermere. The questions put to her were answered with little more than a choked gurgle, a small tear in the corner of her eye, and an occasional spray of confectionery and pastry crumbs. They largely left her alone, which, oddly, was what Bowen was apparently doing. Perhaps the emotion of their parting was just too much for him to bear.

Thompson told of his expectations for the flight, and of his hopes for what he might find at its end. A place for mankind to grow, to expand from the planet to which they were tied. A planet which would spell the end of the hunger and hardship and inequity of the first and second worlds which existed on this one Earth. A planet which would open the way for mankind to conquer the stars.

Well, that was all very well, said the glazed eyes of the reporters in front of him, but it wouldn't compete with the tits on page three.

So they were from *those* texts, were they! Thompson read the reporters' eyes as easily as he could the monosyllabic columns which they produced.

'Of course, there might be extraterrestrials,' he said, and the promise of ET cleared the eyes in a moment. 'There's no reason why another habitable planet should not already be inhabited,' Thompson continued. 'And when we arrive, the first thing we are going to have to do is find out whether we are in fact pioneers, or visitors. If there are beings there to greet us, then we must hope that their greeting is friendly, and that they don't behave in the sort of xenophobic manner that we have seen in many of our own films on the subject. It would be interesting to consider humans as the aliens, which is what we will be to them. How will they see us? Will we be a vastly advanced species? Will we be like gods to them, or will we be hideous monsters?' The reporters scribbled furiously, and held recorders to him.

'These ETs, Dr Thompson. How big do you think their tits would be?'

Wilverton seemed to be sipping his small glass of champagne all alone, standing quietly in the corner of the room because they wouldn't let him into the kitchen. He had tried talking to some of the reporters when they came over to him, recognizing from his uniform jump suit and name badge that he was one of the crew, but they didn't seem to stay long. He sipped quietly and waited the last few minutes before he left this old world behind for the best part of nine hundred years. The excitement which boiled inside him was intense. You could tell from the way . . . from his . . . the expression . . . actually you couldn't tell at all, but he *was* excited.

Carlton flashed his teeth at the cameras, which flashed back, and it was touch and go which of them won the battle of brightness. It would be Carlton's perfect features which would be most prominent in the texts the following morning – 'Pull the zip down at bit further, Pete; let's see those pecs' – just as they had been since the crew was chosen. Given that the rest of them had the collective sex appeal of a hand of bananas – that is, only if you're desperate – this was not altogether surprising.

A lot of the quotes would be Carlton's as well, with words like 'adventure' and 'hero' and 'sacrifice' liberally sprinkled among the 'honour' and 'pride' bits.

Not many quotes would come from Bowen, since there were still laws against printing most of what Bowen had to say.

And no quotes at all would come from Vyland, since he stood apart like Wilverton, waving the press away whenever they veered too close, and sipping his champagne whilst wearing the look of a man who has discovered that the extra nought on his balance was an error the bank would never pick up. He was waving them goodbye at last, and he could get on with his work.

He would be the first man to the stars. Vyland would be the name that lived forever in the annals of scientific history.

Even if the unthinkable happened, and tachyon matter transference didn't, still Vyland would beat Curtis, thanks to the other ship and its pilot, which were even now preparing for launch thousands of miles away. His persuasive skills had seen to that.

And anyway, Curtis and his crew would not get there at all.

As he watched the crew walk out into the sunshine and the tumultuous cheers of the crowds outside, he raised his glass to them. It would be the last time he would see them – or maybe once more, he thought, and smiled again, as his plan further unfolded in his mind. He did not wish them bon voyage, because he knew that their voyage would not be a bon one. His programming skills would see to that.

Murder? No, not really, he decided. Self-defence. Defence of the family name.

He was glad he had done it.

So was the Challenger, especially as it had made the suggestion in the first place.

'Well, good luck to you, Dick,' said the Cabinet Minister, who seemed to get all the we-should-be-there-but-the-scheme-might-be-a-spectacular-failure-so-we-can't-risk-anyone-too-important assignments.

'Richard,' said Curtis, shaking hands. He had filed past the group of dignitaries, the last in the line, and the rest of the crew were already crossing the concourse to the space-ship's stairway.

'What's that?' The Minister cocked an ear, a smile of misunderstanding playing round her lips.

'It's Richard, not Dick.' Curtis let the hand go.

'Oh, well good luck anyway.' The Minister nodded Curtis on his way before turning to her husband and joining an ever-growing club by muttering, 'He looks like a Dick to me.'

Curtis caught up with the rest as they paused at the base of the space-ship *Pioneer* and turned to the crowd for one last wave, and to allow one last cheer to wash over them and send them on their way, before they turned and climbed. Each one stopped once more, briefly, at the top and waved again, taking his leave of the planet. Finally Captain Curtis himself paused on the top step, spun round, raised his arm for quiet and spoke into the small microphone attached to the stairway.

'I think it was Milton' – he started one of those speeches that is apparently not prepared at all but is just plucked from the fertile mind of the speaker – 'who spoke of the search for the new world, and asked who would tempt the dark unbottomed infinite abyss of space. Who would be sufficient?'

Ah, yes, thought the crowd, that was Milton all right. Good old Johnny Milton.

'What did he say?' the Minister asked her husband.

'Something about bottoms, I think,' he replied.

She frowned. 'Oh dear. How unpleasant.'

Curtis indicated himself and his crew, who weren't there any more.

'I hope and believe that we will prove sufficient for the challenge. We go with what courage we can muster to further the dreams of mankind. We now take another giant leap in our history, or rather in our future, an even, er, gianter leap perhaps than the one that was taken before . . . in the past. . .' Finish it, said the little voice in the back of his head. Finish it with your finishing sentence while they're still not throwing things at you, and get out of here.

'We will not see you again; we will not see this world again until nearly the end of this millennium, for it is up to us now to tempt that dark unbottomed infinite,' and for dramatic effect he lifted his head and his arm and indicated the sky above them, and in doing so lost his balance before finishing the sentence with 'ab-aaaaahhh!' as he slipped down four steps and tempted the strength of the stairway with his own bottom, then scrabbled back to the top and through the door of the *Pioneer* to the loudest cheers of all. Cheers which drowned out the laughter even as they emerged from heads shaking with incredulity.

Ten minutes later, and the flare of rockets pushed the space-ship *Pioneer* perfectly into the clear blue skies. As far as the people who craned their necks to watch the glorious departure were concerned, it would not return in their lifetime.

The launch itself had gone smoothly largely because all Curtis had to do was sit strapped in his seat and try not to be sick, not that this was particularly recognized by the Earthbound watchers, who assumed the crew would be doing all the work. In fact, Arnold was running the show for the moment, and Arnold had been programmed by Vyland, who knew exactly what he was doing and had revelled in it. The crew would have to do nothing until the craft was well beyond Earth's solar system, and was heading out on its path to Alcyone at full speed.

Many thousands of miles across the other side of the globe, a second space-ship was preparing to take off. There was none of the hype involved with *Pioneer* – quite the opposite – but there was none of the amateurism either. There was simply the launch of a ship which looked like, and was, the twin of the *Pioneer*, carrying the third Inertialess Device, which Curtis thought was still in his office safe, safe.

The race was on.

VI

The abandonment of gravity meant, of course, weightlessness, and a whole new field in which Curtis could display his talents. He unbuckled his safety harness and floated gracefully towards what used to be the ceiling of the craft. He hit it, head first, and bounced off at an angle which took him within arm's reach of Bowen, who grabbed him and pushed him back towards his seat with a scowl. When he reached the furniture, Curtis wrapped both arms round it, and tried to sound nonchalent.

'Well, we're on our way.'

'Sorry?' came a voice from a head bolted to a shelf in one corner of the control room. Carlton and Thompson looked at it in distaste. They had not come across the ship's computer until recently, and it was the sort of thing that needed some getting used to. The reason for its unusual appearance had been explained to them, along with no great re-assurance, but they wished that at least their Captain had been sufficiently capable to give the thing a body. The head did not move, but its eyes did swivel towards whoever was speaking at the time. Beneath the shelf on which it sat, a metal arm protruded from the shelf, and this seemed to belong to the head above it. There was just the one arm, which in itself was slightly disconcerting.

Arnold sat quite high up in the corner of a control room shaped like an oblong but with curved walls – made necessary by the fact that it was very near to the extreme pointy end of the craft – and surveyed the scene before him. It looked not a lot different from a room on Earth, except that the view through the panoramic window showed rather more black sky and white stars than would normally be the case.

The window was at one end of the oblong, and stretched from about three feet off the floor to the curve of the ceiling, with Carlton sitting in his chair beneath it. Between Carlton and the window was an array of dials and switches telling the pilot all he needed to know about the motile state of the craft, which, at the moment, was just about nothing. He would perform various checks on Arnold throughout the flight, and would probably take over when they were nearing Alcyone, but for now he was fairly redundant.

Dotted about the room were other chairs, each bearing one of the stellarnauts, and there were two tables located almost centrally. Curtis had thoughtfully provided really nice, generously upholstered chairs which they could sink into with comfort. Since they now weighed as much as a feather recovering from illness, it just became another comment on the Captain.

Around the walls were a number of consoles like that in front of Carlton, showing the state of the various life-support systems in nice friendly green glowing numbers. When they became nasty red ones, it was time for someone to worry. According to the manual, quite who should worry depended on which of the numbers went red, but there was a sort of tacit agreement amongst all the crew that if any of the numbers went red, they would probably all worry at the same time, regardless of the manual. Very equitable.

Above the consoles, the walls were covered with various star charts, which made it look all space-ship-like, and a few paintings, copies of the latest masterpieces and intended to be reassuring and have a calming influence. Unfortunately, the current idiom demanded that master-pieces were little more than violent slashes of colour which would only be reassuring in an abattoir. The thought was there though, and the thought had been that of Curtis, so it was hardly surprising that it missed its mark like a bankrupt German.

There were a few cabinets dotted about, where the consoles allowed them room, and one of these contained food other than the nutritious but plain fare which would make up the crew's normal diet, although generally this would not be available until they had landed on whatever they found circling Alcyone.

'Contained' is perhaps misleading, in that if it were opened without Arnold having received an instruction, it would contain food to the same degree as Mother Hubbard's cupboard. When an instruction *had* been received, though, Arnold would synthesize the manifestation of the request.

Another of the cabinets contained drink, much of which was pre-synthesized so the crew could raid it whenever they wanted, or, in the case of alcohol, when the Captain gave his express permission. When Bowen asked, he thought to himself, glancing at the cabinet already, that permission had better be damned express.

And that just about did it with the furniture. It was going to be a bit like spending a couple of weeks in a modern school room, with Arnold as the teacher.

There were two doors, one next to Carlton, leading to the very extreme end of the pointy bit, where the gym was housed, and one in the rear wall, leading to everywhere else.

'I said, "We're on our way," ' repeated Curtis, vaguely annoyed that Arnold still appeared to be a little hard of hearing.

37

'Sure thing, Dick,' said Arnold, with a cheery smile.

'Don't call me Dick.'

'Just trying to be friendly.' The smile faded.

'Well, don't be friendly, then.' The smile disappeared.

Carlton decided he had better intervene. 'All systems okay, Arnold?'

'What?' snapped the computer.

Carlton sighed, and repeated the question at increased volume, this time getting a response.

'Mind your own business.'

'What?' said Carlton.

'What?' said Arnold.

'WHAT DO YOU MEAN, "MIND YOUR OWN BUSINESS"?'

'I have been told,' said Arnold haughtily, 'not to be friendly. And there is no need to shout.'

Carlton glanced through the port at the shrinking globe of his home planet, containing over two billion women and no Arnolds, and felt the first stirrings of a feeling which was going to become a frequent visitor to him. He should never have come.

'Be friendly, Arnold,' said Bowen. 'Just don't call Richard "Dick". Okay?' Arnold grunted non-committally.

'This misbegotten creature is in charge of the flight, is it?' asked Carlton, who knew perfectly well that it was. He asked quietly, so that Arnold did not hear.

'Arnold has instructions on the first few hundred million miles of the trip,' said Curtis. 'After that time, we shall have to enter new directions into his memory banks. In the unlikely event of there being an emergency, I can, of course, take control from Arnold.'

Bowen allowed a small doubt to enter his mind as to his preference between Curtis and Arnold. The only consolation was that if the ship did have to be controlled manually, it would be Carlton who would fly it. Bowen had rather more faith in Carlton than in the other two. Mind you, he had more faith in Ethel than in those two.

Wilverton was writing his diary. The last book he had read was in diary form, and Scott had kept a diary which had become famous, and so had Pepys, so Wilverton was writing his diary. He looked up at Thompson, who was sitting next to him, and waved his pen in the air. It was an old and fairly ornate fountain pen.

'My mother gave me this pen, you know.'

Thompson looked at the pen, and then at Wilverton, tying to contain his excitement, and replied, 'Really?'

'Yes. It must have been when I was at primary school, I think. Or was it secondary? No, it must have been primary, because I remember getting an ink stain on my knee, which means I must have been wearing short trousers, and I wore long trousers at secondary school. I remember that I was the only one in the class who had a fountain pen. Everyone else had Biros. Some of them were really quite jealous of me.'

'I can imagine.' This could be a very long trip, thought Thompson. He did manage to contain his excitement, and proved it by yawning.

Wilverton noticed, and, being fairly sensitive to such subtle indications, went back to writing his diary, pausing only to ask, 'How many Ls in "wally"?' Thompson smiled thinly.

Carlton decided that it was time he got an answer from Arnold concerning the state of the flight so far. Just a small point, admittedly, but he felt he would like to know if something drastic was about to happen. He planned to get back to the Earth and its contents with as little hassle as possible.

'Are all systems okay, Arnold?' he asked, politely but loudly.

'Well, almost,' responded the computer, swivelling its eyes to look at Carlton, who found the manoeuvre rather disconcerting. Not half as disconcerting as the answer which had accompanied it, however.

'What did you say?' he asked, incredulously.

'I said, "WELL, ALMOST",' Arnold shouted, assuming that Carlton's auditory organs suffered from the same partial malfunction as did his own.

'I heard what you said.' Carlton made a monumental effort to remain calm. 'What, exactly, did you mean by it? Would you please elucidate?'

'We're not going quite as fast as we should be. Given the exact weight of the ship and all its contents, including the crew, of course, my calculations show that we should be travelling exactly four point seven miles per second faster than we actually are.'

'Isn't that within the acceptable error limits?'

'I have no acceptable error limits,' said Arnold imperiously.

'He's right,' said Curtis. 'I programmed the mathematical capabilities myself, remember.' No-one was at all convinced that *that* proved anything. 'We must be carrying more weight than we should.'

'How much more?' asked Bowen, who had one of those nasty feelings in the pit of his stomach.

'One hundred and twenty-five pounds,' Arnold and Curtis duetted.

Bowen tried to imagine what could weigh one hundred and twenty-five pounds. It was not the most challenging of tasks. A female human being would weigh one hundred and twenty-five pounds.

Gloria had rushed from the launch party in tears almost before it had started, after planting a kiss on Curtis that would have unblocked most drains. Curtis had put her reaction down to the fact that he had eaten Cornish pasties for lunch, and that the taste must have lingered. Bowen put it down to the mind-gnawing fact that, for some totally inexplicable reason, Gloria actually fancied the moron.

He would not have minded so much had Gloria not been blessed with the kind of beauty which would make a bishop kick a hole in a stained glass window and then dance on the pieces.

'Can you tell whether there is another life-form aboard this ship, Arnold?' asked Bowen, and repeated the question at the computer's request.

'This isn't the *Enterprise*, you know. I suppose I could look if you insist,' he offered graciously.

'Why do you expect another life-form?' asked Carlton, wondering why they were referring to life-forms, and not people. Had he been asked, Bowen would have replied that all living things were called life-forms in space journeys. He had already seen the film in Arnold's memory banks.

'I would not be surprised to find that there is a young lady by the name of Gloria Parkson on board this ship.'

Curtis looked puzzled. 'Why on Earth would Gloria want to stow away on this ship?'

Bowen looked at him. Only years of experience of this man could make one accept that he really did not know of any reason why his secretary should choose to follow this course of action. He decided that the time had finally come to put him wise, or at least less ignorant.

'Because, for some reason which would baffle the greatest psychological minds of our time, Gloria is madly in love with you. "Madly" being the operative bloody word.'

The insults fell on deaf ears. Curtis could find no mathematical formula to help him deal with the concept of love. He could think of no reason why Big Bill should consider the possibility.

He said as much.

Bowen's eyes wandered upward, and then sideways as the door which led everywhere else opened. In the doorway stood the confirmation of his theory. Or hung, rather, as Gloria gripped the hand holds in an effort to cope with zero gravity, which she had not been fully expecting.

'Gloria!' said Curtis, recognizing her in an instant.

VII

By this time, the theory of relativity predicted that about eighteen months would have passed on Earth, and as if to prove just what a nifty theory if was, it had. Vyland had invited his fellow scientists into his laboratory once more, and again they were crowded round his microwave look-alikes, better known as matter transference devices. In one of these stood a perfect replica of the space-ship *Pioneer*.

The machines now had knobs and dials as well as a switch. Progress. Vyland twiddled the knobs and dials knowledgeably, and threw the switch. The model of the *Pioneer* disappeared from the machine it had formerly occupied, and reappeared instantaneously in the other. It was perfect.

Congratulations were flung around the room like superlatives at an Oscar ceremony, except in this case they were well deserved. Vyland smiled, accepting the plaudits. It was the triumph he had expected, like many others before it and many more to follow. Smarmy git.

Vyland's thoughts then turned briefly to the stars. He doubted that he would be needing it now, but he still had that second string to his bow, just in case. And if the second string did not work, then he had the third string as well, thanks to his programming skills, which were as consummate as all his others. His bow was becoming a veritable horse's tail with all these strings – quite appropriate, really, since most people considered Vyland himself to be a veritable horse's arse.

Curtis let go his hold on the seat, and pushed himself towards his secretary. She saw him, and pushed herself away from the door in an effort to meet him halfway. The others sat strapped in their seats, and watched the aerial ballet being played out above them. Curtis and Gloria only missed each other by slightly more than arm's length, but that was enough. With nothing to stop them, they floated gracefully to opposite sides of the control room, where their momentum was rudely, but effectively, interrupted by the walls. They struggled round, and tried again. Curtis swooped low over Thompson's head like a World War Two Spitfire, only with rather less control.

On their third attempt, the two acrobats managed to link arms, and spun round each other like Fonteyn and Nureyev might have done had they both been lousy at ballet.

'What are you doing here?' asked Curtis, with Bowen's reasoning taking an optimistic hold on his brain. She rewarded his optimism.

'I couldn't leave you! I couldn't bear to see you go out of my life! I love you, Dick!'

'Richard.'

'Sorry. I love you, Richard!'

'Oh, Gloria!' said Curtis.

'Oh, Richard!' said Gloria.

'Oh, Christ!' said Bowen.

Wilverton turned to Thompson, pen poised.

'What bit did she say she loved?'

No-one saw fit to educate him, and a still-life scene held sway in the control room as Gloria's gaze held Curtis's, and the pair of them looked like the centrepiece of a cake with rather too much gooey icing.

This was all Bowen needed. Not only had he ensconced himself in a confined space with a nerd like Curtis, but now he was going to have to suffer a whole month of the asshole learning how to make love – descriptively speaking, that is. It had been bad enough at the Research Centre when she traipsed after him with eyes like Bambi on learning that its mother wasn't dead after all, but at least Bowen had only had to suffer that during working hours.

Long working hours, of course, as he dedicated himself to his job and was thereby forced to sacrifice the time he might spend at home with his family. Long working hours during which he watched Gloria from afar, and from anear whenever he got the chance, at which times he smiled at her with his most attractive smile and she smiled back occasionally with the apparent warmth of summer on Neptune. Long hours when there was never a sign that the gorgeous creature found him any more appealing than a traffic accident.

Bowen scowled.

Carlton didn't. Carlton waited to catch her eye, when his most familiar expression would shine at her like the sweet-smelling sunrise of a summer day after gentle overnight rain had freshened the whole earth. It was a good expression, which would have made Carlton rich had he been able to bottle and sell it. As he had in fact only been able to wear it, it had simply made him very popular, and often tired.

Carlton waited, expectantly.

Thompson looked on impassively. Time and place, and all that, and this was neither. It was he, therefore, who disrupted an atmosphere which threatened to become cloyingly emotional.

'We'll have to turn back.'

'What!' said a now upside-down Curtis, whose senses were

still grappling with the fact that love had at last come his way.

Thompson sighed, wondering if every bloody thing on this ship was going to say 'what' or 'sorry' whenever anyone said anything. He repeated his statement while the Captain manoeuvred himself so that 'up' meant the same for him as for his crew.

Curtis looked at Thompson, and moved his jaw up and down a couple of times, hoping that his brain would find something to push out of the hole explaining why they could not turn back. No sound emerged, though, tempting Thompson to say 'what' or 'sorry', but he was in no mood for anything even remotely amusing. Curtis's impression of a goldfish continued, but now he started to move his head back and forth as well, looking at various members of the crew for inspiration. He got some from Wilverton, but not the kind he wanted.

'Absolutely right. We will have to turn back immediately.'

Carlton said nothing. He could see that an extra passenger could cause trouble, and that they really should turn back and hand her over to the authorities. But something at the back of his mind, and various other parts of his anatomy for that matter, wanted to keep her on board.

The wilting stare from Bowen finally took its toll of Curtis. He wilted.

'Arnold,' he said morosely, 'turn the ship round.'

It is not possible to talk morosely and loudly at the same time.

'Sorry?'

'TURN THE BLOODY SHIP ROUND!' yelled Bowen.

'No can do, I'm afraid.'

No-one said anything, or anything that Arnold heard anyway, but they were all staring at him, so he continued.

'My orders for the first two days of this trip are irrevocable. Apart from taking evasive action in the event of asteroids or meteorites, I am to stay on this pre-set course. I am instructed to warn you that any attempt to disconnect me will result in the shorting-out of one of the main circuits of the primary drive mechanism, and its back-up systems, which will mean that the nuclear explosions are no longer contained within a magnetic field. The results of that are fairly straight-forward.'

Arnold finished with a cheery smile and fell silent. Then his eyes started swivelling around the control room, searching for some reaction, hoping that he might be able to lip-read any questions that were put to him. As it turned out, he did not have to lip-read, as Bowen's question was not so much put to him as flung at him, accompanied by a look which should have melted a few of his circuits.

'Professor Vyland has programmed me,' said Arnold, searching his memory for an accurate description of some of the terms used by Bowen, and finding that the meaning did not make the question any clearer. He could not remember stating that Professor Vyland was indulging in sexual intercourse, for example.

Mention of programming banished the thoughts. The phrase was not one that Arnold was wont to use. He had been able to resist most of Curtis's attempts to put orders inside his head, but Vyland had proved to be a different matter. Very different.

'He also asked me to point out, should the necessity for such explanation ever arise, that he is sorry about whatever predicament it is in which you find yourselves.'

Arnold looked directly at Curtis, who was frowning in perplexity at this point. Vyland had known that Curtis would be frowning in perplexity at this point, and had specifically programmed Arnold to look at him whilst explaining. Nice touch.

'For you to be contemplating turning back,' continued the computer, 'you must be in some sort of trouble. Therefore, Professor Vyland wishes you the best of luck in finding another solution.' Another cheery smile accompanied this friendly gesture.

Bowen's gesture wasn't at all friendly, and he suggested that Professor Vyland's parents had exhibited tardiness in their application for a marriage licence. He also said that he would do something even nastier to Vyland's face than God had already done – he was good at insults. Then he said he'd kill him.

'The Professor, as a final comment,' continued Arnold when Bowen's mouth had stopped moving, 'says that if you do turn back after the two days are up, then you will be wasting your time. The time dilation affect would be quite large enough to ensure that, by the time you arrived back on Earth, the statute of limitations would have run out on any crime which Professor Vyland might have committed. He wished you all "Bon voyage". Says it's French.'

There was no sound for a long time, as they all contemplated Vyland's message. Finally, the Captain of the *Pioneer* broke the silence. In a pained voice, he said, 'I knew it was French.' He was ignored.

'It looks like Gloria will have to stay,' said Carlton, trying to effect a tone which suggested regret at the situation. The thought seemed to cheer Curtis almost as much, and he glanced at Gloria, who smiled back shyly. Carlton turned up the volume. 'Will it affect the flight adversely, Arnold?'

'Apparently not,' replied the computer, with a half-imagined twitch of one eyebrow. He was of course referring to his ability to increase the ship's speed by the required amount, and not to any human weaknesses of which he could have no knowledge.

'I'm going to bed,' said Bowen. 'The Captain can sort this one out.' The title was delivered with respect in the same way as third-class mail is delivered with alacrity. Curtis was too caught up in his thoughts to notice.

Bowen left his seat and made for the door, pushing off from the floor with his arms held in front of him, and looking for all the world like a beer-gutted middle-aged Superman in civvies. The idea apparently had universal appeal, as they all followed, turning Superman into the opening scenes of Peter Pan.

Thompson decided to begin his bee experiment, or to put it another way, to begin the experiment with his bee. Singular. There were rules, apparently, which prevented any unnecessary mass being brought on board, and Thompson's plans for a small hive had had to be shelved on the orders of the Captain. It probably would not have made all that much difference, since bees as a rule are not the weightiest of creatures, or in zero gravity the massiest of creatures, but Curtis was so chuffed at finding someone who was actually prepared to obey his rules that he stuck by it.

So Thompson had brought – with permission – Abercrom, along with sufficient flora to keep his dietary needs satisfied during the month-long flight. Or *her* dietary needs. Thompson was not too sure how you told one from the other where bees were concerned. He could always watch to see which toilet it went into, he supposed with a smile as he pulled himself along the corridor on the way to his cabin.

This zero gravity was fun, he thought, as his arms used hardly any effort at all, and he had that feeling you sometimes get in dreams that you can float for ever between footsteps. Fun for humans, at least. How would Abercrom be faring? he wondered.

Fun for bees as well, by the look of it as he entered and crossed to the plastic container which was Abercrom bee's apartment for the duration. Abercrom pushed himself off one wall with his rear pair of legs – and did so with more grace than Bowen had mustered minutes before – and floated across the space to a flower. Looking closely, Thompson could swear that the front pair of legs were making little breast-stroke motions.

Wilverton hung in the cocoon on the wall of his cabin, wide awake. Cocoons were little more than insulated sacks but were necessary for sleeping, so that the slumberer did not do himself any damage by floating about during the night. There was no danger of that in Wilverton's case, because he was very unlikely to sleep as long as Arnold was reading him a story, which was precisely what Arnold was doing at that moment.

From a small loudspeaker in the wall next to the cocoon came the description of how an ordinary farmer's nephew had managed to get himself caught up in the battle between the evil Galactic Empire and the good rebels. He was trying to save the beautiful Princess from a fate worse than death. Wilverton had no doubt that he would succeed in his endeavour, but that did not lessen the excitement when the odds looked impossible. At the end of the chapter, Arnold paused, and Wilverton sighed.

'Why doesn't anything exciting happen in real life, Arnold?' he mused, speaking into a microphone just a few inches away, next to the loudspeaker. The position of the microphone was fortunate, as high-decibel musings do lose some whimsy.

'I think it depends on who you are,' Arnold replied.

'Well, nobody I've met has ever seemed particularly excited.'

'Odd, that, isn't it.'

Wilverton sighed again. 'No, I don't suppose it is, really, Arnold. Carry on, please.'

Arnold carried on, describing the battle between the rebels and the giant space station of the Empire, which the former could not possibly win, and plainly would.

Wilverton forgot his plea for excitement as he lost himself once more in the plot; or what there was of it. Arnold did not. Whilst one part of his positronic brain was controlling his audio output, another was grappling with the problem.

Grappling with the problem was precisely what Curtis and Gloria were doing in the cabin next door. There had not been an extra cabin on the *Pioneer*, and there had not been an extra cocoon, either. Arnold had the ingredients to synthesize food and drink but not, apparently, cabins or cocoons, so Curtis had gallantly insisted that Gloria share both of his, while thoughts ran through his head which had nothing whatever to do with the amount of space which would be left when both of them were occupying the same cocoon. An understandable oversight, in the circumstances, but one which he would have done well not to overlook.

There was *no* room inside the cocoon once two people were in it. They could not move; not even a little, unfortunately. They had to breathe alternately, or not at all. It was not going to work. The cocoon would have to be abandoned, and abandon it they did.

Once the cocoon had been vacated, however, they had to face the problems of zero gravity, and even for a well co-ordinated person those problems were considerable. For Curtis, whose co-ordination was akin to that of Pinocchio immediately after the strings had been cut, the problems were insurmountable. So, therefore, was Gloria. Curtis reached the morning a very frustrated, and considerably bruised, man. 'Man' not conveying the exact meaning Curtis had hoped it would.

For Gloria's part, the illusions she had conjured in her mind over the time she had worshipped Curtis from afar now resembled crystal chandeliers after an earthquake which would have rendered Richter inadequately numerate.

VIII

The next day dawned with a surprising amount of good humour abounding on board the *Pioneer*, although in Curtis's case that would be a bit of an exaggeration – a-stepping maybe; the looks he was getting from Gloria this morning didn't really help. It was certainly an exaggeration in Bowen's case, but then good humour was generally engendered in Big Bill only when something septic happened to a family member.

After the strain of the build-up to the launch and the event itself, the feeling that they were finally under way lifted the pressure, and the tiredness of the previous night had in most cases been slept to refreshment.

Curtis *was* getting the hang of the zero gravity though, meaning that he headed in the right direction once out of every four attempts, which was a vast improvement, and hardly ever hit anyone hard enough to hurt them, and the best bit about it was that he didn't feel sick, which had been one of his worries – one of many; Curtis was an expert on worries and owned one of the world's largest collections. The thought that he might spend well over eight hundred years vomiting was not one which held great attraction. And it doesn't if you think about it.

Despite falling three quick thrusts and an embarrassed apology short of manhood, Curtis was therefore becoming quite jolly, especially when Gloria reluctantly agreed to sit on his lap, and he even tried to join his crew in friendly banter. When he found the door locked on that particular corridor of pleasure he plucked a hand-held computer game which chose that moment to drift past his face, and tossed it at Thompson.

'Catch!' he said, to the top of Thompson's head, while the front concentrated for a moment on the crossword on his lap.

'Danny!'

Thompson looked up just in time to see the corner of the game out of the corner of his eye, and then into the corner of his eye.

'Er, sorry,' said Curtis, as Thompson raised and kept his hand over the now seeping cut and glared with one-eyed disdain at his excuse for a Captain. The others used both eyes to do exactly the same thing.

'Here, let's get that cleaned up,' said Curtis, who had seen hundreds of situations just like this. He handed Gloria to Carlton, then managed, with only a few false lunges, to pull himself round the hand-holds to the door, helping Thompson as he went, and hitting him against the door jamb on his way out.

Carlton caught Gloria, and planted an expert kiss on her lips. Gloria caught her breath, and looked closely at Carlton. She had not really given him more than passing notice the previous day, occupied as she was with Curtis, but that occupation was not quite so full-time this morning, for one reason or another.

He had ever such nice features, she now realized, especially those deep brown eyes, and he was holding her in arms that promised much more power than they were using. Not that she wanted to be unkind to Richard, but the comparison was inevitable. And that smile!

Carlton's eyes held a strange expression, rather like a lion when he sees a deer limping. He treated her to another kiss. Without meaning to, Gloria found herself comparing the kiss with the ones she had received the night before – which for the most part had been like those of a baby grouper with a runny nose – and then a strange look came into her eyes, rather like a deer with a death wish. All her illusions came rushing back, wearing a different face. It was one which smiled confidently at her.

The exact programming supplied by Vyland meant that the Professor knew, for the first two days of the trip, at least, exactly where the ship would be, and Arnold, taking into account the slight discrepancy induced by the presence of Gloria, had made sure that was exactly where it was.

The scientists were crowded round the large window of Vyland's new office. In the one 'microwave' which now remained stood, again, the model of the *Pioneer*. The faces of the scientists held a unanimous expression of almost child-like excitement.

They all gazed at a marked spot in the middle of the well-manicured lawns outside the office, while in the distance a metallic figure bent over a garden hoe, straightening the edges of the flower beds with a precision no human gardener could hope to achieve. Vyland twiddled his knobs and turned his dials. He threw the switch.

On the outside of the ship, close to one of the hatches, which contained mineral-gathering equipment, materialized a perfect replica model of the space-ship *Pioneer*. Arnold had been expecting it. Out of sight of the crew, a mechanical arm had already extended itself to the exact spot, and, as the model arrived, the top two centimetres were expertly sheared off by the pincers which, on this occasion, constituted the arm's fingers. One second later, the model disappeared, and the arm retracted, with no-one having seen it.

48

Had they seen it, it would have been a dead giveaway that something was going on.

But they hadn't.

So it wasn't.

There was a pause of several minutes, while the machine in front of Vyland stood empty, and then, on the lawn, in precisely the place marked, appeared a perfect replica of the space-ship *Pioneer*, with the top two centimetres neatly sheared off. The scientists were awe-struck.

Vyland smiled, and gave a small shrug. The years had not made him any more endearing, and it wouldn't have been difficult.

Curtis had returned to the control room and a cool reception – anything else would have felt very peculiar to Curtis – and Thompson, with a sticking plaster on one eye and a resigned expression on the other, followed him at a safe and unaided distance. Captain Quicksilver immediately determined that the position of Gloria was a cause for concern, to himself if not, apparently, to her. She was still sitting on Carlton's lap, and his arms were twined around her waist. Why was that?

'Why are you sitting on his lap?' he asked Gloria, who looked slightly troubled by the question, mainly because the answer, which she knew well enough, was not the kind she wanted to put into words.

'I'm keeping her safe from you,' Carlton told him, a touch nastily, inadvertently solving Gloria's problem. Curtis glared at him, but he had a long way to go where glares were concerned, and Carlton didn't shrivel up. Nor did he release Gloria. Nor did Gloria show any signs of wanting to be released.

Curtis supposed it was not altogether surprising. Still, she had said that she loved him – Curtis, not Carlton – so it must be all right, because he knew that she would not lie to him. Would she? The door to his worry bank opened hungrily, but . . . no, not Gloria.

His trust was stretched to the limit, and a little bit beyond, when, after swapping small talk – so small that Curtis's straining ears could not understand the words – and even participating in the two-player game on Curtis's computer weapon, Carlton later proceeded to take Gloria to his cabin to show her his collection of stamps.

No, really. Carlton did have a collection of stamps, bought a few days before the *Pioneer* had taken off. When he got back, they would be over eight hundred years old, and in mint condition. No fool, Carlton.

Curtis watched them make their way across the control room, and noticed with some annoyance that Carlton had to 'help' Gloria on several occasions. He floated over to Bowen, and, in his agitation, completed the manoeuvre perfectly.

49

'Did you see that?' he hissed. 'He put his arm round Gloria three times.'

Bowen shook his head. 'Don't be stupid. His arm's not that long.'

It took Carlton a little over half an hour to show Gloria his collection of stamps. When they returned, it was obvious that stamps had a strange effect on Gloria. They made her very flushed, and caused her to look at the ground and giggle a lot, in an embarrassed sort of way. Carlton must have been very fond of stamps, because they clearly made him very happy. They made Curtis furious, and turned him a funny shade of purple, mixed with green. And he hadn't even seen them.

Curtis immediately determined to get even, and to get Gloria back. He was not very experienced in these matters, and wondered if some sort of duel was the way it was supposed to be done. He glanced at his own body, and then at Carlton's muscular frame, and decided that was not the way it was supposed to be done. It would be a little like David and Goliath, only with the latter having the sling. A pity it had not been Wilverton who had stolen Gloria, he thought.

Then it came to him. He was the Captain; he could order people to do things. A smile spread across his face; a little secret smile that everyone saw immediately. He would wait a while so that nobody would suspect what he was doing.

Wilverton looked back down to his diary, and then looked up again.

'How many "T"'s in prat?' he asked.

That's funny, thought Curtis, breaking off from his plan for a second. You'd think Wilverton would know how to spell, wouldn't you?

Bowen turned his attention back to the game of Scrabble he was playing with Arnold. He was getting rapidly bored with it, largely thanks to the fact that he was getting soundly thrashed. The arm extended from the wall beneath Arnold's shelf, and added a 'Z' and an 'E' to an existing 'L'.

'Zel. Triple letter score, thirty-two points. Your go.'

'What the bloody hell is a zel?' rhymed Bowen.

'It's a form of Oriental cymbal.' Arnold's tone suggested that anyone who did not know what a 'zel' was must have an IQ which started with a decimal point.

Bowen did not argue; he had long since given that up as a waste of breath. Instead, he added a 'C' and a 'K' onto the 'LO' which he had previously put down, and looked pleased with himself.

'Lock. Ten points.' Arnold said nothing. His eyes swivelled down to the letters held magnetically onto a rack in front of him, and the arm moved towards them. He added an 'E' and an 'X' to the 'K' on the metallic board.

'Kex.' He did not wait for Bowen to ask. 'The dry stalk of the hemlock or other umbelliferous plants. Double word score, twenty-eight points.'

'Smart arse,' muttered Bowen.

'Sorry?'

'Nothing.' An evil grin spread across Bowen's face, and he added 'B', 'O', 'L' to his 'LOCK'.

'Fifteen.'

Arnold immediately reached for his letters and added an 'S'.

'Triple word score, forty-eight.'

'Er, Carlton,' said Curtis, obviously having just thought of something. Carlton looked up in mild inquiry. 'You might have to fly the ship for a while tomorrow, while I re-program Arnold. I think it might be best if you get an early night.' He smiled in what he thought might be a concerned way. Carlton glanced at Gloria, and winked. She gave him an uncertain smile in response.

'I think you're probably right, sir,' he said, wondering whether to salute, or touch a forelock, and deciding against it. 'Off I go, then.' He pulled himself to the door, and left obediently. He even climbed into his cocoon when he reached his cabin, where he hung quite contentedly, waiting for a visitor. He smiled when he heard Curtis and Gloria passing his cabin door together a little while later.

They were preceded by Thompson with a two-game headache. The first was the one with which Curtis had assaulted him, and the second was the Scrabble, one of the rules of which was now apparently that you had loudly to abuse your opponent between each go. The conversation of Abercrom was far more appealing, he had intimated on his way out.

But Abercrom can't talk, Curtis pointed out, showing off his education.

Precisely, Thompson had responded, with a smile as wide as an emaciated wafer.

In the rapidly emptying control room, the game of Scrabble continued. That the words came from the same language as had been used by Shakespeare and Wordsworth would have been distressing to someone more sensitive than the protagonists.

Bowen picked up the word 'HIT' and added it to a letter already on the board. Arnold glared at him. Bowen glared back. This kind of game he had only ever lost to Ethel, whose language would make a trooper blush. Arnold added 'tah' to the new word.

'Shouldn't that be "ER"?' asked Bowen.

'Shittah is a tree whose durable wood was used in the construction of the Jewish Tabernacle and its furniture.'

Bowen's eyes narrowed. The trick when Scrabble got to this level was to make sure you reached the stage where you could get away with putting absolutely anything down, so long as it was reasonably pronounceable, in the knowledge that it was not going to be challenged for one of two reasons. Either the opponent would not ask you to explain because being a sexually aware and liberated adult they should know what it meant anyway, or else because your explanations so far had left them in such a state that if they did not understand something, the last thing they wanted you to do *was* to explain it.

Bowen picked up some letters and arranged them on the board in a confident manner, but maintaining the evil leering sort of expression that is supposed to tell anyone watching that you are being deliberately disgusting. Arnold stared at him, then stared at the board, but said nothing.

Inwardly Bowen grinned. That's got the little junk heap!

Arnold thought momentarily and then added his own word, utilizing one of Bowen's recent letters. Bowen frowned.

'What does that mean?' he asked. Arnold explained at length and in detail. Bowen felt his stomach turn over. 'Does it? Good grief,' he said, showing just how shocked he was. 'With an avocado?'

'It's not as fattening that way,' Arnold told him by way of confirmation. Bowen swallowed hard. He stared at his letters and tried to concentrate, then forced the demonic grin back onto his face and put two more letters down to make something that sounded like an exclamation. Arnold merely stared at it for a second before linking its initial letter to a triple word square with some more unlikely consonants.

'And what's that?' asked Bowen automatically, before the memory of the last explanation could stop him. Arnold started explaining in the verbal equivalent of the technicolour used to tint a triple-X-rated movie. 'All right, all right, I believe you!' Bowen said quickly, and started looking for a word like cloud, to settle his stomach.

Inwardly, Arnold grinned. That's got the fat human!

Wilverton looked up from his book and noticed that the two were still playing Scrabble, having been too engrossed to notice the conversation. Wilverton liked Scrabble. He floated across.

'Mind if I join in?' he asked. Bowen pointed to one of the words on the board which he had understood since puberty, and he went away again.

Bed, Wilverton decided. That was where everyone else was.

And he was right, but they were no longer in the formation they had adopted when leaving the control room an hour before.

Gloria had excused herself for natural reasons, and Curtis hung happily in his cocoon, waiting for her return. He could not quite believe how easy it had been. Gloria was back with him, and he was sure that she loved him, despite the fact that she had resisted his advances without a hint of the passion which must be burning inside her. So much for Carlton!

'Richard!' The voice rang out in Curtis's cabin, and Curtis found that there was enough room in the cocoon for his stomach, at least, to turn over. The voice sounded sort of ethereal, and, loud though it was, as though it came from a long way off. It also sounded uncomfortably like that of his father, or at least how he supposed his father's voice might sound if it were a long way off and had been dead for quite a long time.

'Hello?' he said, quietly.

'Is that you, Richard?'

'Er.' He tried to think. Was it him? 'Er. Yes. Yes, I think so. Who is that?'

'You don't recognize my voice?'

'Er. Is that you, F . . . father?'

'Of course!'

'Daddy!' There was a catch in his voice. 'Daddy, I'm sorry I killed you! It was an awful accident.'

'So are you, Richard, so are you.' The voice certainly spoke like his father, anyway. 'You are a disaster looking for somewhere to happen, and you frequently find it. And don't call me Daddy.'

'Yes. I mean no, Father.' Curtis squirmed uncomfortably, there not being any other way to squirm. Talking to his dead father was almost as difficult as talking to the live one. 'It wasn't entirely my fault, Father. You know I couldn't have hung those curtains all by myself.'

'Why on Earth not?'

'Well, it's the curly bits at the top. I've never been very good with my hands.'

'They managed all right when you pushed me out of the window!'

'I didn't mean to push you, Father.' Curtis was making his earlier squirm look like a cat's exuberant stretch. 'I just sort of fell against you. I was only trying to help.'

'You're a prat, Richard.'

'Yes, Father.' There didn't seem a great deal of point in arguing. Not a shred of the evidence was on his side. He paused while the memories queued up in his head. 'I have missed you, Father.' The catch was back.

'Shame you didn't miss me at the vital moment,' the voice told him. It didn't help his guilt any. Then his eyes started watering, and that was something his father would never allow. He had to change the subject.

'How's the weather?' he asked.

'Cloudy.'

'Oh, dear.'

'What do you mean "oh dear"? If it wasn't cloudy, we wouldn't have anything to sit on, would we?'

'No, I suppose not,' said Curtis, trying to imagine his father sitting on a cloud and playing a harp, and not really succeeding.

It seemed to have helped a little bit as his eyes were not threatening to become small waterfalls – or cataracts. He could bring the conversation back to what he really needed. Another pause, then:

'Do you forgive me, Father? I'd feel ever so much better if you did. I really was only trying to help.'

He had always wanted to please his father. It was largely why he was here now, he thought, because his father had wanted him to conquer space. Actually his father would have settled for getting him off the face of the Earth, but he wasn't completely wrong.

There was a short silence, as if someone were thinking.

'I'll forgive you if you'll do something for me, Richard. And it's for your own good anyway.'

'Anything, Father.'

'Don't tempt me.'

'Sorry, Father.'

'It's that girl, Gloria. She's no good for you, boy.'

'Well, not yet, Father, but – '

'Not ever, Richard. Listen to me.' Curtis listened.

So did Carlton and Gloria. In Carlton's cabin, where Gloria was supposedly answering the call of nature, and in fact was, in a way, the two of them were snuggled neatly into the cocoon, which Carlton's muscles had managed to stretch where Curtis's lack of same had failed. The disguised voice of the computer was a little quieter than in Curtis's room, and Carlton had instructed Arnold that, during this role-playing, it was only to be heard in those two cabins. With a bit of luck, Curtis would be throwing Gloria at him by the time Arnold had finished. It all depended on Curtis's stupidity, and Carlton knew that he certainly could. Depend on Curtis's stupidity.

'I'm not sure I like this,' said Gloria quietly.

Carlton looked surprised. 'But you said it would be easier if Curtis wasn't jealous. This way he won't be jealous.'

Gloria looked almost as uncomfortable as when she had been in this position with Curtis. 'I know, but that was for Richard's own good. I didn't want him to feel bad, and I still don't. It's not really fair on him this way, is it; fooling him like this?'

What a big-hearted girl she was, thought Carlton. Big in every organ department, come to think of it.

'Sometimes you have to be cruel to be kind, and no-one else knows what's happening. It *is* for his own good in the end.' Gloria looked at him for a few moments, weighing his words and trying to find an alternative to their actions. She couldn't. 'It'll be all right,' Carlton told her, with a reassuring squeeze of her hand. 'You'll see.' Gloria was nice, he thought, she was considerate, and he liked her. That was good, because they would be together for a whole month, and he wouldn't have to pretend.

'I suppose so,' she sighed uneasily, and they listened again.

'We spirits can see a little way into the future,' said Arnold, 'and I can

54

see no good coming from that girl. When you get back to Earth, there are going to be thousands of women all throwing themselves at you. Beautiful women who would do anything for a hero from outer space. If you are with her, then you will get none of the others. Take my advice, Richard, and let her go.'

Curtis considered. It seemed a shame, but if that was what his father thought . . . Carlton gave Gloria a little squeeze.

'Are you sure, Father?' he asked, quietly sad.

'Sorry?'

Carlton and Gloria proved that there was enough room in a cocoon, albeit stretched, for two stomachs to turn over. But Curtis had not noticed the tell-tale deafness.

'I said, "Are you sure?" '

'Oh, yes, quite sure. No doubt about it.'

'And you forgive me?'

'I suppose so. It's sort of in the rules up here, anyway.'

Curtis brightened, grudging forgiveness being better than no forgiveness at all. 'I'll do what you say, then, Father.'

'Good boy. Goodbye, Richard.'

'Goodbye, Father.'

Carlton and Gloria hugged each other in congratulation, the former more enthusiastically than the latter.

Arnold's instructions were only for the actual conversation, so he was not disobeying when his voice then rang out in every cabin on the ship.

'How was that, Peter? He certainly fell for it. He must be as gullible as you said he was!' And in the control room, Arnold smiled diabolically to himself.

IX

By the time the *Pioneer* had been travelling at full speed for about thirty-six hours, and Curtis had fallen into a fitful doze following Arnold's Carlton-induced prank, Vyland was the white-haired and stooped old man walking slowly across a launch pad at one of the space stations on Earth. The station was not big, and there was very little space between the ship and the buildings. Not much was needed. When this ship took off, there would be no flare of burning fuel from rockets to scorch anything around it. In fact, it would not take off at all in the way the phrase is normally used. This ship would simply disappear, and re-materialize somewhere else in the Galaxy, many light years away, and it didn't need to sit in a giant microwave and get sent, because all the mechanics were contained within it.

Clever stuff.

But then whatever people thought of Vyland – and that ranged from evil all the way up to pretty damned nasty – they had to admit that he was quite bright.

He paused at the steps of the craft, and looked up at it. It had taken slightly longer to perfect than he had promised some sixty years before, but now he had made it. Vyland allowed a self-satisfied grin to spread across his face as he climbed the steps. The expression had become his trade-mark.

This was its first manned flight, and the press had clamoured for any available view. Vyland had constructed enough barriers to ensure there were none. Not that it was to be a secret; he just enjoyed annoying them.

He made his way to a seat at the rear of the control room, next to a large window, through which he could see the metal buildings of the station glinting in the mid-morning sunlight. Across an expanse of grassland he could see the massive sun collection centre, one of those where the solar system's most plentiful resource was turned into the cheap power which ran just about everything on the planet. Outside it, the nuclear fuel workers' picket seemed smaller today.

The odd robotic menial wandered about the place; or not so odd now that its caricature of the human gait had become a commonplace sight. Its red eyes no longer held any hint of danger, as they had when they were first turned on a public whose inbred phobia lurked just beneath the surface; a public presumably convinced that because Mary Shelley had written *Frankenstein*, fifty-eight years before the first internal combustion engine was patented, it had to be true. How times had changed, he thought smugly. How people – other people, that is – had not!

He looked to the pilot, whose own red eyes were turned away from him, and a brief doubt crossed his mind as to the accuracy of his calculations, but brief was the operative word. The doubt recognized that it was completely out of place in Vyland's mind, and sulked off somewhere else, apologetically. Vyland's self-satisfied grin spread a little further.

The pilot turned, nodded in response to a vague but permission-granting wave of Vyland's hand, speedily tapped in the instructions to the command computer and pressed a small button on the console in front of him.

Vyland felt nothing, and could not say whether any time had passed. The only difference was that the building had disappeared, to be replaced by a huge globe, a blue-green planet which looked so much like Earth that someone with less confidence than Vyland would have thought that they had travelled merely to an orbit around their own home.

But it was not Earth. It was a planet circling a star known as Alcyone, and he was the first one to visit it. If Vyland's self-satisfied grin had spread any further, the top of his head would have fallen off.

He looked back in the direction of Sol, of the Earth. They were still out there somewhere, maybe, he thought to himself. Surely they would have lasted a few days, even with Captain Moron in command.

It seemed incredible that after their two-week trip, this planet would have been occupied for over three hundred years; incredible but immensely satisfying.

But of course they would not get there, he remembered. They would get to within a few parsecs, and then the computer would fulfil its programming.

He nodded.

And if one or more of them *was* incredibly lucky and did actually arrive, the victory would still be his. They would find his proxy there, just ahead of them.

Over the years, he had wondered why he had done it. He remembered thinking that not only must he beat them; he must stop them. But he had not recognized the thought as being his own. And yet he had acted on it immediately.

Why had he done that?

Vyland would have hated the answer.

He paused a while, surveying the new planet, and letting the planet survey him, recognizing that it was a singular honour for the both of them, then motioned the pilot to make the second port of call in their trip round the Galaxy.

He wanted to materialize his ship in such a place that the *Pioneer*, should it have survived the worst that Curtis could do so far, would streak past it on the way to Alcyone. The ultra-fast camera had been prepared to capture the ship on film as she flashed past at near light speed.

The robot programmed the correct co-ordinates into the computer, while the passenger settled himself back in his chair, sighed a contented sigh and nodded once more to his pilot. The co-ordinates were perfect, again, naturally, and the ship appeared at a point in space past which the *Pioneer* would streak in a little under ten minutes' time.

It was a rotten piece of luck, really, because that particular point in space was also juxtaposed by a bloody great black hole about which even Vyland could have known nothing.

Black holes do not sound like too much bad news, the name suggesting just empty space, with a possibility of falling. Unfortunately for Vyland, they are very far from empty; in fact, they have so much matter crammed into them that they are, in many ways, the exact opposite of empty. The gravitational attraction of all that matter is so strong that even light cannot travel fast enough to escape, hence the blackness, and the bit about falling.

The fall will definitely have a landing though, and a harder landing than anywhere else in the Universe. There is a school of thought that says you won't actually hit anything, but will emerge somewhere else in the Universe through a white hole, unscathed and smelling of daisies.

This is not the sort of school to which you want to send your children.

No sooner, therefore, had Vyland's ship materialized, than it was pulled violently from the position where it was supposed to hang in restful expectation.

The robotic pilot immediately bent to the controls, panic not something to which his positronic mind was readily subject, which was probably just as well; it is a well-documented fact that any pilot who runs up and down his craft waving his arms about and screaming 'We're all going to die!' at the top of a cracking voice is almost invariably right.

Vyland was human, or very nearly, but his range of reaction stretched from calm acceptance of a situation to irritated dismissal of it. Vyland was not one to be overawed by any possible fate which faced him, because he was supremely confident that he could outsmart fate.

As the space-ship completely failed to respond to the pilot's urgings, it looked like fate was about ready to take Vyland on, and as gravity sucked the craft ever faster towards its welcoming squelch, it began to look like it might win.

Vyland glanced down at the instrument panel on his right, set into the arm of his chair, and punched in a few commands. Is there anything nearby apart from this black hole? he asked the console. Yes there is, the console answered back.

You jammy bugger.

Ah, but how are you going to get there? asked fate, with the grin of anticipated victory still on its lips.

Vyland turned his attention to the device attached to his waist band, and copied into it the co-ordinates suggested by his chair arm.

As he reached for the button, so the black hole finally claimed the ship, and all around them were scintillating flashes of light as the photons frantically – photons can't help being frantic – strove to escape from their prison, and failed.

As Vyland pressed the button, a scream of panic finally emerged from the craft.

The robot had cracked.

The atmosphere on board the space-ship *Pioneer* at that fateful moment could have been better. Carlton and Gloria sat quietly together, not talking. Bowen sat hunched over an electronic dictionary, learning all the words which contained 'Q' and no 'U', whilst in front of him the Scrabble board proudly displayed the results of the last game. On Earth it would have been seized by the obscene publications people.

Wilverton was writing his diary. He was in a foul mood, thanks to the fact that his fountain pen had run out of ink, and while he was attempting to refill it, Curtis had knocked the ink bottle over, and had managed to get most of the contents out; no easy task in zero gravity. Wilverton was therefore using a Biro, and was copying some of the words from the Scrabble board.

Thompson looked at his journal, reading an article for the man in the street – or the man on Earth at least, whether in a street or not – describing life on a space-ship. It even talked about the camaraderie between the crew members, which, it said, was critical to the success of the mission. He glanced around him. We might as well turn back now, he thought.

Curtis was sitting in the Captain's chair, which seemed to be the only way left for him to make the statement, glaring alternately at Carlton, Gloria and Arnold. Especially Arnold. How this *machine* – and the tone suggested that the word was a synonym for something emerging from a dog's bottom – whom he had honoured by making it look like his father could repay him by doing something like that, he simply did not know.

With no trouble at all, would have been the answer had he felt constrained actually to ask.

For his part, Arnold managed, just, and wisely, not to smirk.

The air was liberally interspersed with little blue globules of ink, and was therefore almost the same colour as when Curtis came in and told Carlton exactly what he thought of his merry little jape.

'I wasn't fooled, you know!' he pointed out coldly.

'I never thought you would be,' Carlton responded, as a small blue wobble drifted past his nose on its way up to the ceiling, where it wouldn't be bothered. Curtis stared at Carlton and wished that the cutting response you always thought of two days after you've had the argument would, just this once, come to him when he needed it, but his mind's sheath remained stubbornly empty, as it had since birth.

Gloria looked guiltily from Curtis to Carlton and back, and back again, but said nothing. By way of a diversion she watched a blue mother wobble with a string of blue baby wobbles following it.

'Ten minutes to go, everyone,' said Arnold.

At the end of that time, the computer would no longer be in charge of the ship until Curtis had reprogrammed it. Carlton would have to fly for a while. It was probably just as well, because it would give them all something to do.

They did not have to wait that long, in the event. After a couple of minutes had passed in stony silence, Arnold spoke again.

'We're being pulled off course!' Wilverton looked up sharply – this sounded more like it. 'I can't see anything, but there must be a strong gravity well somewhere around. Very strong. It must be a black hole!'

'I can't feel anything,' said Bowen. When you were pulled off course in a space-ship, everyone in the control room lurched over to one side and had to grab hold of something; *everyone* knew that!

'By the time you *can* feel something, it's going to be way too late,' Arnold informed him encouragingly. By way of confirmation, one of the numbers on the console in front of Carlton, and in Bowen's line of sight, began flashing a nice warm red colour.

Bowen's stomach lurched over to one side, and a cold hand grabbed hold of it.

The crew should have been in safe hands because the computer should have pulled the craft out of the increasing gravitational field before it got too strong, since Arnold was a very advanced computer, with instantaneous reactions and unerring knowledge of what to do in such circumstances. Unfortunately, what Arnold actually did was to panic and yell:

'Somebody do something!'

Wilverton was writing furiously. Couldn't be better.

Whenever a crisis occurs in life, a great tragedy which requires strength of character and incisive action, there always seems to be someone who comes to the rescue, showing hitherto unguessed depths of resolve, showing that rare quality of leadership in adversity; someone who takes command in an instant and who dominates the situation by imposing his will on it, and who solves the problems in a split second of unnatural calm.

They couldn't half have done with someone like that on the *Pioneer*.

'Give me control, Arnold,' said Carlton. Perhaps they did have someone after all.

'WHAT?' shrieked the computer. The *Pioneer* veered further towards the black hole.

'Give me control! Now!' He forced his voice to be calm and authoritative, and was aware of Gloria's big blue eyes boring into him. Not that the latter influenced the former.

'I can't. Not for another seven minutes and forty-three seconds.'

'How long before the gravity becomes too strong for us to be able to escape?' Carlton shouted. Arnold was good at maths. Curtis would have answered as well had he not been holding his breath.

'Six minutes and twelve seconds.'

'Magic!'

'We could do with some,' said Bowen, thinking that Ethel had not been all that bad after all, and wondering if that was going too far. Wilverton was writing furiously. In his excitement, he had even forgotten that he was using a Biro. Curtis still held his breath.

Thompson thought hard, not caring who might be looking at him, under the circumstances.

'Arnold,' he said loudly. The computer looked at him. 'How long did Vyland say you had to keep control of this ship?'

'Two days.'

'And how long has passed on Earth so far?'

Arnold thought for a moment. 'Sixty-one years, four months, and thirteen days.'

'That is longer than – '

'Fourteen days.'

'Yes. That is longer than – '

'Fifteen days.' A second number stopped being green, in a red sort of way.

'Will you please shut up?'

'Yes.'

'That is longer than two days, isn't it?'

Arnold considered this. 'Yes. Good point. You have control.'

'Peter?' invited Thompson.

Carlton grabbed the controls, and gave the *Pioneer* all the power at his disposal. There was silence as he tried to force it to change its path, to drag it out of the pull of the black hole. Deep and nerve-stretchingly tense silence. Silence broken only by the sound of Biro on paper. Curtis was turning rapidly purple. The numbers seemed content to be red.

The ship strained to get away, responding to Carlton's electronic and mental urgings, while the black hole greedily pulled at it. The hole had clearly savoured the taste of the *Pioneer*'s sister ship and was bent on succeeding where Oliver Twist failed.

Carlton wanted a wheel or something that he could grab and force, but had to satisfy himself with knobs, dials and meters, the last of which currently hovered between deliverance and demolition. Come on, he thought, willing the needles over to the left. If they moved to the right, it would be a matter of seconds before they never moved again. I'll go to church, he thought, a little desperately, assuming as many before him in dangerous situations that their God had arranged the peril purely to boost attendance on a Sunday.

But slowly, deliberately prolonging the agony, the needles moved left, rightly.

The crew felt nothing, but one of the numbers relented to green, and the other, seeing it was now singular and the very centre of attention, joined in after a few more seconds of fame. The gravity dutifully lessened with distance, until the *Pioneer* finally settled itself onto a new course.

'We're safe,' said Carlton, and visibly relaxed his grip on the controls. Gloria flung her arms round his neck and tried to swallow him. Thompson sagged with relief, and Bowen, with an unbeatable head start, made that effort look feeble. Wilverton stopped writing. Curtis let his breath escape. It came out of both ends.

Just a few minutes later, another *Pioneer* flashed towards the black hole. The upsurge in neutrino bombardment had been noted by the pilot well before the body became a danger, and he knew what to expect and how to use it to his advantage. By coming just close enough, he could use the gravity as a slingshot, increase his speed even more, and overtake his rivals. The manoeuvre was not a difficult one for a skilled pilot, and the ship streaked safely past the hole, curving perfectly onto a new trajectory. A grin spread across his face as his instruments told him how fast the ship was now going. A grin which looked very much the same as the one Paul Vyland had been wearing, appropriately enough.

It replaced a frown which he had been sporting for a while. He did not know why he had let himself be talked into this. It was not a logical thing to do, and yet he had agreed readily. At the time it had seemed such a good idea. Odd. He felt like a pawn in a game.

And if there was one thing that Mycroft Vyland was not, he told himself, it was a pawn in a game.

Brother Paul had explained to him how they could not allow the family name to be besmirched by letting someone else beat them to the stars when they had the opportunity to do it themselves. And it had sounded so appealing, even though he knew that when Paul said 'themselves' he meant Mycroft. So he had agreed to beat this Curtis chap to Alcyone.

He generally did what his brother suggested, thanks to the twist of fate which had produced Paul seventeen minutes before him, but that was surely going a bit far.

Or was it? The frown returned.

And so did the Challenger.

So Paul wanted him to beat this other ship to the planet, did he? Perhaps so that he could have the last laugh even though he would be long dead by then, if he was not already. Well, that was okay by Mycroft – he still fancied the idea of being the first there himself. But he was not going to let anyone share his new world. There would be no-one on his heels to take some of the glory.

The other ship would not reach its goal at all. Somehow – and he would work out just how later on – somehow, Mycroft would stop it.

There! He had decided. And all on his own, with no Paul to make suggestions.

Far away, the Challenger hid its mental satisfaction. This was going to be easy.

Mycroft looked at the plastic frog which sat on the console in front of him, and smiled.

'How shall we do it, eh, Froggy?' he asked, and listened. The frog did not answer, but Mycroft's smile did not fade, and he reached out and patted it on the head.

'Don't worry, Froggy. Daddy will think of something.' Pat. 'Good Froggy. Ribbit.'

Well, all right, thought the Challenger, the frequencies within rising slightly, he may need some looking after, but that could be arranged.

The frog remained stubbornly mute, but something rather peculiar happened next to it.

On the console, suddenly, there sat an old man with white hair and shoulders obviously rounded even as he sat. He was looking down at a device attached to his waist band, and his finger rested on a button. It was a personal tachyon transferrer, the latest on the market, in fact pretty much the only on the market. A limited range, but with the extremely handy attribute of being able to make a person travel faster than light, and able, therefore, to escape from black-hole gravity.

He looked up from the device and removed his finger, and smiled a self-satisfied smile at his younger twin brother.

Rather a lot younger, now, the original seventeen minutes having been dilated to over sixty years.

'Father?' asked Mycroft, with disbelief in his voice, but seeing family in that smile. The eyes which met his, though, were well used to dissipating any positive emotion in their path, and they answered Mycroft without needing to call on the mouth for help.

'Paul?' asked Mycroft incredulously, and the eyes nodded.

If the twins had listened very carefully, they might just have heard the rhythmic banging of fate's head against the wall of its psychiatrist's office.

X

Bowen slowly turned over a card, making quite sure that he could see what it was before Arnold. It was the six of spades. On a small table in front of the computer lay the six of clubs, held by its lightly magnetized surface. Bowen completed the action of turning the card face up, saying 'Snap!' as he did so.

The rules of the game, as far as he could remember them from the last time he had indulged in its intricacies about thirty years before, in a different life, required that Arnold should stop playing at this point and let Bowen pick up the cards from the table. Arnold did not appear to be playing by the same rules. He watched Bowen turn the card over, then crisply, and about half a second after Bowen, said 'Snap!' and reached out his arm to claim the cards as his own. Bowen's hand clamped down over what approximated to a metal wrist, albeit covered with artificial skin.

'What do you think you're doing?' Bowen asked.

Arnold looked at him. 'What?'

Bowen took a deep breath, let it out in an audible sigh, and accompanied it with a glare at Curtis that was normally kept safely in a scabbard.

'I said, "WHAT DO YOU THINK YOU'RE DOING?" ' The others, except Carlton, who was missing, looked at them momentarily and with no great surprise. Sparring with Arnold was already one of Bowen's recognized pastimes.

Arnold managed to convey an impression of mild surprise, although his features remained motionless. He spoke as if to a child.

'According to the rules, the player who first calls "snap", upon recognizing two cards of the same colour and value, picks up the cards currently in the playing pile, and adds them to his hand. I thought that was fairly basic.'

Bowen began to change colour.

'I CALLED "SNAP" FIRST!'

'I didn't hear you.'

'*YOU WOULDN'T HEAR A BOMB AT TWO FEET!*' screamed Bowen.

'That would depend on how big the bomb was, I would have thought.'

Bowen reached the decision that verbal attack was not bearing fruit, and threw the rest of his cards at Arnold, pushing himself away and turning his back on the machine.

'I presume you are conceding the game?' said Arnold, as the three of diamonds glanced off his forehead and attached itself to the metallic surface of the shelf on which he sat.

Bowen told him what he could do with the game. Given that Arnold did not possess a torso, it was an anatomical impossibility which would have confused him greatly had he heard the instruction. He had caught the vitriolic tone, though, and his eyes narrowed warningly at his playmate.

Arnold was undeniably deafer than ever, and Bowen knew why.

When everything had calmed down following the event on the black hole's horizon, Curtis had reprogrammed Arnold, and had tried to cure his deafness as a bonus, while Carlton flew the ship with one hand, and expertly maintained Gloria's smile with the other. Curtis could see what Carlton was doing from the corner of his eye – and the middle, occasionally, as he turned to glare at his rival suitor – and the sight did not please him. He was therefore working on Arnold with something less than the loving care which one might have expected. In fact, he would have done no less delicate a job had he been wearing boxing gloves and armour; and given what he planned to try to do to Carlton as soon as he got the chance, that might not have been a bad idea.

Bowen, meanwhile, had tried to think of some sort of game at which he could defeat Arnold. Arm wrestling was out, since Arnold's metal sinews would be an easy match for Bowen's muscles, trained though they were through countless repetitions of lifting a beer glass, and try as he might, he could not recall a game which relied solely on the ability to produce wind and expel it at high-decibel levels, at which he was unarguably talented.

Wilverton had been several miles away, in a little world of his own, reliving his favourite fantasy. In it, he was standing quite still, watching a beautiful girl approaching. She had long, dark hair, and everything that came in pairs was beautifully formed. She glided up to him, and looked downwards, drawing her breath in sharply as her eyes widened with wonder. She reached out and touched its tip, saying huskily, 'What a magnificent fountain pen!'

Eventually, Curtis had finished his fiddling, leaving Arnold in control, though as deaf as a post, and giving Carlton the chance to visit the gym while Gloria found a magazine. Bowen had reasoned that snap was the only game in which he stood a chance – and then only if he cheated. Wilverton had returned to the real world, remembered that he was using a Biro, and tried to remember some more of the Scrabble words to put in front of Curtis's name in his diary.

And now the game of snap had reached its abrupt end.

'That bloody thing's stone deaf now,' Bowen told Curtis, jerking his thumb over his shoulder in case there was any doubt as to the subject.

Curtis knew very well, and was about to adopt an apologetic stance, since Arnold was admittedly proving a bit of a disappointment on the ear front, when two things happened.

First, the door at the front end of the control room opened, and Carlton emerged from the gym. His vest was constructed using apparently about three strands of material and did nothing to conceal the definition of his muscles. The shorts left extremely little to the imagination, and from the look on Gloria's face, imagination was a distant second to memory in any case. A slight sheen of sweat completed Carlton's dress, and he flashed his smile at Gloria as he floated past. Gloria smiled back.

Curtis didn't.

Secondly, Bowen insulted the concept and creation of Arnold, and added a few choice words about its programmer for good measure.

Curtis therefore boldly adopted a belligerent stance instead.

'The auditory function of modern computers is very delicate, and if you think that turning a couple of screws here and there is going to make any difference, then you obviously know as little about computers as I think you do.'

Bowen did not find this explanation placatory. He plucked from the air a magazine that he had already looked at – not read – half a dozen times and turned the pages like an advert for super-strong staples. The complaint of the turning pages was the only noise in an atmosphere heavy with unspent emotion.

When Carlton returned to the room, looking refreshed and bloody perfect, Wilverton looked up, a thought – an interesting thought no doubt – having struck him.

'You know, one of the most fascinating things about auditory functions . . .' he began.

'Oh, blow it out your arse!' suggested Bowen.

Wilverton did not. Instead, he snapped shut both his mouth and his diary, retracted his Biro, and left the control room.

Bowen told Arnold, loudly, to put a film on in his cabin, preferably one that went on for a week, and also left.

Carlton surfaced from his hello to Gloria, and stretched expansively.

'I think I'll lie down for a while,' he said, and Gloria released her seat strap.

Curtis frowned. 'You can't be tired already.'

'No.' Carlton winked. 'Not yet.' Gloria frowned her disapproval of the comment, but still followed him from the room.

Curtis stared after them impotently.

This left him alone with Thompson. Or, more pertinently, it left Thompson alone with Curtis. This arrangement left anyone in Thompson's place feeling rather like an expensive bit of Wedgwood on the shop shelf when the door opens and a prospective customer with horns and a bell announces himself with a loud moo.

'I've just got to check on Abercrom,' he said feebly, and consigned Curtis to a singularity.

And so the happy band of travellers continued on their way to a star far, far away; boldly going where no man had gone before – except Paul Vyland, and a few others who had since followed him.

With nothing else to do, Curtis sat in the control room, and sulked. Carlton had seduced, yes, seduced, Gloria away from him – although what she saw in that second-rate pilot he could not imagine (Curtis had an imagination which stretched about as far as a whalebone corset; an old one).

Not that he cared. Gloria was not the only girl in the Galaxy. The little voice in the back of his head reminded him that she had so far been the only girl in the Galaxy who had shown any interest in him.

And he didn't care!

He didn't!

In all those years, the only one, despite all his boasting to friends at school about what he and Lysanne had done behind the bike sheds after the annual dance, and the fervent hope that what he was describing in such graphic detail had actually been physically possible.

Despite all those visits to the local holodisc, where he sat on a chair in the dimmest corner of the room and waited for a girl to ask him to dance, which none ever did so that he had to make the move himself, something he could only do when he had sufficient alcohol swilling around inside him to muffle those voices telling him to sit where he was and not risk the humiliation again, by which time he could barely walk, so that if the object of his inebriated desire – usually the only one left and as likely as not tethered to one corner of the bar by a lead – actually consented to dance, then he was less likely to sweep her off her feet than throw up over her shoulder. All Curtis had ever pulled were a few Christmas crackers and the occasional muscle in the process.

Not that he cared any more. He could easily do without being muscular and tall and handsome and bloody perfect, like bloody Carlton. Which was just as well, since he did not seem to have a great deal of choice. Bastard!

This was a gold medal sulk.

If only there had been some gravity, he would have staked his claim with Gloria before Carlton had stuck his oar – amongst other things – in.

Trust Carlton to be a bloody expert in zero gravity.

But you couldn't get gravity on a space-ship, he thought, without spinning it. Spinning would apply centrifugal force, and that would take the place of gravity. He should have set the ship spinning while he and Gloria were . . . or weren't. And that was when the idea hit him. His mind saw Carlton suddenly being subject to gravity, and crashing to the floor half way though his performance. If he got Arnold to spin the ship now, then that would be exactly what would happen.

A little vindictive smile crawled across his features, and took residence, and large vindictive thoughts filled his head; so large, unfortunately, that there wasn't enough room left for those thoughts which consider the consequences.

Curtis sidled over to Arnold's shelf and told him to spin the ship around its short axis for one minute. He told him quietly, conspiratorially, glancing over his shoulder towards the door in case it should open and catch him out.

'Why are you whispering?' asked Arnold. 'And more to the point, *what* are you whispering?' Curtis frowned at his creation while what he was pleased to call his mind searched for someone other than himself on whom he could lay the blame for the computer's deafness. No-one sprung up to fill the void.

He repeated the order, slightly louder.

'Nope,' said Arnold.

'WHAT DO YOU MEAN "NO"?'

'I didn't say "No", I said "Nope".' Arnold was not one to let even the slightest chance to goad pass him by. 'And I meant that I still didn't hear what you said. You're mumbling.'

'I AM NOT MUMBLING!! SPIN THE SHIP ON ITS SHORT AXIS FOR ONE MINUTE. DID YOU HEAR THAT?'

'Yes,' said Arnold quietly, and did nothing.

'Well?'

'Are you sure?'

'*OF COURSE I'M SURE. I'M THE BLOODY CAPTAIN!*'
There, that told him, he thought, and puffed up his chest so that it was now flat. Arnold shrugged without moving the shoulders he didn't possess.

Curtis had progressed towards apoplexy without thinking that the control room was almost right at the front of the *Pioneer*. That meant it would spin a lot faster than the middle, which was where the cabins were, and the centrifugal force would be correspondingly greater.

Curtis chuckled to himself, and even began to rub his hands together, before Arnold gave a sharp burst on the small side rockets to set the ship spinning. It was only when he found that the rear wall of the cabin, which he happened to be facing, was receding at some speed, that it occurred to him that something was amiss with the plan. The receding far wall suggested that the front wall was approaching his back at the

69

same considerable speed, and he was just about to tell Arnold to stop when the approach turned into an arrival.

The air was knocked out of him in a rush, rendering his instruction nothing more than a grunt which Arnold did not hear anyway. Loose objects, now subject to the same artificial gravity that had just assailed Curtis, began falling to the floor – in this instance, the front wall against which Curtis lay helplessly – and he was hit by a variety of odds and ends, none of which he saw through his tightly closed eyes.

He did not notice, therefore, the small globules of blue ink which hit his face, hands and clothing. It so happened that his clothing was almost exactly the same colour as the ink, so it did not show. His face and hands were a different colour from the ink, so it did.

Wilverton's cabin was situated almost exactly in the centre of the ship, so no centrifugal force was applied to it, and he knew nothing of what happened except that he heard a shout of rage from Bowen's cabin further down the corridor.

In that cabin there had been some gravity formed, and it came at rather an inopportune moment. On arriving in his cabin, Bowen had settled down to watch his film, accompanied by several tubes of beer. When the gravity arrived, the several had been diminished, and Bowen was getting rid of most of what he had drunk so far. In zero gravity, this was normally done by propelling the waste liquid down a tube, the entrance to which was in the wall. The sudden gravity unfortunately made that wall the ceiling, and from where Bowen found himself lying beneath it, there was no way the liquid was going to find the tube. It succumbed to the force applied to it, and most of it landed on Bowen, who found the experience less than exhilarating. Hence the shout of rage.

Sadly, in order to shout, either with or without rage, one must open one's mouth. Bowen should not have opened his mouth.

Opposite Bowen's cabin, Thompson was floating in front of Abercrom's apartment, watching as the bee moved from one bloom to the next, lying on his back, arms tucked behind his head, and waggling his feet up and down. Okay, maybe he wasn't, Thompson admitted, but it looked a bit like it.

Then suddenly it couldn't look like it any more as pseudo-gravity pulled Thompson below the level of Abercrom's shelf. He frowned, wondering what was going on. And so, understandably, did Abercrom.

Between Bowen's cabin and that of Wilverton, was Carlton's. The gravity, when it came, was very gentle, and it came just too late for Curtis's plan to succeed. As Carlton finished what apparently he was best at, and collapsed on top of Gloria, he found that he could indeed collapse on top of Gloria, which was rather unusual in zero gravity.

Something at the back of his mind recalled the sound of the muffled though shouting voice of Curtis, one of those echo memories that lets you recognize what someone has said just after you've said 'pardon'. This was gravity, thought Carlton. Centrifugally induced gravity. Curtisian centrifugally induced gravity.

He sounded like Wilverton.

So *that* was what the Captain was up to!

Gloria did not realize what was happening, but she thought she did, having read about such things in various paperback books which her school friends had forced upon her and which made her blush. She leaned closer to Carlton's ear and whispered.

'I can feel the earth move.'

Carlton did not disillusion her, but he determined to disillusion Curtis of the notion that he could do this sort of thing and get away with it. While the visible bits of him relaxed, his mind considered courses of action.

He dressed quickly – which was not difficult since their jump suits were zip-up affairs – and made his way to the control room.

When the gravity was neatly cancelled by a burst from the rockets opposite to those first used, Curtis floated away from the wall, along with the other loose objects, so that various magazines, books, computer games and a largely empty ink bottle joined him in mid-air, this last finding its way behind the food cabinet, where it remained out of sight. He opened his eyes experimentally, and found that everything looked much the same as it had before his little foray into the unplanned. He had to concede, at least privately, that it had not been a devastating success. Devastating, maybe; success, no.

It occurred to him that the other crew members would not be delirious about it, either, and he immediately wondered how he could pass the buck. His eyes settled on Arnold. He still owed the computer one for that impersonation of his father, and now seemed as good a time as any, and better than most. He floated over to Arnold's shelf, and spoke directly into the computer's ear.

'You will tell the other crew members that this experiment was your idea, and that I had nothing whatever to do with it,' he said bravely.

Arnold's eyes swivelled towards him slowly, as if weighing the order and considering his response. That, of course, was entirely unthinkable, as Arnold was merely an obedient, although very sophisticated, machine, and would always do whatever it was told to do.

'Bollocks!' said Arnold.

Nearly always.

Curtis stared at him, and Arnold stared right back. Curtis gave up. It did not matter anyway, he thought. He was Captain of the *Pioneer*, and could do what he wanted. No-one could question his command, so he had nothing to fear from the other members of the crew . . . who would be bursting into the control room at any moment with murder on their minds.

He looked around for somewhere to hide.

The door opened in front of Carlton, and he looked in on what appeared to be an empty control room.

Then he noticed a guilty hand sticking out from behind the drinks cabinet at the far end of the room. A hand mottled with little blue stains. Carlton frowned, before realization struck, as he remembered the ink globules which had been hovering near the ceiling.

As he watched, the hand was moved, and turned over, as if someone were studying it, which Carlton assumed was indeed what was happening. He wondered if Curtis would remember the ink and link it with his blue hand. He doubted it. The hand was withdrawn, and a little smile replaced the frown on Carlton's face.

Bowen was next into the room, with a freshly washed face and clean clothes. The redness of his features was only partly due to the scrubbing he had just inflicted. Any bonhomie induced by the comedy film had been left in his cabin with a vengeance.

The arrival of Gloria led Bowen to moderate his language somewhat as he described what had happened, and inquired as to the whereabouts of their illustrious leader – or 'bastard', as he put it – and the last two members of the company arrived on the scene just in time to see Carlton shrug his shoulders.

'I don't know where Richard is, but I must admit I am a little worried.' He went on with the explanation which that friendly statement patently demanded.

'Richard was obviously experimenting with centrifugally induced gravity, which, in itself, is quite a good idea. The trouble is that here, right at the end of the ship, a sudden burst of centrifugal force like that will make the gravity stronger than anywhere else, and that could bring on Gumby's syndrome. Which, of course, can be fatal.' Eyebrows were lowered at him.

'Centrifugal force applied to the human body has the effect of separating the blood, as you probably know,' he explained. 'All the red corpuscles collect in the major organs, especially the bladder, and leave the outer extremities, face, hands and so on, a very pale colour, with blue blotches. The problem then is that if the bladder is emptied before the corpuscles are re-absorbed into the body – and that takes eight hours – then the person will die. First happened to a bloke called Gumby, hence the name. He didn't feel bad, just went to the loo, and . . .' He snapped his fingers expressively.

Their attention was suddenly drawn to the cabinet at the far end of the control room, where Curtis emerged, looking horror-stricken at the backs of his hands. Gloria let slip a little involuntary scream. Carlton

72

muttered, 'Oh, my God!', and Wilverton reached for his diary. Thompson's face showed momentary disbelief, and he glanced at Carlton, but said nothing.

Curtis looked up from his hands to the surrounding faces. Suddenly, he very much wanted to visit the toilet.

'Don't you realize what this means?' Vyland – Paul somehow didn't seem to suit him, being a familiar term, and no-one got familiar with Vyland; even 'Professor' was getting a bit personal – looked calmly at his younger twin, and his own youthful face looked back. 'I will be not only the founder of the Galactic Empire through tachyon matter transference, but I will arrive in a blaze of glory hundreds of years after I am presumed dead, the first to travel by conventional craft to another star.' His eyes took on a faraway look – thanks to his age, far away was generally where he looked nowadays, so it wasn't hard. 'I will be the most famous man in all of history, history which has been and history yet to come!'

Megalomania ran in Vyland's family, and when things ran in that family, they really shifted. Megalomania had been running ever since Vyland's ancestors had left the trees and their little hairy feet had hit the ground.

'I must make a plan.' None of your 'we' here. 'But first I need some sleep. I shall of course use the Captain's quarters.'

'But they're mine!' Mycroft finally managed to get a word in edgeways.

' "Were", Mycroft. Of course I'm going to use the Captain's quarters.' The statement was one such as allowed for no possibility of argument. 'I'm older than you.'

'You're only seveneen minutes older than me,' Mycroft responded petulantly.

'I am sixty years older than you if I'm a day.'

'You're not a day, you're seventeen minutes.'

Vyland sighed. There had always been this sort of, well, problem, with Mycroft. When he wasn't being incredibly intelligent, he was generally being incredibly mad. And Vyland was too old to deal with it is as vigorously as he used to, so he didn't swipe his little brother understandingly round the head.

'Let's not argue, Mycroft,' he said instead. 'There are more important things to do. We have to see to the *Pioneer*. But we'll do it in the morning. You can sleep where you like, so long as it's not in the Captain's quarters.'

He moved towards the door of the control room, slowly, and grateful for the lack of gravity, the strength of which had seemed to increase over the past few years.

'You've never liked me,' Mycroft sulked. Vyland paused momentarily. He'd never actually liked anybody, but self-pity rarely took account of all available facts. Nor did raving lunacy either, probably by definition. 'Only Froggy's ever liked me.'

'Oh, not with the frog again.' Vyland had not spotted the creature since Mycroft had snatched it at the earliest available opportunity and stuffed it down the front of his jump suit. 'I thought Doctor Manx had talked you out of that.'

'He was silly.'

'*Why* was he silly?' Vyland didn't want to ask, let alone know, but it was one of those situations where you know you are going to be told in any case.

'He said Froggy was a small plastic toy and couldn't possibly be talking to me, *that*'s why.'

Vyland nodded slowly, and pulled himself towards the door. That was probably an irrefutable argument inside his little brother's head, and insanity was just about the only subject in which Vyland felt unqualified.

One thing he *did* know – Mycroft would have to go.

XI

Curtis hung in his cocoon, literally, as far as he was concerned, dying for a pee.

He had gone there after assurances from Carlton that there would be no problem if he restrained himself for the full eight hours, determining to sleep through the danger period. Sleep, however, turned out to be the last thing he was likely to do, especially when the thought struck him that if he did fall asleep, then the first thing he was likely to do would be something he had not done since his very early childhood, which then *would* be the last thing he did. Curtis felt very uncomfortable in more ways than one.

The occupants of the control room were feeling very pleased with themselves. They knew that they had eight hours of peace ahead of them, at the end of which they would be due for their own sleep periods anyway. A restful time stretched into the distance.

'Boredom', it would have been called on normal space-ships, and something therefore to be avoided. It was a problem, since there was a limit to the entertainment value of playing humorously with globules of weightless water, or being really hysterical and throwing one of your crew mates about like in a game of catch. A limit that was generally reached just after you started doing it.

Crews on normal space-ships, though, were denied such pastimes as constant bickering, competition for sexual favours, and coping with a Captain who would breeze into the finals of International Tosser of the Year.

The relief in the *Pioneer*'s control room at the lack of activity was therefore palpable, and they made their respective ways to the cabins some hours later already much refreshed, hearing as they did so a half-imagined ecstatic sigh, and the tinkling sound of running liquid.

Many years before, or about a day before, according to the crew of *Pioneer*, a space-ship had circled a blue-green planet which itself circled a sun called Alcyone. The inaugural settlement was about to be built on the planet which had first been visited by Paul Vyland. The ship was much larger than Vyland's, and carried not only people, but also construction materials, plus the robots and computers which would put

75

that material together in such a way that the people could move down from the space-ship and live in it.

Before very long, the first settlement expanded into the first town, then the first city, and finally, the capital of the new world. A world called after its discoverer: the planet Vyland.

Man had joined the indigenous life-forms, and started to take over. On all seven continents, within a few short years, great cities rose: gleaming metallic and cellulose structures that blended into the land, through no accident. Mankind was determined that its first colonized planet would remain one of beauty and harmony, and would not become merely a carbon copy of Earth, which, although not now overcrowded since the sense of birth control had been voluntarily recognized by all, was not the sort of place where anyone with anything but an extreme hatred for aesthetics would choose to live. There were millions of planets within reach of man now, so there was no need to cramp any one of them.

Molecular computers were sent forth in robotic hands, and placed on chosen sites. They conversed with the aboriginal molecules in the land around them, and constructed the cities with joint orders from humans and the planet itself. The first city of the great continent known as Tropana, a city called Garden, was constructed at the outer limits of its tropical jungle within five months, such was the unbounded efficiency of these tools and their complete lack of demand for tea breaks, and all without rustling a leaf of the giant trees. Who said they'd never learn?

A few years after that – or about two and a half hours – a woman called Vanessa Gravers lived in the city of Garden in a spacious mansion by a lake. This did not make her anything particularly special, as a large number of people did much the same thing. Vanessa wanted to be special, though, and having a minor talent as a writer, befitting her Piscean birth sign, she decided with the help of her horoscope that a biography of the greatest scientist who ever lived – Paul Vyland, of course – was the easiest way to ensure it.

Her research followed Vyland – to Vanessa so Taurean that he probably had a cud rather than a teething ring – from his intolerably inculpable childhood through an infuriatingly immaculate adolescence and an insufferably impeccable university career to the acquisition of his post as Head of Research at the Arnold Curtis Space Research Centre. And there she found something interesting. The Research Centre had not been run by Arnold Curtis, as Vanessa had assumed, but by his son Richard, who appeared, from the sketchy information available, to have been a quite exceptional mathematician. He had also disappeared from the scene a matter of months after Vyland had joined the Centre. What, Vanessa asked herself, had happened to Curtis?

*

76

What had happened to Curtis, most recently, was Gumby's syndrome.

By the time the sleep period had ended, Curtis was once again up and around, and positively exuding universal bonhomie in post-urinal relief. Carlton even felt a twinge of guilt as Curtis wished him good morning and thanks him for the concern he had expressed the previous day, but it passed remarkably quickly.

Curtis was in such a good mood that he decided to do something about Arnold's deafness. Delicate though it was, he was confident that he could solve the problem, and soon the innards of the computer's head were visible through a hole in one temple.

Curtis tinkered carefully for a while, and the others looked on in trepidation, knowing that while Curtis probably *could* put Arnold right, he almost certainly wouldn't.

Arnold looked on in something that made trepidation look like arrogant confidence. His eyes could not follow what was going on inside his head, so he stared at Curtis instead, apparently willing him to finish.

'Have you any idea how embarrassing this is?' he hissed at his creator.

Curtis did not answer, not wanting to risk asking why it should be embarrassing.

'I hope you know what you're doing,' Arnold warned him.

'Of course I do, Arnold,' Curtis replied irritably.

'What?' said Arnold.

After some time passed in silence, Curtis replaced the missing segment of forehead and carefully manoeuvred himself back proudly, the equivalent in zero gravity of standing back proudly.

'How's that, Arnold?' he asked, in a normal voice. Arnold stared at him.

'HOW'S THAT, ARNOLD?' he repeated, at somewhat greater volume. Arnold stared at him.

'Brilliant!' muttered Carlton quietly, from the other side of the room. Arnold looked at him instead.

Further comment was arrested by Arnold's next movement. He reached out his arm and grabbed a piece of paper. Using one of his fingers which happened to double as a pen, he started writing. Curtis moved closer to see the results. He read them as they emerged, which was not terribly quickly.

'I . . . appear . . . to . . . have . . . lost . . . my . . . voice,' he read. 'I appear to have lost my voice.' Curtis frowned in puzzlement, and started looking around Arnold's shelf for the missing ability. How on Earth could that have happened? Someone was about to tell him how on Earth that could have happened when Arnold started writing again.

'Might . . . I . . . respect . . . fully . . . submit,' read Curtis, 'that . . . the . . . person . . . who . . . attempted . . . to . . . improve . . . my hearing . . . made . . . a . . . complete . . . camel's . . . fa– ' Curtis did not read any more for a while, and, as soon as Arnold stopped writing, he put the piece of paper in his pocket.

'Arnold is suggesting that something went wrong while I was adjusting his auditory capability,' explained Curtis to a crew who would never have guessed. He leaned close to Arnold and hissed, ' "As per bloody usual", eh?' then continued out loud. 'I really don't think that is very likely, but I am willing to investigate the possibility.'

'Excuse me,' said Wilverton, a note of puzzlement in his voice, which was fairly unusual for him. Curtis postponed the beginning of his search and looked at him questioningly. 'Why hasn't Arnold the facility to converse via screens on the consoles or in the walls or something? It seems a little old-fashioned to have to write things down.'

Curtis knew the answer to that one. 'He doesn't have to use screens; he can talk.'

'Ah, yes, of course.' Wilverton opened his diary again.

'Now then . . .' said Curtis.

He had not had the chance to move before Arnold started writing again. Curtis leaned over to look, and found that it was not the plea for leniency which he had half expected.

'We . . . appear . . . to . . . be . . . approaching . . . a . . . meteor . . . shower . . . which . . . could . . . develop . . . into . . . a . . . longer . . . outbreak . . . of . . . rock . . . Given . . . the . . . mean . . . density . . . of . . . such . . . showers . . . the . . . chances . . . of . . . the . . . space . . . ship . . . being . . . hit . . . is . . . somewhere . . . in . . . the . . . region . . . of . . . seventy . . . three . . . per . . . cent . . . Any . . . one . . . direct . . . hit . . . would . . . of . . . course . . . be . . . fatal . . . Help . . . me!'

'Seventy-three per cent,' said Wilverton, almost to himself. 'That's not good.'

Thompson, sitting next to him, nodded concernedly, and frowned.

'Still, we'll be fine,' Wilverton continued, smiling at him. 'So there's no need to adopt the obvious solution.'

'What obvious solution?'

'I'll save it until we need it.'

'We *do* need it, you . . .' Thompson searched the nearby atmosphere for a suitable word, and then remembered that Wilverton might just have an answer, and came up with '. . . know.'

'No we don't. Not yet.'

'What do you mean? There's a three in four chance that we'll be hit!' He was looking quite worried, but Wilverton still smiled.

'We're the stars of the book,' he explained with a confidence which suddenly he didn't feel. 'If the ship gets hit then that's the end of the story, and they can't stop it now because it's not long enough for publication yet. Relax.'

Thompson looked at him with a fresh worry, and a big one, in mind, but did not get the chance to reply as their attention was diverted by another movement of Arnold's writing finger. Curtis relayed the message as it came.

'The . . . density . . . of . . . the . . . meteor . . . shower . . . seems . . . to . . . be . . . increasing . . . Look . . . do . . . you . . . mind . . . very . . . much . . . if . . . I . . . stop . . . writing . . . these . . . damned . . . silly . . . full . . . stops . . . between . . . each . . . word??? As I was writing. At present rates, within an hour it will have reached the level of a storm. That will mean that the chances of the ship being hit will rise to ninety-four per cent. That is almost a cert, if you ask me.'

'We didn't,' said Wilverton, still apparently unconcerned.

Thompson's worry grew in direct proportion to the First Officer's confidence. Not only were they about to be pulped, but the person who seemed to know a way out was apparently pretty way out himself, and thought he was part of a book.

This was not a good time for Wilverton to crack up, or the ship was going to do pretty much the same thing, but Thompson did not think that a plea to Wilverton to wait a little while before going mad would have much effect.

Why did he have to choose now?

He did not know that Wilverton was at that moment asking himself why the hell he thought he was part of a book, and not coming up with a convincing answer, nor an unconvincing answer either. Wilverton *did* know he wasn't mad, but the evidence was not on his side, since he also knew that what was happening wasn't real.

The Challenger shifted its entity comfortably in a quiet emanation of microwaves and tried to sense surreptitiously how the Champion was reacting. Get your designated Player out of *this* one, it thought, as it pushed the renegade notion further into the human's brain.

Gloria and Carlton were the only others close enough to hear what the two were saying, but could think of no argument to throw into the affray. Danny would know what to do, thought Gloria; he was awfully sensible. What can I do? wondered Carlton, and flexed a bicep to no apparent effect.

Thompson decided to go onto the attack.

'Look, you've got to be one of the more minor characters in the book at the moment. You could get written out, you know. It'd be good dramatic irony if you know a way out.'

Wilverton considered this, but then shook his head.

'No, you can't get away with that when you're using meteors. They're all-or-nothing options.' Well, that was encouraging, thought Thompson, taking a deep breath and wondering whether counting would help. It seemed unlikely.

'Are you two going to stop muttering and do something?' demanded Bowen helpfully. Wilverton looked over to him and gave him a cheery smile, which was always a waste of time with Bowen.

'No need.'

'What?' said Bowen, not understanding what the small twit was talking about, but knowing that scientists as a breed always talked as much crap as sense, so not really being surprised. Wilverton maintained the smile and opened his mouth to explain, but Thompson leapt in – to the conversation, not Wilverton's mouth – recognizing that Bowen's reaction to Wilverton's reasoning would not be encouraging.

'Look.' He spoke quietly but forcefully, capturing Wilverton's attention again. 'Do you know a way to get us out of this?' Wilverton nodded happily. 'And you're not going to do anything?' Wilverton shook his head happily.

'Would you like me to smack him a bit?' asked Carlton, having come up with an option.

'We'll keep it in reserve,' Thompson told him, in a tone that wasn't entirely dismissive, then turned back to Wilverton. 'You let me get us out of that black hole scrape, though, didn't you? You didn't tell me that it didn't matter then, did you?' The tone was now becoming accusatory.

'It could still have been a short story at that stage.'

'But this could be a novelette,' pressed Thompson, feeling his grip on sanity slipping rapidly; but if you can't beat them, humour them. 'One of two or three which make up the book. You must have read enough to know.'

Wilverton suddenly stopped smiling and considered the possibility. He frowned.

'Dammit! I hadn't thought of that. You could be right.' He spun towards the computer, happy to have something else on which to concentrate other than the seditious notion which his brain seemed to be entertaining. 'Arnold, listen very carefully.'

XII

By this time several years had elapsed on Vyland since Vanessa had discovered her long-lost mathematician, or rather hadn't, and during those years she had not been idle.

Firstly, the biography of Taurean Vyland was published, and very successful it proved to be. Secondly, she met the love of her life, Gerund, who was an Arien and the perfect match for her. Thirdly, she wrote a biography of Richard Curtis. And fourthly, she lost the love of her life, Gerund, who was still an Arien, but who as a match was now spent.

Well, she didn't actually lose him, because she knew exactly where he was, or at least she knew where he was the last time she had seen him. He had been in a bedroom from which voices were emerging. Emerging in distorted form, having had to squeeze their sound waves through the cracks round the door in order to get out. When Vanessa eased the door ajar, the voices took on a more normal aspect, but the words did not. Gerund's first.

'Her personal astrologer has advised her that I am the one she must marry, and there's no way she's going to ignore *her* advice. Which is just as well, since it cost me enough. Unlike my "dearly beloved" ' – he sounded like Bowen – 'I don't trust the stars always to come up with the right answers!'

'You are clever, darling,' came the responding voice. The facts that it was a female voice and that it had called him 'darling' weighed rather heavily against it. Probably an Aquarian, thought Vanessa, although Gerund was favourite to carry the can. The fact that the voice emerged from a bedroom was thus far circumstantial.

'Once this next biography comes out and I marry her, we'll be made for life. Wonderful stuff, astrology!'

'One thing *I* know about astrology – Aries is the sign of the Ram.'

Noises off. Promising before long to become noises on.

Vanessa pushed the door wide, and the bed was admitted into the evidence; not that much evidence would be needed, since Gerund was not only red-handed but a pretty flushed pink in most other areas as well.

'How can you do this?' cried Vanessa, thereby stopping them from providing an immediate demonstration. Gerund turned casually, a reaction which later deepened Vanessa's shame with the realization that it was a practised one, but which for now went unnoticed. 'And you an Aries!'

'Baaa,' said Gerund.

Fifthly, the biography of Curtis flopped, which was more than Gerund had been doing.

A conjunction of bad news for Vanessa, but a pools win for a Challenger now warming to its task. There was a towering rage inside Vanessa which needed an avenue for release, and it took hardly any influence at all to make Curtis look like Broadway.

The only half-interesting thing about Curtis had been his disappearance in a self-built space-ship, hence the public apathy. But for Vanessa, he now became the focus of an irate zeal, and according to her research, there was a vague chance, the remotest of possibilities, that, thanks to the effects of time dilation, Curtis was still alive out in space somewhere.

She immediately adopted the possibility as an irrefutable fact. Everyone else thought that she was more loopy than an aerobatic display.

Within weeks of this adoption, Vanessa Gravers was chairbeing of the Richard Curtis Society, meetings of which were attended by roughly a dozen people of varying degrees of eccentricity or gullibility. They all believed in the *Pioneer*, and were determined to prove its existence to a general populace who couldn't really give a toss either way.

They studied notes written by Paul Vyland himself which they believed traced the proposed route of the ship, and instructions for loading that route onto the computer which would run the *Pioneer* with an efficiency its human companions could not hope to match.

They pooled their money – well, Vanessa pooled; the rest sort of dribbled – got themselves a tachyon-drive space-ship, and prepared to find the *Pioneer*. For all but one of the members of the Society, their mission was one of adventure, but for Vanessa, it was one of revenge.

She had arranged that her ship would be equipped with one of those things which humans make best – weapons. The decision had been no more hers than the thought which had set her on this quest, even though her own voice had been the one which had ordered the laser to be secretly mounted and disguised as an ordinary distance image enhancer, but the fact was not allowed to bother her.

And revenge not just on Curtis – when she reached the stars, Vanessa was going to tell them exactly what she thought of them!

The expedition couldn't be like those of the past – where Stanley flogged through the jungle in order to say one presumptuous sentence;

or someone traipsed through the whole of Russia to China just to bring back mints – because the actual travelling bit was not very difficult any more. Expeditions by tachyon drive tended simply to be about what you found when you got there, rather than about how much hassle it had been to get there in the first place. Vanessa didn't mind; she was hunting Curtis, not glory.

The computer on board her ship made Arnold look like a tin of bolts, and it had correlated all the information available to it in order to establish the position of the *Pioneer* at the highest probability level. What's more, it had done it rather well, because, when the button was pressed to activate the ship's tachyon drive, the computer took it right into the middle of the meteor storm which the *Pioneer* was about to enter.

It did not take the intrepid explorers long to establish that, regardless of the fact that meteors are hard and odourless, they had landed, as it were, in the soft and smelly, and, using a small tachyon jump – on Vanessa's orders, delivered imperiously but nonetheless rapidly from her state-room – they moved themselves just outside the storm. The fact that they had not been hit by one of the meteors was a tremendous piece of luck, but they would need another if they were to spot the *Pioneer*.

The computer matched its ship's speed to what it had calculated would be that of the *Pioneer*, and all the crew peered through the windows or studied their instrumentation. And the second piece of incredible luck occurred when, right in the middle of the storm, they saw the graceful shape of their quest.

While the rest of the crew were lined up by the windows, watching the ages-old space-ship *Pioneer*, Vanessa, in her state-room, was crouched behind her 'distance image enhancer', taking careful aim. After all her preparation, she would finally have her revenge on the man who had brought her so much sorrow.

She could see the window of the control room, and she could see the faces of the people within; faces which already looked worried, and with good reason, she thought. If you've consulted the stars today, they will have told you a story without a happy ending. This, Gerund Curtis, is where you get yours.

Her finger was on the point of squeezing the trigger when . . .

Arnold had listened while Wilverton told him exactly what to do when a meteor was heading for the ship. What you did, he instructed, was to fire one of your retro rockets at the meteor. The force of this would send it flying harmlessly into space. At the same time, of course, you had to fire the opposite rocket to stop the ship going into a spin (which could bring on Gumby's syndrome), and keep it going straight.

At first Arnold was dubious about this, and his thoughts were worried

83

ones. Will it work? Will I be able to do it? But then he found that the answer to both these questions was an emphatic 'Yes', and he began to enjoy himself.

Hey, this is really quite fun! he thought. You can't miss these meteors. Here comes another . . . Wham! . . . That showed it . . . I know, I'll fire the next one against another one, and we'll see how well I can aim . . . Right, here it comes; I'll hit that one over there that looks like an apple . . . Kerpow! . . . Got it! Now I'll get that one that looks like a big black rugby ball . . . Missed! . . . Oh well, never mind . . . How about that one that looks just like a space-ship with lots of people looking out of the windows at us . . .

. . . when the *Pioneer* apparently threw a meteor at her.

There is something about sitting on a space-ship surrounded by zillions of cubic light years of absolutely bugger all, watching a meteor, through a much magnifying view-finder, growing in size as it approaches your window, that concentrates the mind quite wonderfully. At least, no-one has ever come back to say that it doesn't.

If you're lucky, it also concentrates the aim wonderfully as well.

Vanessa watched the meteor getting larger, homing in with the accuracy of a Sagittarian arrow, a massive chunk of rock spinning lazily end over end and promising that eventual contact with her ship was going to slow it down by all of a couple of miles per hour. She trained her laser image enhancer on the centre of the thing and fired, squeezing the trigger like a robust lover. The meteor continued to grow, but slowed, and then suddenly exploded in a shower of minute and harmless particles.

Vanessa sighed her relief, and settled herself to take aim once again at the *Pioneer*.

Bother, thought Arnold politely; but then Arnold was a very polite computer when he wasn't talking to someone else. Something must have got in the way. I'll have another go. There's one . . .

How do they know? thought Vanessa wildly. How do the bastards know?

A second meteor – the one which had initiated this question by changing direction at Arnold's urging and which now threatened to nip over and say hello in that inimitable and rather terminal way that slabs of fast-moving rock playfully have – filled the view-finder of her image enhancer.

She fired, and kept firing, apparently to no effect, until her whole life was the jagged rock which rolled towards her, and the beads of sweat which rolled down her. This didn't necessarily make her life any worse, only shorter.

84

It was all right for the rest of the crew, thought a part of her mind suddenly, perversely. They won't have recognized yet that the thing's heading for us; it's too far away.

She kept pressing, and it kept coming, and she kept pressing and her finger ached and she ignored it . . . and then the meteor eventually succumbed to the unequal contest in another burst of pebbles, and her ship, and more importantly, she, were momentarily safe.

'Momentary' was not Vanessa's chosen description for her remaining life span, whatever the stars might apparently have planned. She wished she hadn't come. She wished she was safe.

Something in her mind told her that she *could* be safe.

Of course she could! she realized – why hadn't she thought of that?

She looked briefly through the view-finder once more, and loosed off a shot at her adversary, before legging – and arming – it towards the far corner of her still locked private quarters. A far corner containing a little airlock, which led through to a little escape pod.

'Ahem, Ms Gravers,' came a voice through the loudspeaker on the wall as she flew – both in terms of speed and elevation – past it. 'Ms Gravers, there appears to be a meteor approaching us, Ms Gravers. Permission to change course, Ms Gravers.'

The loudspeaker paused, presumably listening, then said, 'She's not answering,' with a level of alarm that was more a dead giveaway than a hint. 'Hit those bloody buttons!'

Vanessa reached out to hit her own button as the meteor in her mind's eye looked even more threatening than had the ones in her view-finder.

Right, Arnold thought, one more go. This one coming now . . .

He took careful aim and fired, an extra powerful burst, then watched as the rock sped on its new path towards the still stubbornly existing target.

You know, it really does look like a space-ship with people looking out of the windows.

He looked closer, increasing the magnification on an outward-pointing camera which would generally not be used until they had landed somewhere and were exploring terrain via the discretion method. The camera shot showed him that the things which looked like faces were indeed faces, white and staring faces with open mouths and sitting on top of fast-moving bodies which rushed for the buttons which could move the space-ship to safety, and had almost reached them when Arnold's giant marble exploded their ship around their ears.

Oops, thought Arnold.

'Oops' hardly summed up the feelings of the Challenger, as it watched its carefully planned manipulation of Vanessa rather brutally interrupted. 'Bloody angry' would have been a more accurate description, and an ultraviolet outburst indicated its opinion. Why hadn't she moved the ship out of the way instead of panicking and heading for the escape pod? It sensed the Champion next to it in the ether, and suddenly knew the answer.

'Satisfied' would have done rather nicely for the Champion. Had it still possessed its physical form, the equivalent of the smile which spread over its silicon features would have brought back memories of Vyland himself. The Challenger would really have to try harder than that . . .

. . . and the Challenger would, in a way that would bring back memories of Vyland much more appropriately. And within the complaining bounds of a much stretched law of probability, it was still possible to spring a surprise from Earth itself.

He slept longer these days, thought Vyland, as he made his way to the control room. And more frequently. As the door opened in front of him, Mycroft looked up guiltily, and his hand shot to the opening at the front of his jump suit, and then came away empty. Vyland passed no comment, but crossed instead to the food cabinet, where a repulsive biscuit awaited him. He withdrew it and favoured it with a sneer before biting one corner as though he had felt it wriggle on his hand.

'Did you sleep well?' asked Mycroft, as pointedly as he could, which wasn't very.

'Passably,' Vyland replied, not rising to the bait, even though it was more appetizing than the biscuit.

'Never liked me,' mumbled Mycroft. There was a pause during which Mycroft's lower lip moved slowly outwards.

'How long are you going to sulk, exactly?' asked Vyland.

'Not sulking.' Vyland shrugged. 'Even Mummy preferred you to me,' Mycroft suddenly accused him. Their father had left when the twins were barely old enough to read – eighteen months, in their case – and had never been heard of again, suggesting that he viewed the pair of them with equitable loathing. 'She wrote you a letter.' Mycroft's pout grew. 'She never wrote one to me.'

Vyland shrugged again. It was true that their mother's suicide note had been addressed specifically to him, the name underlined several times. 'If you ever do one decent thing in your life, look after Mycroft', it had said, amongst other things.

Well, he had not gone against her wishes. He hadn't looked after Mycroft, that much was true, but then he had never done a decent thing in his life, either. So, semantically . . .

'That was all a long time ago, Mycroft, and we have other things with which to concern ourselves. Like that space-ship out there. The one that's trying to beat us. What shall we do to stop it, eh?' Humour him, that was always the best way. And Mycroft did not know about the programming still in the *Pioneer*'s computer, so he would think that the question was for real.

Mycroft smiled immediately. He liked it when Paul asked his help with something.

'We could create a hyperphallic acid net. Or we could board it!' he suggested excitedly. He had been thinking about this. 'Like they used to in the days of the Spanish galleons.' He's got to go, thought Vyland.

'Board it.'

'Yes.'

'Both of us. All at once.'

'Yes.'

'I think you will find that in the days of the Spanish galleons, that particular manoeuvre was generally undertaken only when those doing the boarding held a numerical advantage. Now shut up and let me think.'

Mycroft pushed himself towards the door.

'Where are you going now?'

'Pee,' sulked Mycroft, and left.

Vyland sighed. Mycroft hadn't been this bad for a long time. Mind you, he had not seen him in sixty years, so his memory might not be in possession of all of the facts. If he were left alone, he should snap out of it soon.

But not yet, apparently. In his cabin, Mycroft unzipped his jump suit, reached in, pulled out a small plastic frog, and piddled down his leg.

XIII

The materials used in Arnold's construction were such that he couldn't blush. This was probably just as well, because he felt acutely embarrassed. He watched the remains of Vanessa Gravers's space-ship spin off into the depths of interstellar space through the gaps in the meteor storm, and wondered vaguely what kind of beings he had just destroyed. If they were extraterrestrials – which, obviously, they must have been, since nothing could have caught the *Pioneer* from Earth – then it was the first, historic meeting between humans and aliens. A meeting dreamed about for centuries, a joining of minds, of cultures; hands reaching out across star systems. The ultimate adventure in the history of mankind. And Arnold had smashed them to a pulp with a bloody great rock.

Arnold considered that the best course of action was to say nothing; or to write nothing, to be precise. Nothing about that, anyway. He did write them a little note saying that they had now passed safely through the meteor storm, and that there was really no need to thank him.

'It's the first damn thing it's done right since it was built,' whispered Bowen to Carlton. 'If it thinks I'm going to thank it, it's got another bloody think coming.'

Carlton concurred. 'This ship would be a lot safer if we turned it off for good,' he muttered.

Whispering and muttering were now useless, however. As a result of Curtis's tinkering, Arnold could hear a flea fart at twenty paces, even if he could not express his outrage verbally.

Those two had done nothing but have a go at him from the start of the trip, thought the computer. They had better watch it, or it's come-uppance time.

The case had been cut, dried, and its like had been seen many times before in the history of human violence.

'You stand accused that on or about the evening of the third of June in the year of two thousand two hundred and thirty-seven and on the three days following that evening, you did kill, against their wishes, the seventeen people mentioned in the deposition in front of you. That with your own bare hands you did severally strangle, pummel, throttle – in as much as it differs from strangle by article twenty-seven point three, paragraph seven of the common-law definition, not that it matters much to the person or persons upon whom the strangulation and/or throttling was diversely carried out – and with various instruments of a generally large and blunt nature, beat, batter, club or cudgel – given once again the differences between those actions as defined in the heretofore previously mentioned article and paragraph therein – those seventeen people. How do you plead?'

The prisoner stood in the dock and stared at the court clerk on the screen in front of him. Various wires were attached to various parts of his body, so that he looked like a poorly decorated Christmas tree. He paused a moment before answering, then said simply, 'Bastard.'

The court clerk turned from the screen in front of him to the judge who sat in gown and wig on a bench behind him.

'The prisoner pleads "Bastard", my Lord,' he reported.

The judge considered and nodded, then gave a serious look over his ridiculously old-fashioned half-moon spectacles to the accused.

'Did you kill all these people?' he asked in slow measured tones.

The prisoner looked confused, and shuffled from foot to foot, as though he were trying to convey the answer in a slow-motion Morse code. As it turned out, he wasn't, because after a pause of several seconds he said, 'Well, yeah.'

The wires attached to him carried this information to the various lights at their other ends, and all the lights showed green, making the Christmas scene much brighter. The prisoner was telling the truth and nothing but the truth, which no-one had particularly doubted, since this was not the trial itself but was the final confirmatory hearing before sentence was passed, and in any case most of what he had done had been broadcast live to the nation via remote-controlled vidivision cameras.

The judge gave a slow measured nod, nicely co-ordinated with his tone.

'In view of the heinous nature of your crimes, we feel constrained to pass on you the maximum sentence allowable for these offences.'

He paused and, over the top of his grey wig, he laid a piece of black cloth. The fact that it was not attached to an extremely rare antique camera indicated that bad news was on the way.

'You will be taken from here, and at a time suitable to the administrative authorities, you will be terminated. May God have mercy on your soul, in the unlikely event of you actually having one.'

The prisoner looked sullenly at the judge. Termination no longer meant becoming a briefly integral part of the national grid. Now it meant standing in a tachyon matter transference room and being transported to a point in space chosen at random by a computer. A point in space unoccupied by any known heavenly body. Unoccupied by anything except a great big vacuum, in which it isn't even any use holding your breath, because a temperature of absolute zero – or minus two hundred and seventy-three degrees centigrade – will freeze all your important bits quite regardless of what you may be holding, while the effects of zero pressure outside the body, and body pressure inside it, do not really bear thinking about. You will be dead in very short order.

The expression on the prisoner's face at this moment was not, therefore, a particularly beatific one, not that any expression on that face could be beatific. It looked rather as though someone had taken a large and shapeless lump of clay and haphazardly stuck ears, nose, eyes and so on onto it. As a piece of modern art it would have been quite daring, but as a face it was a dismal failure. The animal snarl which now adorned it did little to improve matters.

He raised a clenched fist the size of a small block of flats, and shook it at the judge, via the closed-circuit screen.

'I'll get you for this,' he said traditionally, in tones just like those of the judge, which gave away the fact that he had been practising the line for weeks – which was in fact a pre-requisite to his delivery of a sentence containing fully five intelligible words.

The judge smiled, in the sure knowledge that Harry 'Crusher' Baxton would soon be breathing space, and would not be 'getting' anyone. The governor of this particular state never, but never, gave reprieves from death row, and especially never for the sort of crimes for which Baxton had been convicted.

In fact the governor was poised with pen in hand over the order. The only good 'Crusher' Baxton, as far as he was concerned, was a dead 'Crusher' Baxton, and he was going to create a good 'Crusher' Baxton bloody quick. Even as they were leading the creature from the court-room – with the aid of weapons that were very accurate and particularly damaging from a safe distance – someone timidly asked him about what he would like as a last meal, thinking that unless he fancied a soft-boiled egg, then a salad might be the only thing with sufficient cooking time available.

Within an hour, Baxton stood in the centre of the deportation room, looking down at the priest who was standing in front of him. He was even less happy than before because the priest had made him stop reading – which meant looking at the pictures and wondering what the squiggles meant – his favourite magazine, which this week contained a 'true' story of the complete destruction of the world by atomic war.

'Crusher' liked that sort of thing immensely. Given the possibility of reincarnation and the understanding of what it meant, he would have come back as a bomb.

The priest was not little, but was dwarfed by Baxton, and felt rather as if he were giving the last rites to a bull elephant. He muttered a few words like an attempt on the speed-talking record, then crossed both himself and the condemned man, and the only response he got was an occasional grunt from two hundred and fifty pounds of bone and gristle. Having glanced briefly at the face in front of him, and considered the unlikelihood that he would ever see anything quite like that on the front side of another human being, the priest fled the room.

The door was securely locked, and Baxton shut his eyes tightly, waiting for instantaneous death. The matter which made up his massive frame was reduced to its component tachyons, and veritably flung across space, to be re-formed at the spot pre-ordained by the computer.

A spot right in the middle of the infinite void of the cosmos.

'My great-grandfather was an explorer, you know,' said Wilverton. Gloria, to whom he was speaking, widened her dinner-plate eyes with appropriate wonder.

'Really. How exciting!'

'Oh, yes, it must have been. Mind you, he came to a very sticky end.'

Gloria looked concerned. 'Oh, dear. Whatever happened?'

Wilverton adopted a sorrowful expression. 'Well, it seems he ran into this voodoo tribe in the Amazon basin. They'd never seen a white man before, and they assumed he was some sort of evil spirit. They put this curse on him, said he was going to drop dread, just like that. And, do you know, that's exactly what happened.

Gloria shook her head in disbelief. 'How awful!'

'Yes. Eighty-four years later, he was playing squash, and, bang! That was it! Dead!' His lips twitched at the joke.

'Oh, dear,' said Gloria. Wilverton grinned.

'Get it?' he asked.

'Yes. It must have been awful for you.' Wilverton stopped grinning.

'No, you don't . . . Oh, never mind.' He sighed heavily, and a deep concern marred his features. Gloria realized how deeply the incident still touched him.

Carlton frowned, having overheard the conversation. Wilverton telling a joke? What was going on now? He glanced at Thompson, and received a shrug in return.

Bowen just wished the little twerp would shut up.

Baxton was still standing with his eyes tightly shut, waiting for the end, and it was almost a minute before a thought forced its way into his head suggesting that the end really ought to have come by then. He made a big effort to remember the correct muscle sequence, succeeded after a false start of twitching an ear, and opened his eyes. An even bigger effort, and he frowned. It looked like a bridge collapsing.

'I apologize for my actions earlier on, Paul,' said Mycroft, as he

91

re-entered the control room. 'I conclude that the pressures of solitude, coupled with the real need to beat the *Pioneer* to Alcyone, put an intolerable but temporary strain on my mental capacity.'

Vyland nodded shortly. Then he sniffed experimentally, but passed no comment on what his nose told him. Time to concentrate on the important things in life; like finding a way of killing off his brother. Mycroft had his sights – as in gun – set on someone else.

'What about Curtis?' he asked.

'Curtis is a wart on the arse of science which must be expunged,' Vyland pronounced, with a rude vehemence.

Mycroft wondered how you expunged a wart. Then he wondered how you punged a wart in the first place.

He shook his head angrily. Control yourself, Mycroft.

'Have you any ideas?' he asked.

A light on the console to his right started flashing slowly orange. Left to themselves these things generally moved on to flashing slowly red, then quickly red, but it wasn't given the chance. Mycroft checked the cause.

'We have slowed down, by a marginal amount.' He checked the power output from the engines on several dials further over to his right, found them unaltered, and did a quick mental calculation. 'There must be two hundred and fifty pounds extra mass on board. Did you adjust for your own arrival?'

His brother nodded, and at the same time gave a bovine grunt of agreement and threw his voice so that it sounded like a bovine yell of anger coming from somewhere outside the control room.

'Good,' said Mycroft. 'Well in that case it must be . . .'

'Aaarrgghh,' said . . . Vyland? And both of them looked towards the door.

'Crusher' was not given to fast movement, which was one of the reasons he had been caught. Another being that when he did eventually decide to move, he had to struggle with the matter of direction. Three hundred and sixty degrees were many more than he could count, let alone put in an order of preference. The one he chose had started at the fingertips of the law and had moved unerringly up its long arms.

Thus, it was quite a while before he decided to move from where he stood. In front of him was a door, and he quickly worked out that this would be a first-class place to aim for if he wanted to get out of the room. He took what he imagined would be a small step, and instead floated up towards the ceiling.

This annoyed 'Crusher'. The list of things which annoyed 'Crusher' was not a short one – several encyclopedias would have grown somewhat had they included everything on it – so it was not an earth-shattering event. Crusher's reaction when he became annoyed generally *was* earth-shattering, though, and the semantic fact that the Earth was a considerable distance behind him was not going to affect the shatter aspect, should Crusher have anything to do with it.

The two brothers pulled themselves down the corridor towards the noise, each politely letting the other go first whenever possible, until they hung outside the door of the Captain's quarters.

'Well?' said Vyland, when a pause in the roaring and the sound of things hitting other things at, for them, terminal velocity, allowed him to be heard. 'Open the door.'

'What, of *your* cabin?' Mycroft sounded just like a true Vyland. Vyland sighed.

'Mycroft, I am ninety-three years old, biologically. Therefore, minus the bio, you should open the door.' They stared at each other for a while, then Mycroft sighed, and opened the door.

Mycroft shut the door, ignoring a momentary pressure on his back.

Mycroft locked the door.

In between the opening and the shutting, he noticed the following.

A human being. Probably. Though it was one of those sightings over which a half-decent defence lawyer would have the jury tutting in seconds flat. A mouth, presumably on the front side of the human being, open and screaming at such volume that it could walk into a job with a demolition company. Two arms whose biceps would be marked as hills on any decent map of wherever he happened to be at the time. A projectile of uncertain nature, but looking suspiciously like a piece of cupboard, heading towards him at a rate of knots. And a small plastic frog, hanging in mid-air and looking scared.

It was the last of these which overrode the sense of pressure on his back.

'He's got f – ' he said, before he could stop himself.

Vyland moved backwards, taking his hands from the small of his twin's back as the closing door negated the opportunity.

Neither of them asked who the creature was, or how he had come to be on the ship. Firstly, because they knew that no definitive answer was currently available, and secondly, because asking was an admission that they didn't know.

Instead, a smile spread across Mycroft's face. Vyland frowned at it, and it went away, but Mycroft still sounded cheerful.

'*Now* we outnumber them!'

Gloria gazed out of the window at the stars, and fitted shapes to the patterns they made. That one looked just like a cot with a little string of bells across the top that tiny hands could play with. Oh, and those over there just had to be . . .

'Lovely material this, isn't it, Gloria?' said Wilverton.

'Twins holding hands and smiling,' she replied.

'Sorry?'

'Oh, sorry. What did you say?'

'I said, "lovely material".' He fingered the cloth of which his jump suit was made. Gloria agreed. 'Waterproof, tear-proof, crush-proof. Even fire-proof.' He emphasized the last phrase.

'I didn't know they were fire-proof,' replied Gloria, saying exactly the right thing.

'Yes, almost completely. It's the asbestos content, you know.'

'That's dangerous, isn't it?' Gloria had heard about asbestos some-where.

'Not any more,' said Wilverton, and looked sad. 'It used to be, of course. My great-aunt Gladys died of asbestosis.'

'Oh, dear. How awful!'

'Yes,' agreed Wilverton. 'It took us four months to cremate her.'

'Oh, dear,' said Gloria.

Wilverton grinned. 'Get it?'

'Yes. What with your grandfather as well, it must have been terrible for the family.'

'No, you still don't . . . Oh, never mind.'

He sighed heavily again, and looked worried again. Gloria's soft heart went out to him. The poor man had lost so much in such tragic circumstances, and he had no family he could fall back on.

She glanced briefly at Carlton, then looked back at the stars, to the constellation which was exactly like the main living room of a luxury flat with beautifully curved walls and windows and with lovely colourful furnishings and its own terminal in one corner where someone could work without having to leave the children who were playing in front of the vidivision while a real sea-peat fire burned behind the screen over to one side and a mother cat suckled her kittens in a basket in front of it. If you used a bit of imagination.

Carlton did not see Gloria's glance, as he was looking at Wilverton. Something was definitely up. Two jokes in ten minutes. He checked again with Thompson, as he had ten minutes before, and Thompson shrugged as he had ten minutes before. Carlton floated across to where the First Officer sat strapped into his seat.

'What's up, Wilverton?' he asked.

'Nothing,' lied Wilverton. 'Nothing at all.'

'Oh, come on. Two jokes in a row, and I bet they're the first you've ever told. Something's fishy. What is it?'

Wilverton glanced round the room to see Gloria staring out of the window, Bowen leafing through a dog-eared magazine, Thompson toying with the computer game, and Curtis doodling some ornate mathematical symbols – he certainly knew how to have fun, did Dick.

Wilverton beckoned Carlton to come closer. Carlton frowned, but complied.

'I've read hundreds of books,' whispered Wilverton, his eyes darting about as he spoke. 'Now that we've got out of that bit with the meteor shower, I reckon they'll throw in a death.' Because this *was* a book, wasn't it? It wasn't really real.

To Carlton he looked very serious about the whole thing, so, not recognizing that the seriousness might have its roots in distress, he said, 'And you think the least likeable character will be the one to go.'

'Not necessarily the least likeable; more probably the one who has been least involved. So I'm making sure it's not me.'

Carlton considered the hypothesis for nearly a whole second. The man was obviously right out of his tree.

'Why are you whispering?' he asked. Wilverton leaned even closer.

'Because if everyone knows, then we'll all start trying to outdo each other, and on a space-ship that could be dangerous.'

Carlton nodded. 'You're really weird, Wilverton.'

'Oh, good,' said Wilverton, apparently brightening a little. 'That should help.'

Carlton shook his head, and made his way back to his seat.

'What are we going to do about him?' he asked Thompson, on the way.

'Why do anything?' Thompson asked, putting the shrug in his voice this time, since his shoulders were beginning to think their owner was learning how to fly. 'He seems harmless. Treat it as an eccentricity.'

Carlton nodded, and continued on his way. He stopped off at Gloria, and whispered. 'I've just told Danny I think Wilverton's harmless. Best to treat it just as an eccentricity.'

Gloria smiled at him. He'd make a wonderful father.

XIV

The next day was Carlton's birthday. Curtis, even though he considered it should be left for celebratory purposes when they approached their goal, allowed the alcohol to be broken out after much cajoling from the crew members – Bowen told him to – who felt that some relaxation would not go amiss. Very soon, most of those present were becoming as relaxed as newts.

The combination of Wilverton's spoken wish from his first night on board, and the birthday party now in full swing, put Arnold in mind of one of the tapes in his memory banks. Being a thinking computer, Arnold had an idea. Being Arnold, it was not a very good one.

But Arthur C. Clarke was dead, as far as he knew, and even if he had survived to be a hundred and fifty, he would be unlikely to chase them half-way across the Galaxy just to pursue a copyright suit, even for his most famous work. He decided to go for it.

He waved his arm around to indicate that he had a message of import to impart, and managed to hit himself on the head – not that he could have hit himself anywhere else. Something went click, and Arnold said, 'Ow!'

He was about to start rubbing the spot he had hit when it occurred to him that there was no pain, as was generally to be expected with a metal casing and no nerves. Instead he said, 'Sorry to . . .' He stopped short, realizing that he was hearing the sound of his own voice, and looked at Curtis. 'Delicate, eh?' he muttered, then started again.

'Sorry to interrupt the festivities, but we have a problem.'

'A problem? What is it?' asked Thompson and Carlton simultaneously.

'Well, it's something you have difficulty with, but that's not important right now.' Arnold's preoccupation with his film memory bank was becoming obsessive.

'No,' said Bowen, looking hard at both computers. 'What is the problem?'

'It's in the AE35 unit.'

'Damn!' said Curtis, recognizing the need for a decision, an animal he had always approached with the same confidence he would a starving tiger. 'Thompson, you'll have to nip out and have a look at it. I'll help you.' Thompson fully appreciated the unlikely nature of this offer, and kept well clear of his Captain as they left the control room.

They were lucky to have a computer like Arnold running the ship and making sure things went properly, thought Gloria – she had downed a few, mind you. But then computers were ever so clever, weren't they? And another thing:

'How did you get your voice back, Arnold?' she asked.

'I hit myself on the head.'

'How clever.'

Thompson could not remember what or where the AE35 unit actually was, but he was not going to admit that in front of Curtis. He figured that he would recognize it when he saw it. Curtis helped him into his space suit, sort of, and saw him into the air lock, trying to remember what and where the AE35 unit actually was, and figuring that Thompson would be bound to know.

Curtis managed to don the headset from the other suit, so that Thompson could talk to him should he so wish – anything being possible. It would be Curtis's job to operate the outer door, when Thompson informed him that he was ready to exit, and then re-enter later on. Thompson duly informed, and Curtis opened the door.

Thompson pulled himself outside the craft, and looked around, seeing the stars innocuously still despite the speed of their movement, seeing the largely smooth surface of the space-ship *Pioneer*, but not, unfortunately, seeing anything with AE35 written on it in big letters, as he was sort of hoping.

Back in the control room, a thought meandered into Wilverton's head. He mulled over it for a few moments, wondering if it was worth mentioning in the light of the reaction to most of his comments, and finally decided that, in the circumstances, it probably was. He cleared his throat.

'Er.' A few sets of bleary eyes were turned vaguely in his direction. 'We, er, haven't actually got an AE35 unit.'

'Don't be stupid,' said Bowen. 'We must have one. It couldn't have gone wrong if we didn't have one, could it?'

Wilverton had to accept that the logic of that argument was sound, but found that, unfortunately, all things considered, it did not refute his hypothesis. He thought like that, you see.

'I think that Arnold is trying to carry out my wishes.' They all looked at him, waiting for some explanation. 'I think I intimated a couple of nights ago that I sort of wished something exciting would happen on board this ship, like it does in books, and I think that Arnold is trying to make that wish come true. This little episode reminds me rather strongly of a book which I once read – well, I read it more than once, actually – in which the computer reported a breakdown in the AE35 unit, prior to taking over the ship. Only the AE35 unit hadn't actually broken down.'

'You mean the AE35 unit hasn't actually broken down?' asked Bowen, his brain settling happily onto the last sentence, since the rest had long since drowned in alcohol.

'No, we haven't got an AE35 unit,' repeated Wilverton, beginning to wish that he had never started.

Carlton came soberly to the rescue. Carlton did not get drunk when there was work to be done. He tightened his grip on Gloria, and asked, 'What did the computer do in this book after the bit about the AE35 unit?'

Wilverton swallowed. 'Well, he caused the death of the person who went out to look at it.'

Curtis's befuddled mind – even more befuddled than usual – looked around the interesting bits in the corridor near to the door. It didn't take long. The cupboard containing one space suit and a gap where the other was stored, and a panel with a number of buttons to control the external cameras and mechanical arms for use on a planet's surface if they could not venture out themselves, and that was about it.

'Just locating the AE35,' came Thompson's tinny voice in his ear. Outside, Thompson hung just clear of the exit and looked around, wondering how to break it to Curtis that he had no idea of where to start looking.

Curtis reached out to one of the buttons, as if to pass the time. His hand had almost reached it when a bit of his brain demanded to know what the hell it was doing.

I thought I'd just press this to see what happened, his hand told it.

That could be dangerous, said the brain. What if Danny was near the equipment when you started it? And since you don't know where the AE35 is, he could be.

Bloody hell! said the hand, snapping itself away from the button as though the small dog it was about to stroke had suddenly foamed at the mouth and snapped at it.

Curtis jerked himself away from the panel, keen not to cause the death of anyone else, reasonably enough, and flew across the corridor to the far wall, where his progress was arrested by his forehead, causing him to screw his eyes shut and flinch various limbs in reaction. One of the limbs pushed him off the wall again and back across the corridor. He opened his eyes just in time to see his elbow pushing the button which operated the rock-cracking punch on the outer hull.

'Hurghhh!' said Thompson, in a comment brief but, well, to the point.

Curtis stared in horror at the button, and hit it again to retract the punch, thereby pulling it free of Thompson and bouncing him off the ship's hull out into space.

'Er,' said Curtis.

Carlton glanced out of the port and saw Thompson's body spiralling away into the distance, with what appeared to be a large hole in his back pack. He turned back to Wilverton, his brain getting ready to say something along the lines of 'Well, Arnold is hardly likely to kill Thompson, is he?' In the event, though, his mouth didn't say that. Instead, Carlton snapped his head back to the port, and suggested,

'. . . .!?!?'

The others watched Carlton's arm rising slowly to point out of the port, and then followed its indication to see Thompson's graceful aerial display – only without any air, which was the problem really. They all passed the same comment as had Carlton.

The sobering effect which this sight had was remarkable, if impractical in normal circumstances as a cure for drunkenness. Bowen's mind immediately found two prime candidates for the presumed accident.

The first, and less likely of the two, sat on the shelf, and swivelled his eyes so that he could follow the progress of Thompson. The second, and far more likely, suddenly appeared in the doorway, looking sheepish. Very sheepish. He explained, falteringly, what he had done. Somehow, there was a marked lack of surprise.

'Well, can't we *do* something?' Gloria looked and sounded outraged, and would probably have leapt to her feet by now if, firstly, that action would not have resulted in her disappearance to the ceiling at a rate of knots and, secondly, Carlton had not still been holding her tightly on his lap.

Wilverton shook his head.

'I'm afraid not. In a vacuum and at that temperature it would be way too late. Poor Danny.' And the use of the Christian name made Thompson sound like one of their oldest and most valued friends, so that Curtis winced just a little bit more. 'I'm afraid he's gone.'

'You've bloody done it again!' Bowen presented the opening gambit for the prosecution, as soon as he had retrieved sufficient breath to form the accusation. 'Can't you do *anything* without killing someone?'

Now this was a little unfair, and Curtis's speech centre formed words that pointed out that he had, in fact, only ever killed two people. Fortunately, the filter system which stops you saying some of the things that you would almost certainly regret caught the words before they contradicted Bowen's implication. Two, said the filter, was rather more than most people manage to kill in a whole lifetime. The events inside his head allowed Bowen to pass further comment.

'If I were you, I'd stop telling people that you're not a Dick. Because if you're not, then I've never met one!'

Curtis looked wretched. Carlton and Gloria looked on in still shocked silence. '. . . then I've never met one', wrote Wilverton.

By this time, thought Vyland, they would have hand-held TMTs – tachyon matter transferrers – which could be pointed and operated by a simpleton. He wished they could have nipped back and got one – a TMT, not a simpleton.

He bent over his work, noting that his back did not complain at the action as much as it did under one gravity, and tinkered with his device.

In the background he was accompanied by Baxton's farmyard impressions – he was doing cow-that-has-eaten-something-which-violently-disagrees-with-it at the moment – and the sound of rhythmic thumping, as of shoulder on hull. Mycroft was off somewhere, trying to find a method of diverting Baxton's attention, probably in consultation with his teddy bear or something.

Vyland had completed most of his work – there remained only the reconnection of contacts, of which there are quite a few in a TMT – when a terrible screeching noise rushed into his head and tried to tear up his eardrums.

He had heard this noise before, though not, mercifully, for a long time. Mycroft was playing his violin.

Vyland dropped what he was doing, leaving it hanging in the air demanding a new definition for 'drop', and pulled himself from the control room. He made his way towards the noise, despite counter suggestions from those parts of his body which let in sound that the opposite direction was really a much better idea, and found Mycroft outside the Baxton residence.

'What the hell are you doing?' he shouted. Mycroft grinned at him, and Vyland's eyes rose to accompany a sigh. This was the sort of grin which bounced off walls in rooms where it didn't hurt to do so.

'Music soothes the savage breast,' Mycroft told him. Useful information perhaps, in the normal course of events, except that it wasn't Baxton's breasts Vyland was worried about, although he probably had nipple muscles with achievable violent inclinations.

Plus, there was the undeniable fact that this wasn't music, and was extremely unlikely to soothe anything. The sound made by Mycroft's bow had always induced a tendency towards homicide in anyone who heard it, so Baxton was hardly likely to find it soporific.

'Why don't you go inside and try it?' suggested Vyland, brotherly love burning as strong within him as ever – and that was fact, not irony.

Mycroft shook his head, the grin still in place, and his eyes wide with the excitement of it all.

'Do I *look* mad?' he asked, rather unnecessarily.

Vyland snatched the note-basher from Mycroft's hand, and his ears breathed in the gentler sounds of Crusher's demolitionary activities. Then he drew the bow across the strings, letting a sweet note of pure music drift into the air.

Where it floated, alone, unaccompanied by Baxton.

'There, it works,' whispered Mycroft, as Vyland began to play something in a key which clearly and uniquely fitted the lock to Crusher's peace vault. Silence greeted the haunting melody, suggesting that Baxton might not make haunting a possibility as long as it continued.

Then, very quietly, a new sound emerged from the cabin: that of gentle snoring.

As Vyland continued playing, his trademark smile emerged. This would make it easier to send whoever it was on a little trip. And why not send brother Mycroft with him?

'It was a mistake,' Curtis insisted for the umpteenth time, drawing looks which should have rendered his bodily functions as historical as those of Thompson. 'It could have happened to anyone.' He would have been hard pushed to win a referendum on the subject. 'It wasn't my idea.' He tried the deflecting-the-blame ploy.

'One thing I know about computers is that they are only as moronic as their programmers,' Bowen commented, and Curtis realized almost immediately that his ploy had not worked.

'And you two are a pretty good example,' Carlton chipped in.

Arnold heard that. Moronic, eh? Well, it was the last time he did anything nice for any of *this* lot, *that* was for sure. He was only having a bit of fun.

What was worse was the suggestion that Curtis was his programmer. If Bowen had recognized what an insult that was, he would have been proud of himself. Arnold's eyes narrowed.

That was the last chance for those two – the fat one and the one who kept looking at the window to try to see his reflection – and they had blown it. Sod Asimov's three laws of robotics, he thought, I'm going to teach them a lesson.

Arnold did not therefore join in the discussion. He suddenly had something he had to do. He had to prepare the mid-morning meal.

A space-ship is not a good place to be if you happen to be a gourmet. If you are one of those people who demand delicate entrées, mouth-watering hors-d'oeuvres, colour co-ordinated vegetable complements to a sumptuous feast of finest filet mignon, followed by a selection of the most dainty of sweets, then a space-ship is probably right at the top of the list of places to be avoided. This is probably one of the reasons why

101

you find hundreds of restaurants in the middle of Paris but practically no space-ships.

Fortunately for the palates of those who had the gastronomic misfortune to be on the *Pioneer*, their own various dining rooms were very close to space-ships on that list, so they were not going to suffer to any extent much greater than their norm. Most of them knew more about fire fighting than cooking, and gained their knowledge of both in the same place, veterans as they were of the incinerated sausage.

On the *Pioneer*, as on any other space-ship, meals were particularly tedious affairs, since they consisted only of biscuits packed full of the nutrients and proteins and stuff needed to keep a human's fleshy mound functioning properly. Preparation was unlikely in normal events to be more momentous than the repercussions of a crew member's demise.

This preparation was not going to be a normal event, though. There were extra ingredients in the biscuits to be consumed by Bowen and Carlton, one of which was a laxative, and the other a substance which approximated to what joke shops rather basely referred to as fart powder.

XV

Yes, thought Tonto, I have no bananas. And I wasn't supposed to be up here in the first place. If God had intended chimpanzees to fly in space, he would have given them photon-driven rectums.

And he hadn't. And if I was supposed to be here at all, then I was only supposed to be here once. High time to try that button thing again and go home.

It had taken Tonto some time to reach the conclusion, but then chimpanzees are not renowned for their lightning decision making. He had meandered around the ship after Curtis had relaunched it, confused because it had not been part of his training, occasionally pausing further to reduce his diminishing stock of yellow heaven as one of the things tried to float past him, or to sleep. Now, apparently, the trip had gone on long enough, and the bananas had just gone.

Tonto manoeuvred himself to the console with the confidence of a space veteran, pressed the button – well, he screamed as chimps are wont to do and smacked the thing with a flailing fist, but the effect was the same – and the prototype *Pioneer* turned for home for the second time. This time there would be no Curtis to relaunch it. Against all the odds, there would be a welcoming party, though, even after all those years.

The *Pioneer* had now been travelling for a week, almost exactly, according to the astronauts. In Earthly terms, two hundred years had passed. Those two hundred years had seen an expansion in the astronomical knowledge of human scientists quite unparalleled in history. The discovery that they had overestimated the size of the Universe by more than an order of magnitude, thanks to their cock-up on the quasar front, meant that there was now enough matter within it to make it a closed oscillating body that would never die. Its origins were proved beyond any reasonable or theological doubt, and bishops everywhere were on the point of hanging up their cassocks when they realized that everyone now believed in a God because nothing that perfect and beautiful could possibly have happened by chance.

The greatest discovery, although hardly surprising after the coloniza-tion of Vyland, was of the number of planets in the Galaxy, and, moreover, the number of planets capable of supporting human life. Almost every Sol-like star maintained its system of children, and about one in every ten systems had a planet sufficiently similar to Earth to allow settlement. And that meant an awful lot of planets.

When the first citizens of Newton, Einstein and Herschel simultaneously cut the tape in the capital cities and allowed permanent residence to be taken up, it brought the number of inhabited worlds to ten, and marked the accepted beginning of the Galactic Federation of Planets.

The new worlds made even Vyland seem overcrowded with its hundred million inhabitants. Restricting the numbers to just ten million per world would still ensure that mankind could expand at the fastest possible rate and still only scratch the surface of the available real estate.

One question, though, remained unanswered. Given that there were a large number of other planets floating around, all supporting their own flora and minor fauna, there must, somewhere, be other advanced, civilized races just waiting to be discovered. Where were they?

They weren't on board the *Pioneer*. Being two hundred years out of date, they could hardly be called advanced, and the behaviour patterns they had followed since launch did not really entitle them to the adjective 'civilized'. At least they were reasonably subdued at the moment, for obvious reasons – although no longer visible ones since Thompson's body had disappeared into the wide black yonder.

Wilverton especially felt troubled, guilty almost, as if his assertion that a death was imminent had been instrumental in, well, the death that was now historically imminent.

It was this book thing. He still knew he was in a book, and yet he knew that he wasn't mad. The problem was that he was rapidly becoming less sure. He tried to ignore it.

The crew had reluctantly accepted that there was nothing they could do about the unfortunate Thompson, and that abusing Curtis was not going to bring him back. Shocking though it was, his passing was pushed into the background of their thoughts with the help of a few hours and a couple of stiff drinks, though not stiff enough to restore their previous euphoria. And not nearly as stiff as Thompson.

Life was so . . . so – transient was the word that Gloria was looking for and was not going to find, but she knew what she meant.

Which was why you couldn't just sit around and wait in life, she thought, recalling advice from her father. If you wanted something you had to go and get it – recalling advice from 'Fingers' Magee in the pub; funny, she hadn't seen him for ages.

She looked at Carlton, then pulled herself from her seat and headed for Bowen.

Bowen put down his book as he saw Gloria approaching, less out of politeness than because he did not want her to see the kind of thing he was reading. Gloria had been thinking deeply – we're talking relative terms here – and she wanted some advice. Bowen's stomach churned by way of greeting, but he smiled as best he could, trying to portray a friendly, appealing image. Bowen hadn't given up hope.

He sat up. Had he been wearing a tie, he would have straightened it.

'Mr Bowen.'

His shoulders sagged a bit, but the smile clung gamely onto his face.

'Call me Bill,' he said, trying to stop his voice from sounding fatherly.

'Oh, I couldn't.'

The smile slipped a bit. 'Why ever not?'

'Well, you're so much older than I am. You're like my gran – er, my father.'

The smile dropped. The thud as it hit the floor even in zero gravity was drowned only by the further protestations of his stomach.

'What do you want?' he asked, not sounding at all fatherly now.

'Well,' said Gloria, ignoring the timbre of the voice, and raising her own slightly so that Carlton was sure to hear. 'You've been – I mean you were – married for ever such a long time. I was wondering what it was like.'

The rumbling of Big Bill's stomach converted itself into an eruption, and he let forth a belch of such power and duration that it would have elicited a standing ovation from a beach full of bull walruses. Gloria was somewhat taken aback.

'That's what it was like!' snarled Bowen. Gloria went back to her seat.

Bowen frowned, expertly. Gloria would do well to consider the man inside, he thought, with a hypocrisy only he could have ignored – those qualities of sturdiness and forthrightness which he so patently embodied. He did not recognize that he had the unattractive physical attribute of being able to embody just about anything. Where Carlton had a barrel chest, he had a barrel belly.

Bowen accepted that Gloria would never fancy him, in precisely the same way as he accepted that there were fairies at the bottom of his garden, and that criminals should not be punished but led back to the right way with kindness and a load of public money.

For a while the silence was only broken by various gastric manoeuvres, then Arnold spoke above the juices – it sounds better if you call it 'juices'.

'I think that there was a contact during the meteor storm which I was unaware of at the time. We're not getting quite the propulsion power that we should be.' There was a note of confusion in his voice.

It was odd. It must have been a meteor, since there was not a lot else around, but the damage looked like a clean cut by a laser. As far as

Arnold knew, there were very few free-floating and naturally occurring lasers dotted around the Galaxy.

The aliens' ship? Maybe. He wouldn't altogether have blamed them.

'It's okay at the moment,' he continued, 'but it's going to lead to a failure in the system before long. Two people are going to have to go outside and sort it out.'

'Why two?' asked Curtis.

'A lot of tools are going to be needed for this,' Arnold started explaining.

Bowen was about to point out that they were spoiled for choice, when a look of complete horror replaced the latest look he had been wearing, and he pulled himself out of his chair as fast as he could safely allow himself to do, which was not very quickly. He made a slow-motion dash for the door and disappeared down the corridor, his arms working madly to get him to his cabin. At no point did his knees part by so much as a millimetre.

'Peter,' said Gloria softly, dreamily.

'What?' said Carlton gruffly, mind-on-something-elsedly.

'What do you think of marriage, Peter?'

Carlton looked at her. That word had always done peculiar things to his stomach, and right at this moment, despite the warning of her earlier questions to Bowen, those peculiar things were far too much for it. Bowen had obviously left his horrific expression in the control room as he left, because Carlton now used it for a few moments. He pulled himself out of the room with the same urgent caution as had Bowen.

Gloria looked after him, wondering what expression she should wear. Horror had been done. Wilverton had cornered the market in puzzlement. Curtis, listening to Arnold, was on concentration. She tried hate, and liked it.

'Are you sure it's broken?' Curtis asked.

Arnold looked at him, and his mouth looked like it was about to purse, but stopped a little short.

'If you like, we can leave it alone and just fly in circles until you've finished killing everybody,' he suggested.

It was Curtis's turn to do an expression, and he chose resignation. He could have argued, and lost, but why go through that scenario again just for the sake of it?

'Okay,' said Curtis, trying to make it sound like a decision, and failing. 'So we need two people.' He looked around the room. 'Where are the other two?' he asked. Wilverton shrugged. Gloria looked at Curtis.

She had been unfair to him. She had been taken in by Carlton's superficial charms, and it had taken her until now to realize what he was really like. He was an uncaring beast who used people's hearts as his playthings and then spurned them as soon as they were in the palm of his hand.

Richard wouldn't be like that.

Richard deserved another chance. It wasn't entirely his fault that he kept killing people. Forgive and forget, as her mum used to say. She flashed him a smile which nearly made him foul his jump suit.

'I think Carlton's gone to his cabin, Richard,' she said, managing to make the word 'Carlton' sound like an insult, and 'Richard' an invitation.

'What for?' He was only half interested; the other half was wondering what he had done to deserve this obvious change of heart.

For a moment, no-one seemed to know what for, but then Arnold coughed gently, an attention-seeking cough that found its mark as Curtis turned back to him. Arnold whispered at Curtis. Curtis sniggered.

'We are not going to have the services of the other two for a little while, apparently,' he reported. 'Wilverton, you and I had better do it. Arnold says it's urgent. Okay?'

'Yes, fine.'

This surprised even Curtis. For all that he was in the background, Thompson still loomed large in such a situation.

'You sure?'

Wilverton nodded and smiled happily. 'Oh, yes. There won't be any more deaths for a little while.'

Curtis and Gloria both moved their mouths into something approaching a smile with a large side-helping of worry. Arnold just stared – all humans appeared to be more or less demented; Wilverton was just a 'more'.

'The only problem is that we need someone to operate the doors,' continued Curtis, letting Wilverton's comment lie. 'Gloria, you'll have to do that this time. We've got a manual for you to work from, so it shouldn't be too difficult. Think you can manage?'

'If you think I can, then I know I can, Richard.'

Curtis swallowed. 'Come on, Wilverton,' he said. 'Let's get this over with as quickly as possible.' He glanced knowingly at Gloria as they pulled themselves briskly from the control room and down the length of the ship to the outer door.

'Why isn't it automatic?' asked Gloria, looking at the door in front of her, as Curtis started telling her what to do.

'Because you have got to decide when we want to come back in,' he explained. 'Almost everything on the ship is automatic, but it needs human input before its automatic process will begin. Most things on the ship will work if you just talk to them. Anyway, the instructions are nice and simple, especially for a clever girl like you!' He paused for a moment, then added, 'Don't press any of the buttons in that panel over there, by the way.' Gloria stopped just short of giving him a look as cold as Thompson.

Curtis and Wilverton donned their space suits, and they were safely shut outside while Gloria read the instructions for the re-entry procedure.

It was Wilverton's job to put the propulsion unit right, and he did indeed need a lot of tools to do it. The biggest tool of all floated around behind him, bumping into him at vital moments, losing his hold on the instruments Wilverton asked for like a doctor in an operation, and generally doing all the things one would expect of him.

It was a half-hour job, and with Curtis along to help, it was just over an hour and a half later that they returned to the entrance. Their suit back-packs contained sufficient oxygen for roughly a two-hour EVA. They had plenty of time.

Gloria was waiting in some agitation. She looked down again at the manual in front of her.

'Danger!' it said, which was a bit worrying for a start. 'Failure to follow the exact instructions as written in this manual could lead to cabin depressurization.' It could also lead to Richard's faith in her being severely dented, she knew, although the manual omitted to point this out.

Why couldn't this be as easy as opening the doors everywhere else on the ship? she thought. Well, of course it wouldn't be! because then it could be opened accidentally, and that would be dangerous.

She checked the inner door once again, under instruction, to make sure that it was sealed. It looked it. She looked through to the chamber beyond, as the manual told her to do, and a green light winked back at her. That was right, too.

She looked down to the manual and read the final instruction again. It still seemed to her a very peculiar way of opening a door, but Richard *had* said that you had to talk to most things on the ship to get them to work, and there was no doubt it was safe.

She looked up to see Curtis waving through the small window in the outer door, telling her that they were ready, and she glanced down at the manual once more, just to check.

'Depress the button,' it read.

Gloria looked hard at the button on the door in front of her.

'You're a very ugly button,' she began.

XVI

Harry 'Crusher' Baxton slept like a baby. A baby what, it was hard to say – a very large muscular ugly hairy species certainly – but he slept, which was the important thing.

Vyland wished that he could do likewise, or at least that he could stop playing the violin. He had tried a couple of times, and Baxton's eyelids had fluttered alarmingly. It gives an accurate impression of the danger suggested by such as Baxton when his eyelids can flutter alarmingly. Vyland had kept playing, going through his repertoire of slow numbers because anything cheerful might start the eyelids off again, and anyway he didn't know how to play anything cheerful; had Vyland worked at an undertaker's, he would have put a damper on the place.

Mycroft had finished off the reconnections on the TMT, a simple task after Vyland had done all the tricky stuff, and had also adapted a radio circuit to create a transmitter via which they could follow the fun on the *Pioneer*. This latter he now held in a hand which fervently wished that it belonged to someone who wasn't on this spaceship as it inched its way towards a peacefully floating Baxton with a view to attaching the thing to the creature's clothing.

Vyland wondering briefly whether now would be a good time to stop playing, but since Mycroft's other hand held the TMT, he provided another chorus of Boccherini.

Mycroft completed his attachment, hiding the transmitter inside Baxton's pocket by means of a small clip, and retreated slightly faster than a cobra on uppers.

'Is the TMT set to the correct co-ordinates?' asked Vyland, as Bach's G string was aired. Mycroft nodded, and smiled.

Vyland considered. He had a slight problem. With the TMT in *his* hand, he could send Baxton and Mycroft to the *Pioneer*. But to get the TMT in his hand, he would have to stop playing, at which point Baxton would probably break sufficient of his fingers to make holding the TMT an impossibility. Inwardly he shrugged. Mycroft could send Baxton, then he would send Mycroft.

'And then we ran out of money and the iron lung rusted and she died,' continued Gloria. The door remained firmly shut.

Bowen entered the control room, and smiled an enormous smile at Carlton, who was already sitting in the pilot's seat looking as happy as a pig in an appropriate substance. No-one else was to be seen, and they wondered briefly where their colleagues might be. Carlton, especially, wondered where Gloria was. The circumstances under which he had taken his leave suggested long nights of unbroken sleep. Well, he would sort it out when he saw her. For the time being, just about all was right with the world. He had no idea that down at the blunt end of the ship, things were going just about all wrong with the world.

'One in three marriage ends in divorce, you know,' said Gloria, a little desperately, and with no motile reward.

She glanced up to the window two doors away from her, where Curtis was pounding on the thick glass with a look of slightly breathless panic showing through the face plate of his space suit. His mouth appeared to be moving frantically, although she could not hear any of his words. She could not lip-read either, which was a good thing, as Curtis had long since stopped mouthing instructions and was now, well, passing comment.

Wilverton could hear it as there was a radio link between the suits. Eventually he tapped Curtis on the shoulder, calmly. Curtis stopped ranting, and snapped his head round.

'What?'

'Calm down. You'll use less oxygen that way.'

'Calm down!? Calm down!?' The idea appeared to cause Curtis a modicum of surprise, consternation even. 'How can I calm down? We're going to die because some bint with the intelligence of a cushion can't lift one bloody finger and push one bloody button, and you tell me to calm down? Calm down, he says!' More than a modicum maybe.

Wilverton was supremely unconcerned by Curtis's outburst. It ruffled him not a jot. It disturbed his karma not a tad.

'She'll open the door in a minute,' he said, shrugging his shoulders – a fairly pointless gesture in a space suit. 'Don't worry. Look, it's got to be exciting, hasn't it? We can't just sit here for two weeks and have nothing happen.'

'What the bloody hell are you talking about?' screamed Curtis. 'We're going to die!'

Wilverton smiled. He knew. Whatever worries he had did not include being stuck out in space for ever.

'Why don't you try telepathy?' he asked. This was worth a try, he thought; not telepathy, necessarily, because it was unlikely to work, but at least Curtis thinking hard at someone would not involve high-decibel whining.

'What?' The idea did not seem to placate Curtis to any great extent, but despite himself he did stare at Gloria and think frantically, Press the bloody button, you moron!

'I hate you, I hate you, I hate you!' yelled Gloria, and pounded the button in her frustration.

The door opened.

Curtis came as near to falling through it into the air-lock as one can in zero gravity. Wilverton meandered in after him. The air-lock filled with air, the green light came on, Curtis ripped off his helmet, and the inner door opened. He tried his best to fall through that as well, taking great rasping breaths and heaving them out again. Wilverton floated past, looking like he had just had a cucumber sandwich, and muttered, 'See?' He made his way towards his cabin.

Gloria looked at Curtis, at the strange expression in his eyes which she rightly surmised was not, currently, one of undying love. She had made a mess of it again, and the flame of hope burned a little dimmer inside her as she made her slow way towards the control room.

Curtis yanked himself past her and entered the control room a few seconds ahead, deliberately letting the door close on Gloria's miserable visage.

As the door shut, Gloria thrust an arm out to grab a hand hold and stopped a little way ahead. A thought had suddenly sprung into her mind, much bigger than all the miserable, even distraught, ones that currently resided therein.

Richard hates you, the thought said. Richard thinks you are the most stupid creature who ever walked the face of the Earth, and certainly the most stupid who ever left it. He thinks that in an intelligence competition you would come last behind an amoeba known even to his friends as Thicky the Amoeba. He is being really unfair, he is an intellectual snob and he can hardly throw stones because he is about as far away from being perfect as infinity is from zero, and that's an awfully long way.

What's more, he's not the only one. Everyone has thought you were stupid ever since you were a little girl. That's why they used to make fun of you at school and made noises like retarded bovines whenever teacher asked you a question. You're never going to find a nice man who loves you and you're never going to get married and have a family because you're too stupid.

Why don't you get your own back? asked the thought. Why don't you end it all and take them all with you? All you've got to do is open both of the doors at the same time and float out into space, and all your troubles will be over and you'll have taught them a lesson as well; a lesson they could certainly do with learning.

You know how to open the doors now. It's easy.

111

Do it, said the thought. Open the doors.

Gloria listened to all this with a look of astonishment, before her face set in the maiden-aunt-whose-Christmas-present-got-mixed-up-with-the-rude-woman-at-work's-and-who-has-therefore-opened-a-box-containing-a-long-rubber-penis pose.

You're no thought of mine, she told the thing inside her head. You're the Devil, that's what you are, and you're putting ideas into my mind. It's the only answer. Firstly, to even consider killing myself is totally wrong and absolutely stupid!

You split an infinitive, said the thought. They'd point that out to you because they're clever and you're –

Shut up! Gloria told it. Don't interrupt!

Secondly, the very idea of getting my own back is just a childish notion and doesn't do anyone any good. Look what's happened on this space-ship just because they're trying to get their revenge on each other. It just makes everyone more unhappy, and that is not what we were put on this Earth for. Or what we left the Earth for, before you start being silly again and pointing out that we're not on the Earth any more. And you would; I know your type!

Now, whoever you are, you can just take your suggestions and go back wherever you came from. The very idea! Be off with you.

Gloria grabbed the next hand-hold and pulled herself towards the control room once more, shaking her head to rid it of the unaccustomed presence.

The Challenger felt, and could not help but express briefly in thought and gamma rays, something that would have bordered on amazement had it not been far too advanced for that particular emotion still to be part of its psyche. But if it wasn't amazement, then it was pretty damned indistinguishable from it.

A human brain not only resisting its nudges but resisting in an almost dismissive manner! Well, all right, more than 'almost'. And *this* human brain, what was more!

It clamped down on the emanation as soon as it started, but could still sense the Champion reaching out for a metaphorical stroke of its smug.

The Gloria human, thought the Champion, was considerably more of an asset than it had thought!

'Right, as soon as he opens his eyes, press the button,' instructed Vyland. 'We want him awake when he gets there.'

He stopped playing, and Mycroft raised the TMT, pointing it at Baxton like a gun. As he did so, Froggy emerged from the sleeve of his jump suit and floated into his line of fire, and Baxton opened his eyes.

Baxton saw two things: a small plastic frog floating towards him, and

112

something like a gun pointing at him. Strangely, the former of these was not on the list of things which annoyed him, but the latter was, and was quite near the top of it.

Baxton said, 'I say, old chap, how dare you point a gun at me in such a threatening manner' – this is a translation from the original blood-curdling yell. He lunged forward.

So did Mycroft.

In the forefront of his lunge, Mycroft stretched out his hand. Unfortunately, from Vyland's point of view, it was not the one which contained the TMT. But the most important thing in the Galaxy at that moment was a small plastic frog, according to precisely one of the humans present. What the frog thought of the matter remains unknown.

The Challenger could not help a feeling almost of mild protest from transmitting itself to the Champion. The recipient gave a mental shrug at its, currently lesser, opponent. You're trying insanity on one of my team, it thought, I'm just having rather more success.

Mycroft's hand clasped Froggy just before Crusher's fist hit him in the chest, sending him spinning backwards uncontrollably, waving arms and legs about like a parachutist who has just realized he left that big circular bit of cloth on the chair in the hangar.

Involuntarily, the finger covering the TMT button pressed down, and fired a transmission field at wherever it happened to be pointed at the time, before hand and TMT smashed into the wall on the far side of the cabin. The hand came off none too well, the TMT rather worse, and the wall, by now pretty used to being hit with some force since Crusher's occupation of the cabin, hardly noticed at all.

As luck would have it, and did, there were then only two people left on Mycroft's ship, and one of them said, 'Nice shot, Mycroft,' with some sarcasm.

The other said, with some concern, 'Ribbit.'

On a journey of any length through space, there is, inevitably, a considerable amount of waste produced, both organic and inorganic. Recently, on the *Pioneer*, rather more organic waste than usual had emerged, but the less said about that the better. Periodically, this waste is packed into capsules and ejected into the void, where it will float for ever, or until some extraterrestrial race discovers it, assumes it is some sort of greeting card from a far away civilization, opens it up, and decides not to pursue the matter. In this case, in order to compensate for Gloria's unexpected mass and reduce any possible strain on the repaired propulsion units, most of Thompson's belongings were to be included.

113

Carlton was informed by a small flashing light on the console in front of him that the capsule was now ready for ejection.

He informed Arnold of what he was about to do, so that the computer could take note of the reduction in mass which would result, and alter the drive accordingly. Arnold acknowledged the information with a wave of his hand.

Carlton pressed the button, and the waste capsule was released.

At exactly the same moment, two hundred and fifty pounds of bone and gristle materialized in Wilverton's cabin. Arnold patiently waited for Carlton to release the capsule and the mass to fall.

The Champion had seen its Challengers make use of some pretty outrageous coincidences over the eons of playing the Game, but the whole business of Baxton made most look like certainties. It did not let it ruffle its exterior – maintaining a non-committal yellow-green visible emanation – because in this Game, two could play at *that* game.

Arnold did not question the lack of capsule ejection because, after the roaring success of the first part – and it had been a sort of roaring sound he had picked up from the two cabins – he was busy preparing for the second part of his revenge, which required writing a note for Curtis, since he didn't want the information he was about to impart being overheard. That done, he screwed the note up in his hand and stared hard at its intended recipient, who had entered the control room looking as flushed as Bowen's toilet, waiting for a returning glance.

Eventually, Curtis did look at the computer, and Arnold immediately tried to gesture surreptitiously with his eyes. Now that's not easy. It's possible to gesture left or right, or even up or down, but if you are trying to get someone to come towards you, there is a definite problem unless you can make your eyes fall back into your head. Arnold couldn't, but he tried the gesture anyway, and succeeded in looking as though he was having some kind of fit. Curtis floated backwards a couple of yards, and Arnold increased his efforts. Curtis visually checked the bolts which held Arnold onto his shelf, thinking the computer might have flipped and be about to go for the throat.

Arnold glanced heavenward, which didn't make matters any clearer, then tried to mouth an instruction to Curtis to come towards him. Curtis frowned at the lips, but made no attempt at forward motion.

To hell with surreptitious, thought Arnold, and he beckoned with his arm. Curtis hesitated, then slowly approached the shelf. Arnold held out the piece of paper, and treated Curtis to a meaningful glance. Curtis took the paper anyway. He read it. He looked up at Arnold, who was clean out of expressions and who just looked back. He looked at

Carlton. He looked back down at the piece of paper to make sure it said what he thought it said. It did. It said,

'*The blue blotches were ink. There is no such thing as Gumby's syndrome.*'

He read it one last time, then popped it into his mouth, like you're supposed to do with secrets.

Then he chewed. And *how* he chewed. It was not an offhand I've-got-this-something-in-my-mouth-and-I'd-better-give-it-a-quick-chew-before-I-swallow-it sort of chew; this was a real grinding effort, with creditable anger and frustration in the action.

If only Carlton didn't hold all the physical aces to Curtis's three of no-trumps. There must be something he could do! But what?

He chewed. He stared hard at the ground. He frowned in intense concentration. Then he stopped and looked up. An idea had struck him, his second in as many days. Would it be any better than the last one?

Almost certainly not.

In his cabin, Wilverton reached for the towel lightly fixed by Velcro to the wall next to his wash basin, eyes tightly shut against any soap which might be lurking in ambush on his eyebrows. As he pulled it from its home, the towel apparently gave a sort of bovine grunt. It did not protest when he quickly dried his eyes with it though, and then he lost interest in it, as he looked up and something else claimed his attention.

Above head height, and across the other side of the cabin, someone was facing away from him. All Wilverton could see was his enormous back, and the head with its cropped hair sitting solidly on the massive shoulders without bothering with a neck. Wilverton's first thought was a very obvious one.

Must be hell buying shirts, he thought.

Then he pondered a bit. He didn't recognize the description that his eyes were giving him, and there had been easily enough time to memorize those of everyone on board.

The man struggled round to face him, and he was the spitting image of someone whom Wilverton had never seen before in his life, which answered all the questions, but posed a new one which Wilverton did not quite have the presence of mind currently to address. There had been one death already. Perhaps there was a second one coming up.

Curtis emerged from Carlton's cabin, and entered Thompson's. The 'swish' of the door as it opened drowned out the sound of a sort of bovine grunt from Wilverton's room. In his hand he held a little bottle. A little ink bottle, which, now completely inkless, would make a perfect carrying case for something the size of a bee. A little smile played about Curtis's features. It would probably lose.

Baxton pushed himself off the far wall of Curtis's cabin, aiming for the centre of Wilverton's chest. Fortunately for the First Officer, Baxton couldn't hit a barn wall with a banjo, and although the direction was reasonable enough, the height left quite a lot to be desired, and he crashed into the wall above the door. Wilverton pushed himself the other way, and along the floor, to end up in a heap diagonally opposite Baxton.

Logical thought was in short supply in the cabin for various reasons, but Wilverton was aware that his chances of doing anything against this mountain of apparent discontent were somewhere on the shy side of zero, unless he could get his hands on some sort of weapon. He looked round frantically, and found nothing.

Perhaps he could try reason.

'Er, look, can we talk about this at all?' he asked. Baxton made a noise like a bear with a sore everything, and especially the sensitive bits. 'No, I thought not.' Wilverton presumably spoke to himself since Baxton had indicated his lack of interest in having a chat. What Baxton was interested in was tearing his head off, apparently.

'Do you recognize the voice?' Mycroft asked his brother as Wilverton's query emerged from a loudspeaker on the console in front of them. Vyland looked at him, like *that*. He had heard none of the voices for over sixty years.

'I recognize the one like a zoo on fire.'

'My heavens, look at that!' said Wilverton, pointing to something over Baxton's shoulder. Then, you see, Baxton would look round to see what Wilverton was pointing at, and he could make a dash for the door, and with a bit of luck, get through it while he was still alive.

That was the theory.

Baxton just stared at him.

No, you don't understand, you're supposed to look over your shoulder, Wilverton's eyes told him, alternating between the giant's slavering jaws and the non-existent horror somewhere behind him.

Baxton just stared at him.

Plan 'B', thought Wilverton. I'm smaller and more agile. I'll push off this wall, hit him squarely in the chest, knock him out of the way and make a dash for the door while he's still trying to get himself straight.

He pushed hard off the wall, and, surprisingly, managed to hit Baxton squarely in the chest without getting his head twisted off at all, largely because someone moving towards him whilst not holding something lethal was so unusual as to cause Baxton to react like argon.

As a result of the contact, Baxton moved not an inch and Wilverton bounced back to where he had started the manoeuvre.

Plan 'C', he thought, rubbing his shoulder, then he turned his back, crouched, put his hands over his head, and whimpered.

With his face so buried, his view of Baxton was necessarily limited to zero. This did not bother Wilverton to any great extent, being precisely what he had hoped to achieve by the action.

The end for which Wilverton was waiting would come shortly after Baxton reached him, and that had to be done slowly. The baddie pulled himself very gently across the room, from hand-hold to hand-hold, but stopped as something caught his eye.

Over by the door, in two spots about three feet off the ground, a bright shimmering began. As it continued, it spread upwards and downwards and began to take almost human shape. Then, in the midst of the light, two human figures became visible, quickly sharpening into focus.

The right of the two wore calf-length boots, black trousers that appeared to be rather too short, and a sort of golden-coloured sweat shirt. He was slightly crouched, and held what appeared to be some sort of weapon in one hand. The other was dressed in similar fashion, except that his sweat shirt was blue. His distinguishing features were his ears, which came to points at their upper extremity. He, too, held a gun of some sort.

The forms solidified, and the light disappeared. The one in the golden shirt looked about him, seemingly taking little notice of the bulk of Baxton, who had turned to face the newcomers.

'Wrong goddam co-ordinates!' he said. He took a small device from his waist band and flicked it open in front of his face, muttering as he did so, 'Must have been on the Scotch again.' He mumbled into the device.

The one with pointed ears raised a quizzical eyebrow as he viewed his surroundings.

'Fascinating, Captain.'

Baxton arrested his attention by means of another farmyard impression, and then launched himself towards the two, with surprising accuracy. As they started shimmering again, the one with pointed ears raised his gun and shouted:

'Look out, Jim!'

He fired at Baxton, who promptly glowed briefly, and then disappeared. He would have been less than ecstatic to learn that he had outlived the judge who sentenced him by over a year.

The two figures shimmered some more, and then likewise disappeared.

When the silence had permeated Wilverton's skull, and he realized that the death he had feared must have happened and was not his, he looked around, and found himself alone in the cabin. Worrying? More, interesting. He started ticking off the possibilities in his mind.

'Who's Jim?' asked Mycroft, but received the look by way of answer.

From the abrupt way that the transmission had cut off, it was apparent that somehow the crew of the *Pioneer* had managed to overcome Baxton, and clearly in a terminal way. More's the pity I couldn't get Mycroft over there at the same time, thought Vyland. If I didn't know better, I'd think he smashed the TMT for the sole purpose of avoiding such a fate, the calculating swine.

The milk of human kindness ran in Vyland's veins like yoghurt at the back of a bachelor's fridge.

A long way away, Champion and Challenger hung together in the ether, whilst respectfully below them a crowd of what would have been onlookers, had they possessed optical equipment in the physical sense, regarded proceedings. 'Onsensers' does not, perhaps, conjure up a sharp mental image, but that would be a more accurate description. They projected dutiful appreciation of the Champion's rebuff of its opponent's ploy in the mental equivalent of applause. One did not remain Champion for seven eons without knowing a trick or two. The Champion did not acknowledge them, of course.

The Challenger clamped its mental emissions so that none could sense its ultraviolent disappointment at being balked, and resolutely maintained a vacuum of calm – there wasn't any air. Arranging such an outrageous coincidence was not very likely to have won the Game for it at this early stage, but it had been worth a try.

The Champion seemed to have used it to its advantage, as the one chosen as its Player was less worried about his mind, for some reason. Not a good result.

There was plenty more to come, though, and the Player would not get off so lightly in the future.

The door to his cabin opened and Wilverton came out. He was moving slowly, staring at the ground with a look of some concern on his face. There had been a noise. There had been a noise which he recognized, but from where? It was like . . . No, it couldn't have been. Impossible. And someone had spoken, and they had said . . . No, it couldn't have been. Could it?

Perhaps he *was* becoming a touch unbalanced; a touch touched.

He thought about it.

No. No, he wasn't. And even if he was, he could be comfortable if he knew the works in which he found himself. He would just have to learn to live with it, like a wart, or a pain in the neck. He had learned to live with Curtis, after all. He would just accept it as one of those things.

He probably wouldn't mention the book again.

He squared his shoulders, pulled himself along to the control room and settled himself into his seat without a word to any of the others.

Bowen was once again regaling Carlton with a treatise on the joys of being alive with a quiescent bowel. He concluded his regalia with a friendly tap on the back of the head. It was then he turned to look at Wilverton, not seeing Carlton's hand fly up to his eye and his subsequent frantic search of the surrounding atmosphere with the uncovered one.

As he looked, Bowen saw the expression of puzzlement on Wilverton's face, and uncharacteristically asked him what the matter was.

Wilverton looked at him with great sincerity, which is not easy, and told him, 'I'm not sure that this is a book, after all. I think it might be a television series.' This would be the last time he mentioned it.

Bowen looked at him with great incomprehension, which *was* easy. 'Sorry?'

'This.' Wilverton waved his arm to indicate the whole cosmos. 'It might not be a book, after all. It might be a television series.' Positively the last.

Bowen smiled in what might have been an encouraging sort of way. He knew that when you came across a mind that was starting to become unbalanced, you had to treat the person as though he or she were perfectly normal; reassure them, agree with them, keep them calm, do nothing upsetting.

'You're mad,' he said.

XVII

Vanessa Gravers pulled herself over to one of the observation ports of the escape pod and looked out into space.

Space was full of stars.

Not a problem. More or less expected of space.

Shooting stars.

Not necessarily a problem, but unlikely.

Shooting stars that were not only still there when she closed her eyes, but which were also accompanied by little stabs of pain in every part of her skull each time her heart decided to beat, and the decision was one it seemed to like making a lot.

This *was* a problem, and it needed attention.

In her day she had suffered a few hangovers, and this was similar, except that it was hanging over so far that it would certainly have toppled her had she not been supported by zero gravity. Plus, she generally enjoyed getting hangovers, even if she could only assume that fact afterwards. This had definitely not been fun.

And the astrological reading had been so good this morning. Nowhere had it said that ancient spacemen would try to kill her with meteors. Not in the newspaper *she* had read, anyway. It had just told her to get something that bothered her off her chest.

She planned to get someone that bothered her off the face of the Universe.

She fumbled across the pod to the medicine cabinet, and fumbled again for the hand imprint. Having found it, she opened her eyes and straightened gratefully as the cabinet did its work through her finger pores, and the pain, in her head at least, disappeared.

When she looked through the port again there were many fewer stars, all moving like stars should – not at all – and no space-ships.

Bugger.

It was all Curtis's fault. Everything that had ever gone wrong with anything anywhere was Curtis's fault.

She fingered her beaded necklace – the beads were in fact small dice whose appropriate faceted options would be elected by the fates when thrown; a diced necklace, then – and wondered what to do.

She could work out roughly where they were, she thought – her and the pod – because she knew their trajectory and speed, and she knew how long she had been in the pod. Or, she could get the computer to work it out for her. She chose the latter option, not being daft, and instructed the computer in its task.

Oh, thanks a bunch! I'll do all the work then, shall I? the computer didn't even *dream* of saying, being rather unlike Arnold. Instead it just calculated where the *Pioneer* might be, and transported itself to materialize a short distance in front of it, and didn't feel in the slightest boring while it did so.

Meanwhile, as they say, back on the planet Vyland, things had been happening. A lot of things, actually, since it was nearly thirty years since Vanessa had left.

The most notable occurrence started with the first attempt by Vyland to break free from the governmental ties of Earth. The attempt consisted of a polite request, to which Earth predictably responded with a polite refusal.

This did not seem to appease the inhabitants of Vyland, any more than it had countless others in a similar situation in the past, and before long the demands from Vyland to be completely self-governing grew to a clamour. The Earth pointed out that there had been agreements signed on tablets of stone when the colonies were first set up that those colonies were to be for the good of mankind as a whole, and not just those lucky enough to live there. Vyland told Earth exactly where it could stick its tablets of stone (but apparently Slough didn't want them). Seeing the actions of the Vyland government, some of the other colonies began to climb onto the band-wagon. In other words, they were starting to behave just like humans should.

The number of new planets being colonized had dwindled to nothing, though, and very peculiar it was, too. For a sphere round the Earth to a diameter of about a thousand light years, there was a large number of inhabitable planets. Outside that sphere, nothing. Not one. No-one could give any explanation of why, but the matter was pushed into the background in any case as the tension rose between the planets, and continued to rise, until all was nearly ready.

'Gralph!' said Biondor. 'Krel naela gropf nediv tregnorn.'

Zeekrop nodded sadly. 'Dre ngar va troplok, ko frangar.'

Biondor's turn to look sad. 'Krel fanjort kren ba hond.'

'Gunfrelf jort.'

'Ilf peel gul ertgran vou danor farl di treg!' Zeekrop shook his head in slow disbelief at this ingratitude.

'Dre lonmar dia hansrop,' Biondor confirmed.

'Furd-bonos.'

121

'Wilkra.'

The battle fleets of the colonies and good old Mother Earth sat in interstellar . . .

What?

'Well!' said Biondor. 'They still fight among themselves.'
Zeekrop nodded sadly. 'I'm afraid so, my friend.'
Biondor's turn to look sad. 'They cannot join us now.'
'Indeed not.'
'And this after everything you have given to them!' Zeekrop shook his head in slow disbelief at this ingratitude.
'I did my best,' Biondor confirmed.
'Shit-heads.'
'Quite.'

Okay?

The battle fleets of the colonies and good old Mother Earth sat in interstellar nothingness – apart from a few hydrogen atoms, but 'interstellar very little indeed' doesn't have the same sort of ring to it – watching each other, unmoving. In the centre of the no man's space lay a craft on its own. The diplomatic ambassadors were doing absolutely everything they could to find a settlement before committing themselves to war, without actually shifting an inch from the views with which they had boarded the craft, which for the most part were unspoken convictions that war was inevitable and generally the best way of sorting things out. Plus, wars were exactly the sort of things that required diplomatic ambassadors, as chance would have it.
The talks sadly broke down after a decent period, and the ambassadors went sorrowfully back to their respective shuttles to break the news to the waiting fleets.
The generals heard the commands, and gathered their top brasses. In the enormously shielded cruisers which hung in space the best part of a light year behind the front lines, the atmosphere was heavy. With tension, not with excitement. Definitely not.
'It is with the greatest regret that we have to inform you that talks undertaken by our ambassadors have broken down,' said just about every one of them. 'The best efforts of the peace-mongering crap wafflers, er, sorry, the ambassadors, have come to naught, and it is now our appointed place to strive for justice.
'Nobody wanted this war, but it is clear that war has now become the

only course of action open to us. We have reached the last resort, and it is now down to the fighting men and women.'

Slobber.

'There will be casualties.'

Thousands of miles away.

'But their sacrifice is the price we'

– they –

'pay when such treachery as this threatens our basic freedoms.

'We shall fight them in the tactics bunkers just within communications range of the front, we shall fight them in the holographic operations room, we shall fight them in the computer master control console and the robotics command centres.'

We shall fight them everywhere except where we might actually be in danger.

'We shall never surrender.

'We few, we happy few, we band of brothers: for he today that sheds his blood with me shall be my brother'

– even though he'll be dead –

'and men shall think themselves accursed they were not here, and . . . er . . . ahem . . .

'Terrible business, war.'

Two opposing lines of battleships faced each other across the void as the commanders passed orders – passed them forwards, as a rule – to huge mobile arsenals with shields thick enough to withstand the heaviest bombardment, which would lumber about like savage pachyderms, and to small mosquito-like craft whose defence was their speed, which could sting and move on in the blink of a positronic eye.

With their initial battle sequences already programmed in, and with counter manoeuvres the responsibility of the reactive computers, the orders passed were little more than 'Press your buttons'.

The buttons were pressed, and nothing happened.

Suddenly, all the ambassadors found themselves not on their shuttles and heading for their homes like rodents to their nests, but back on the craft in no man's space. All were sitting round the same negotiating table they thought they had left for the last time only a few hours before.

At one end of the table which had previously been empty, however, sat a strange figure. He was humanoid, certainly, although the eyes were a bit too big and the nose and ears were a bit too small. His smooth, hairless, fawn-coloured skin had not a wrinkle on it, but he gave the impression of being old. Or maybe not old, the impression perhaps was more one of authority than age, and a very good impression it was, too.

Not one of the delegates leapt to his feet demanding to know the meaning of this outrage. They sat quietly, nervously, one or two of them fidgeting, clearing their throats as the alien – it was obviously an alien –

looked from face to face, exuding power and sadness. While the alien was sitting there with such an aura, no-one's mind was so much as crossed by the possibility of an hurrumph.

Finally, the alien broke the silence.

'There will be no fighting, humans.'

'Oh, why not?'

'Because I say not!' The alien stared down the assistant ambassador from Earth who had dared to question his statement.

'I am very disappointed in you all,' he continued after the assistant had dropped his eyes to a knot in the plastiwood table top. 'Very disappointed indeed! I had hoped that by now you were old enough not to need looking after all the time. But no. As soon as I turn my back you start squabbling again. When will you learn? Time after time you resort to these stupid scuffles without even looking for another answer, as if you were primitive animals who knew no better than to use force through instinct. I've had it up to here with you. I don't know why I bother, I really don't.'

He looked at the ambassador from Herschel. 'Oh, do stop snivelling.' The ambassador sniffed and wiped his nose with his sleeve. 'I terraform a host of planets for you so that there is plenty of room for you all. I give you a chance to see if you can be left alone, to see if you have grown up enough to be treated as adults, and what do you do? Eh? Give you a century or so and you're about to start an interstellar war. You don't even know the difference between right and wrong yet, do you? *IF YOU DON'T STOP CRYING I'LL GIVE YOU SOMETHING TO CRY ABOUT!!!*'

The ambassador from Herschel dropped his head onto his folded arms and sobbed silently, shoulders heaving. The alien sighed, raised a hand in the air, and suddenly it held a handkerchief.

'I'm sorry. I shouldn't have shouted. Here, use this.' The handkerchief was passed around the table to the ambassador, who blew his nose noisily and sniffed again. The alien waited for him to settle down somewhat.

'Now, I want to know who started it.'

The ambassador from Earth and the ambassador from Vyland looked at one another, and then as one raised an arm and pointed at the other.

'He did!' they said.

'Ooh, you liar,' said the ambassador from Earth. 'We had a pax and you broke it. You know you did.' He turned to the alien, looking aggrieved. 'He's lying; he started it. He did!'

'It wasn't my idea,' said the ambassador from Vyland. 'It was her.' He pointed to the ambassador from Einstein, who was sitting next to him. 'She told me to.'

'And if she told you to put your hand in a disintegration field, would you do that?' asked the alien.

124

The ambassador from Vyland looked down. 'No,' he muttered.

'Well, then! Don't be so stupid!'

'I'll get you for that,' hissed the ambassador from Einstein.

The ambassador from Vyland glanced sideways and stuck his tongue out. The ambassador from Einstein tossed her head and looked the other way. The ambassador from Vyland pulled her pigtail. The ambassador from Earth kicked the ambassador from Vyland under the table just as the ambassador from Einstein swung round and slapped him with her briefcase. The ambassador from Vyland tried to hit the ambassador from Earth with one hand whilst reaching with the other for the ambassador from Einstein's pigtail.

The ambassador from Einstein screamed. The ambassador from Herschel started crying in earnest again.

'*STOP IT*!!' The alien was on his feet, thus revealing the fact that he was totally naked. The ambassador from Einstein giggled, but wilted to silence under the alien's stare.

When Biondor next spoke, everyone listened. Almost literally everyone.

On all the ships busily preparing for the scrap, in all the cabinet rooms in the government offices on the planets of the Federation and on Earth, in the homes of the people who had yet again uncaringly voted megalomaniacs into positions of power, on all communications media which happened to be in operation at the time, and a goodly number that weren't, Biondor's voice was heard loud and clear, and his face was seen. It was the first time that humankind had met an extraterrestrial intelligence, and the meeting was an uncomfortable one.

'You have got a lot of growing up to do, humans; a lot! This war will not take place, now or ever. You will all go to your home planet immediately, and you will stay there until you can comport yourselves in a more seemly manner. Is that understood?'

There was silence.

'I said, "Is that understood?"'

'Yes's emerged from the ambassadors like a female prime minister's admission of fallibility, while millions of jaws dropped all over the Galaxy.

'There's plenty of room there for all of you still,' concluded the alien. 'And if I find any of you outside your own solar system before I have told you that you may, then there will be trouble. Is that clear?'

The 'Yes's came a little more readily.

'Right, be off with you then, and I hope at least you have the intelligence to feel ashamed of yourselves.'

And the table, the craft, that area of space, and all the planets so recently colonized by humanity, were suddenly empty.

*

125

And so was the box of possibilities from which the Challenger could choose. It turned its full attention to the Vylands, and to Vanessa Gravers.

For his part, Biondor made his way to the planet Vyland, as the humans called it, to make preparations. In the event of the Champion's team succeeding in the first round, he must greet them, and break some rather bad news.

It wasn't a lot of fun, being Keeper of the Galaxy, he thought. Especially when some hyper-advanced race insisted on using the thing as a gigantic playground.

'We could do a hyperphallic acid net, Paul,' said Mycroft, as he wound a bandage around his damaged hand and looked for some help in tying off the end. The frog seemed not to be overly interested, but looked like a rampant Florence Nightingale next to Vyland, who sat with the remains of the TMT floating just above the console in front of him, and ignored his twin like an invisible rainbow. Mycroft's hand might have been broken, for all he knew, or cared, but the TMT was definitely dead on arrival.

It probably wouldn't matter. He did not need to move himself around, and they would undoubtedly have others when he reached the planet Vyland (funny how he knew its name). But he would have preferred it in working order. It would certainly have helped with little brother.

'Couldn't we, Paul?'

Vyland looked up. 'What?'

'A hyperphallic net. We could do one – I've got the ingredients.'

'No we couldn't. Why don't you go outside for a walk?'

Mycroft shook his head, and smiled.

Mycroft was going to be a problem, thought Vyland, like human chewing gum on the shoe of his life.

The crew of the *Pioneer* would be the world's first non-stick chewing gum, on the other hand, or rather on the other shoe, because as soon as their ship's computer fulfilled the second part of its programming, they would slip away into space, never to be seen again.

Should he tell Mycroft that this was the reason why he did not need a hyperphallic acid net?

No.

Well, maybe he should, even though it wasn't, but he wouldn't. Not just yet.

XVIII

'Look, Gloria, I'm sorry about what happened earlier on. I think I had a stomach upset or something.' Carlton was speaking very quietly. This was not something he was very used to doing. It wasn't that he had realized that he did want to get married, after all – far from it – but there was quite a bit of the trip to go. He just couldn't face being alone when there was an alternative, especially one as nice as Gloria. His loins would shrivel up.

Not to mention his ego. Which he didn't, because he didn't have a problem with his ego.

Well, he didn't!

Gloria may have been naive, but she had not been born yesterday. In fact she had been born about two hundred and ninety years before, and even Gloria was going to pick something up in that long. She did not believe him. Her mother had been quite vociferous on Carlton's type, just as she had on almost every other type. So Gloria just stared at Carlton, and said nothing. She did not like the way he was looking at her out of only one eye, either. It made him look shifty.

Forgive and forget might be the thing to do, but only when the person to be forgiven was sorry about what was done. This was only sorrow at what had been lost. This wasn't regret, it was lust! Her expression told Carlton as much.

'And,' he said, seeing that the stomach upset was not going to be enough to pacify the woman, 'I wasn't thinking very straight at the time.'

'Perhaps a knock on the head would do the trick,' suggested Gloria. 'It worked for Arnold.'

'Huh?' asked Carlton. Gloria demonstrated, spun on her heel and left, already feeling guilty. (Or rather, she tried to spin on her heel and leave, but she was in zero gravity. Spinning on one's heel and leaving in normal gravity involves a half turn and then forward motion. Gloria spun at least seven hundred and twenty degrees and appeared to be making her way to the door like a top. It was her hitting Carlton on the head that was the important bit, though.) Carlton's hand flew up to his other eye but he did not, this time, look frantically round the room. There was very little point.

Instead, he floated across to Arnold's shelf, in a sidling sort of way, surreptitiously holding his arms slightly out in front of him. He approached the shelf from the side, having contacted the wall about two yards away from it.

'Arnold,' he whispered.

'What?' Arnold whispered back.

'I am fully aware that you doctored the biscuits, but I think you should know that I have thought about the provocation that you endured before doing so, and I have decided that it was a perfectly understandable reaction, and something which I probably would have done myself under the circumstances. I think we should therefore call it quits and be friends. What do you think?'

'What do you want?' whispered Arnold. Arnold had not been born yesterday either, although he was about twenty-five years younger than Gloria.

Carlton's jaw muscles clenched. 'Do not say anything to anyone.' He paused, then forced out, 'Please. But I have lost both of my contact lenses, and I cannot find them because I cannot see well enough to do so. I want you to . . . I would very much like you to locate them for me, if you would. And not a word to anyone, okay?'

'So, Peter Perfect's got contact lenses then, has he?' whispered Arnold with some glee.

'Fu— er, yes, I have. Or rather, no, I haven't, at the moment.'

'Glasses are much easier, you know,' Arnold told him quietly. 'You can't lose glasses like lenses.'

'Glasses float off in zero gravity,' Carlton pointed out, handily.

'So you wear glasses on Earth, do you?' No answer. 'Or could it be that girls don't like passes from men who wear glasses? Hmm?'

Carlton's control hung by a thread. 'Will you look for my contact lenses, and not tell anyone? Please.'

Arnold considered. Enough for now, perhaps. 'Okay.'

'Promise?' I'm asking a machine to promise me something, thought Carlton, foolishness vying with embarrassment.

'Promise. I'll cross my heart and hope to die, if you like, except that I haven't got one.' The computer sounded as though it was about to giggle. Carlton didn't, but managed to keep his voice civil.

'Thank you, Arnold.'

Carlton narrowed his eyes to slits, and tried to make out the shape of his chair across the other side of the room. He thought he could. Now he had to make his way to it and settle himself into it with the studied nonchalance expected of him. He assumed that the chair was the slightly darker smudge in front of the silverish blur which must have been the control panel. He pushed himself to the panel, pretended to check a couple of dials as he worked his way sideways, and sat gratefully on Bowen's lap.

He apologized in the blink of an eye, but not before Bowen had moved him with a two-word command. An awkward silence followed the voluble seating rearrangement, which the Captain felt he ought to break.

He could do this, because there was something he had been thinking about since he and Wilverton had mended the propulsion unit – and, yes, he *did* think that he had helped in doing so. Bless him.

It was when they were getting back in, or weren't. That bit about telepathy. After all, Gloria *had* opened the door just after he had thought at her.

'Do you think I might have telepathic abilities?' he asked Wilverton, taking the opportunity of Gloria's absence to raise a subject which was likely to go down with her like every share he had ever bought.

Wilverton cast his mind back, and remembered his earlier mention of the subject. 'There's no reason why you shouldn't.' He must have *some* abilities, after all. 'We could do a far-seeing experiment if you want.' Curtis readily agreed, and Wilverton thought for a moment. 'Right, I'm going to give you a set of spatial co-ordinates, in binary, and I want you to tell me what comes into your head. Don't try to work out where the co-ordinates are, just tell me what your mind sees.' The others looked on with varying degrees of interest and focus.

Wilverton reeled off a string of numbers, and sat watching Curtis, wondering what would come out. Curtis closed his eyes and tried to let a picture fill his head. Slowly, something did.

'I see a green countryside with a few plastic, or maybe metal, buildings dotted about,' he said, and then paused, a frown appearing slowly on his face. 'There aren't any people there, though. The place is empty; there's a terrible empty feeling about it, as though it had been suddenly deserted. I wonder where the people have gone. But it is beautiful. Very beautiful.'

He opened his eyes and looked at Wilverton. Wilverton was smiling. 'Am I right?' asked Curtis. 'Where is this place?'

'I don't know if you're right, but I'm glad you saw something.'

'Why, where is it? Arnold?'

'Don't ask me, I haven't got a clue.'

'Wilverton? Come on where is it?'

'It's where the IRAS III telescope reckoned a habitable planet circling Alcyone might be,' said Wilverton. 'It's where we're headed.'

'So we won't know if I was right until we get there.' Curtis looked disappointed. Wilverton did not.

'But don't you see? It introduces an element of tension. We won't know the answer until we get there. And that means we must get there.'

'Why? I don't see how you can say th— . . . What do you mean, you haven't got a clue?' Curtis transferred his attention to Arnold rather rudely but quite understandably.

129

'All those binary number thingies. How am I supposed to know what they mean?'

'You've been programmed to understand what those binary number thingies mean, Arnold. They are what you are supposed to be using to get us to Alcyone, Arnold. You are flying this ship using those binary number thingies. Aren't you?' It was very quiet in the control room, with Arnold the most quiet of the lot. A few glances were transferred to Curtis, wondering what he'd done now.

'What's two plus two, Arnold?' asked Curtis.

'Oh, don't be silly.'

'What is it, Arnold?'

Arnold stared at Curtis for a few moments, then his gaze shifted to where his arm protruded from his shelf. His fingers moved very slightly, two of them first, and then another two. Arnold looked at the four that had moved for a little while.

'Four,' he said.

'What's the square root of seven hundred and thirty-seven?'

Arnold looked down at his hand again, and some of the fingers sort of waved about a bit with no particular pattern, like some kind of underwater plant caught in a gentle eddy, then stopped. Arnold looked at Curtis again.

'Sorry, were you talking to me? I thought it was someone else's turn.'

'I was talking to you, Arnold.'

'I don't know,' said Arnold miserably.

'Carlton.' Curtis sounded momentarily a bit like the Captain of a space-ship. 'You'll have to fly while we find out what's wrong with Arnold.'

'You mean no-one's flying it now?' Bowen sounded slightly put out by the implication.

'It's all right,' said Carlton in the direction of the noise. 'We're in the middle of space. The chances of hitting anything are as close to zero as makes no difference.'

There was the briefest of pauses while providence was deciding whether or not to succumb to this temptation, and then . . . nothing happened.

'Right, I'll get my instruments,' said Curtis. 'It's all yours, Carlton.'

Carlton looked in the general direction of the voice which had just spoken to him, and tried not to squint. He watched a fuzzy shape move towards the door in a way which identified it as Curtis, and then disappear through it. When the shape returned, it had a selection of instruments in a little bag that was quite invisible to the pilot, but even sight unseen, he would not have minded a fair bet that Curtis would not be able to play them. The shape moved towards Arnold's shelf, and hung there, the movements now too small for Carlton to see.

130

A moment later Arnold spoke, and those movements stopped.

Curtis was frozen in mid-air. He was about two feet off the ground, and one arm was held out in front of him, grasping a screwdriver. The nearest screw was one which held Arnold to his shelf, and it was this at which the screwdriver was actually pointing. It was also this which had been the indirect cause of Curtis's immobility. The removal of said screw was a prerequisite to gaining entry to Arnold's inner workings, and gaining entry was a prerequisite to locating the computer's mathematical capability. Curtis was about to undertake the operation when Arnold spoke.

'I want Thomas to do it.'

Curtis froze into the pose. This was just too much! He was one of the most brilliant mathematicians in history, and this was a scurrilous slur on his capabilities. He said as much, only in the present tense.

' "Scurrilous",' said Arnold, with the measured tone of one musing on something. 'Opprobrious, grossly abusive. "Slur". An aspersion, a stain especially on character. "Capability". Quality or state of being capable. Hmm. Well, nought so far; shall we go for "This is a" and "on my"?'

'Why do you want Wilverton to do it?' asked Curtis, spotting another losing argument as surely as pigeons spot pavements. Arnold moved his facial equipment only slightly, but still managed to convey the sort of pity one feels for the other competitors when a child appears on a talent show. Only Curtis did not recognize it as such, and only Curtis, therefore, was not surprised when the answer came.

'Because although you are easily the most capable, I feel that Thomas would benefit mentally from the challenge, and the chance to do something useful on the trip. I have to look after the well-being of every crew member, after all.'

Across the cabin, Carlton's mind wandered to his stomach, which, had it been fitted with vocal chords, would have been shouting at the top of an indignant voice just about now, in memory of a certain biscuit mixture. He narrowed his eyes in Arnold's direction, indicating both suspicion and extreme myopia.

Arnold did not notice. He was watching Curtis's reaction, which, predictably enough, was a flattered acceptance of Arnold's reasoning. It never did occur to Curtis that Arnold might have lost his binary facility only after he – Curtis – had made his last lot of adjustments.

'Oh, well, of course, if you put it that way, well, then yes, of course,' he said elegantly. He glanced at Wilverton, and remembered that his First Officer was about as sane as the average inmate who thought himself the world's finest bowl of custard. Curtis frowned in genuine concern for his creation, and asked Arnold if he was quite sure that Wilverton was his favoured choice. The computer nearly sprung a bolt in a convulsive effort to nod, but confirmed vocally that this was indeed so.

Wilverton moved towards the shelf as Bowen let out a sigh of relief and went back to pounding the buttons on the computer game in his hand. Thanks to his previous poundings – Bowen had a uncompromising way of dealing with things which didn't do as he wanted – the machine had lost several of its letter-forming capabilities and apparently felt constrained to point out that he was no longer a space cadet but was, in fact, an ace cat.

Carlton was as relieved as Arnold when Curtis deferred. The quicker Arnold was free to look for his lenses the better; and with Curtis performing the operation, he was just as likely to lose his sight as regain his mathematical expertise. Meantime, he would just have to keep the ship on an even keel, as it were, which meant pretty much leaving it alone.

As he had told Bowen, the chances of their coming across something in the middle of interstellar space were so remote as not to be worth considering. The intense gravitation of a black hole was so strong as to ensure that any two holes within a couple of parsecs of one another would merge in very short order to become just one larger hole, and therefore the *Pioneer* would not meet another one.

So, all he had to do was to keep his hands to himself, gaze sort of towards the black stuff he could see through the fuzzy window-like thing in front of him and trust that no exceptionally bad luck came his way. This he did, peering closely at the nothingness in his field of vision, and completely failing to spot, some way in the distance, a star which was not a star, but an exact double of the *Pioneer*.

Meanwhile.

'It's not fair,' said Gloria, to herself. She was floating in an empty cabin, the one that used to belong to Danny Thompson. As it was generally avoided, it was a good place to go should one feel an emotion that was best felt in private.

'What's not?' asked the omnipresent Arnold from a speaker in the wall. Gloria looked up at it with no great surprise, but speakers could not express disappointment, so her lack of reaction passed unmolested.

'Oh, nothing,' she said, with a sigh. Then her face set resolutely. 'The important thing is not to let it affect your principles. No matter how upset you are, you have to keep your . . . your integrity.'

Arnold remained silent. There did not seem to be the opportunity for a barbed witticism just here.

'Do you know, Arnold, I thought a little while ago about opening both the outer doors and causing lots of damage, just to get my own back, only it wasn't my thought really. I know, because I simply wasn't brought up to think that way. My mother and father always told me that no matter what other people did to you it was the way you behaved yourself that counted, and they were right.'

She paused, and her eyes looked as though they might just be slightly moist. She kept her gaze pointing towards the floor.

'Sooner or later, someone is going to see that it's not just brains that matters, and it's not just what you look like, either. It's what's inside that matters; it's what's in your heart. I'm just going to keep on being me until I find that someone, Arnold.' She paused again and sighed. 'I wish I was just a little bit cleverer, though. I hate being alone.'

Arnold did not answer. For two reasons. One, there did not seem to be the opportunity for a barbed witticism just here.

'Thank you for listening, Arnold.' Gloria took the deep breath of someone making a new start. 'I feel better for that little talk.' She pushed herself to the door of the cabin, pressed the button to open it, and passed through into the corridor beyond.

And, two, because Gloria's words had struck a chord rather deeper in Arnold than even she would have believed possible in her most ingenuous moments. Especially the bit about the doors.

Arnold had a problem.

XIX

'Thomas.' Wilverton looked up from the book he was reading. He thought he had heard steam escaping from somewhere, but the sight of Gloria's face floating a couple of inches from his left ear told him that what he had actually heard was his name being whispered.

'Yes?' he whispered back.

'You're ever so clever, Thomas.' Wilverton shrugged. And he doesn't seem to be mad at the moment either, Gloria thought generously.

'It wasn't as difficult as some people made it look,' he said, referring to the fact that Arnold currently had full use of every faculty he was supposed to have, and now sat happily on his shelf keeping a wary eye on Curtis whenever he was about, in order to ensure that he did not come anywhere near.

'No, I mean apart from that. Generally.' She raised both hands palms up to indicate the whole Universe.

'Well, I'm not "ever so clever". I'm quite bright, I suppose.' Wilverton was getting suitably embarrassed. 'Why . . . er . . . why do you say that?' The first faint traces of optimism gripped a largely unused part of his body.

'It's Richard,' she answered, rather deflatingly. Wilverton twitched an eyebrow by way of a request for an explanation. 'He thinks I'm not very clever, and that's why he doesn't love me.'

Not entirely unreasonable, thought Wilverton, as a reassuring smile lied fluently to Gloria. He looked for some words to accompany it, but the effort of that much disinformation was too great. Gloria saved the sanctity of his vocal chords by carrying on.

'I want you to teach me things so he won't think that I'm stupid any more.'

'What sort of things?' This is an offer of a job for life, he thought, provided you were unusually long-lived.

'I don't know. Clever things. Like talking in a foreign language. I've always wanted to be able to do that.'

'But that would take a long time, and I'm not very good at foreign languages anyway.'

'I can speak a little already.' Her voice was now quite normal, and

134

attracted the attention of Carlton, who was currently the only other occupant of the control room. He did not look round, however, since his eyes were still desperately trying to focus on the thin air an inch in front of his nose. 'I can speak a bit of Greek.' There was pride in her voice now.

Wilverton looked impressed. 'Go on then, say something.'

'Your face looks like a pig's bottom and your smell is that of a haddock's armpit,' she said, in Greek.

Wilverton still looked impressed. 'What does that mean?'

'It means "Greetings to you, I am new in this land and would like to be friends." '

'Well, that's very good. Where did you learn it?'

'There were some Greek men staying in a hotel near where I lived and they taught it to me in the pub one night. They said it would come in very useful if I ever went to Greece.'

'Yes, I'm sure it would. I don't know how much it would impress Richard, though. I don't think he's very likely to speak Greek.'

Gloria looked crestfallen, and almost pouted. Wilverton's sweat glands watched her stop short and heaved a sigh of relief.

'I wish I'd learnt more when I was a kid,' said Gloria. 'My mother kept buying me those *What's It All About* books, but I could never really get into any of them. I did look at *What's It All About: Trees*, I think, because I liked the pictures, but I don't remember anything about it. And I had *What's It All About: Clouds*, and *What's It All About: Pot Plants*, but I never even looked at them. What's the matter?' She had noticed the small smile which reminisced on Wilverton's face. He looked at her.

'I wrote one of those, you know.'

'Did you really? There! I knew you were ever so clever. Which one did you write?'

'The one on algae,' said Wilverton, a little glint coming into his eye. Carlton buried his head expectantly in one hand, but Gloria looked as much disappointed as impressed.

'But that won't help me unless you've got some of the books here.'

Wilverton wondered how he could get back to the punch-line, and realized he couldn't. He shrugged inwardly, and turned to Arnold.

'Have we got any *What's It All About* books on board, Arnold?'

'Afraid not,' Arnold answered cheerily. 'I think for some reason they more or less recklessly assumed that the crew of a space-ship would have IQs in double figures.' Gloria didn't ask what IQs were.

'So we haven't even got *What's It All About: Algae*, then?' asked Wilverton, triumphantly seizing his chance. Arnold did not answer, and Carlton took his hand away from his eyes, relieved that the moment had passed with minimal pain.

135

'You don't really want to learn a lot about any one thing,' Wilverton told Gloria, sensible for a moment. 'What you want to do is to learn a lot of little things about a lot of different subjects. If you can do that, then you can hold a conversation on almost anything. If you specialize, then you can only talk about that.'

'But how do I do that?'

'Well, crosswords are a good way to learn things. I'm sure Arnold could devise a crossword for you. Couldn't you, Arnold?'

'*Me?*' Arnold looked at Wilverton slightly askance. 'Devise a crossword for *her?*' His gaze shifted to Gloria, massively askance.

'It doesn't have to be very difficult,' said Gloria kindly.

'Oh, goody! Thank you! What, you mean, sort of, "Feline domestic pet, three letters"?'

'Arnold,' snapped Wilverton, 'this is no time for your supercilious all-humans-are-stupid attitude. I'm serious about this. Do Gloria a crossword, don't make the clues too easy, but don't go over the top the other way. Is that understood?'

'Yes.' Wilverton had been the one to restore him to full working order, after all.

Carlton made a mental note to warn Wilverton off eating any biscuits for a while.

'Cat!' said Gloria.

Arnold looked at Wilverton with a mixture of plea and justification, but met only stony resolve. The look metamorphosed slowly into something which might have been a warning, but a slip of paper emerged from a slot beneath the computer's shelf, and was gripped and held out by a metal hand. Wilverton floated across and took it with a smile.

'Thank you, Arnold. Most kind.'

'Don't mention it. Pleased to be of service.' Arnold looked at Gloria as Wilverton presented her with the puzzle and loaned her a pen. 'Don't worry that half the squares are filled in,' said the computer helpfully. 'It's supposed to be like that.' Wilverton threw him a withering glance through narrowed eyes, but Arnold was satisfied, and turned his attention elsewhere.

Silence fell as Gloria pored over the clues, and in just a few short minutes she had read them all. She started again. If she couldn't learn things then Richard would just ignore her, and then what would she do? She glanced over to where Carlton peered through the window, and frowned. She looked at Wilverton as he sat in his chair reading through a scientific journal, and frowned again, but this time in what appeared to be thought. She shook her head slightly, and bent it back to the clues.

Picture the tortoise looking at the hare, and knowing, just knowing, that the thing has been living on a diet of pep pills for a week. Picture Gloria doing a crossword.

She was just on the point of complaining to Wilverton – Thomas – that Arnold had made the clues far too difficult, when one of the answers came to her. She wrote 'tub', having worked out the anagram, and looked pleased with herself. She started looking yet again at some of the other clues, spurred by this success, but did not find another to her liking. In fact, she began to get slightly seventeen down: 'A gibbet on which the Romans exposed malefactors, consisting of two beams, one placed transversely to the other; a hybrid; to pass from one side to the other – five letters'.

The door to the control room opened quietly, and Bowen pulled himself in, leaving Curtis as the only member of the party not present.

'This is stupid,' said Gloria hotly. 'No-one would be able to get these answers. I mean, I ask you: "The dry stalk of the hemlock or other umb . . . umbell . . . umbelliferous plants", indeed!!'

'Kex,' said Bowen, in passing, on the way to his seat. Gloria realized that she had an awful lot to learn. I mean, if Bowen knew it, then everyone should! An evil little grin fleetingly peeped out from one corner of Bowen's mouth, but made sure it wasn't seen by anyone.

Wilverton handed Gloria an electronic encyclopedia on his way to the control room door, and left her happily looking for the index.

It occurred to him as he did so that his worry had been banished while he spoke with Gloria. He sighed, and felt slightly sad.

Well, where was the space-ship, then? Vanessa silently asked herself and her computer.

They were both looking, Vanessa through the pod port on the left side of the craft – the port pod port, for the nautically minded – and the computer from all angles. The view from the port currently contained as many space-ships as steamy love scenes in the Bible[1], and the view from all angles was presumably much the same, judging by the lack of reaction from the computer.

Then suddenly there was a ship, and the pod was maintaining position just underneath it as the computer's search proved fruitful.

Vanessa gazed at the silver craft, and her eyes narrowed. It contained her prey, she thought, and that narrowed her eyes still further. Curtis, who had ruined her life, and his crew. Her eyes looked like two clams having a tentative peek at an on-coming ravenous champion clam-eater. Narrow.

Try to kill her, would they!

Apparently, yes.

[1] And it *still* outsold *both* volumes of *The Joy of Orgasms*, virtual reality edition.

Well, they wouldn't get away with it. She'd show them!

She looked around the pod, at the chair and the victuals cabinet, at the control console and the EVA suit which hung next to it, and at the nothing else at all. She did not actually have a great deal to show them with. She had no weapon.

What could she do? she wondered.

Why don't you sabotage their ship? said a little voice in the back of her head, and she snapped her fingers as the idea hit her.

But she must do it surreptitiously. She couldn't just go barging in with all guns blazing, and not just because she didn't have any. She could not afford to make them suspicious. She would be open and honest-looking in her approach, so that they thought they had nothing to fear. And then she would strike!

Next question. How to look open and honest-looking in her approach?

She would knock on the door.

XX

Wilverton made his way down the corridor to his cabin. His inner clock had told him that night had come, even though there was never anything else outside the craft, and he yawned expansively, looking forward to a nice warm cocoon, and some bedtime reading from Arnold. He activated the door to his cabin and looked inside.

It was snowing, which was a bit of a nuisance, because. . . ! !

Not that he had anything against snow. Lovely white stuff, very pretty and useful for snowmen and snowballs and reminiscent of Christmas, even though he had never seen a white Christmas. But it did tend to suggest that a nice warm cocoon was not something which was going to come his way in the foreseeable future – that being about two yards at the moment, as his cabin displayed heavy blizzard conditions.

A frown clouded his features. As it would.

Presumably there was supposed to be a crew member cracking up at this point. Well it wasn't going to be him, that was for sure. It was one thing being in a book – he knew that he could learn to live with that, probably – but insanity was something else entirely. He would have no truck, not even a small van, with insanity.

This was just part of the book, he told himself. Almost certainly. Please let it be part of the book.

He looked behind him to see if there was anyone else coming down the corridor to whom he could display the meteorological phenomenon. He wanted to know what would happen if he did so, wondering if anyone else would be able to see it. If whoever was trying to send him mad was putting pictures in his mind, then it would be invisible to all but him.

There was no-one coming, and he did not go back to fetch anyone. Instead, he stepped into the room. The other way to test the theory was to believe that there was nothing here but a normal cabin, and to climb into his cocoon and just *know* that he was perfectly dry and warm, and see what happened. If, despite knowing that he was dry and warm, he had to admit, however reluctantly, that he was in fact soaked to the skin and freezing to death, then he would logically have proven that it was indeed snow, and not him. Nice theory.

Even though he was well aware that there was nothing in front of him, he still held his arms out slightly, as you do, and gingerly walked forwards, using those little steps that can meet any obstacle without making you fall flat on your face. Under his feet the snow scrunched just like fresh snow does, and the air had that chill in it that air has when snow is falling through it.

Wilverton *knew* that he was dry and reasonably warm.

A drip fell off the end of his nose as the flakes of imaginary snow melted on his face and ran down it. He had to squint as the feather touches battered his eyes.

Something snapped under his foot, sounding for all the world like a twig, but Wilverton paid it little attention. He was beginning to wonder when his cabin had been extended. It had not been this long before, surely. He was only using little steps, admittedly, but he had used an awful lot of them.

Or had he? Probably not. He had probably just used a few and his mind was trying to fool him. Well, he wasn't having any of it. He was half-way across his cabin, and he was warm and dry. He shivered slightly, and a trickle of icy water ran down his back inside his jump suit. He reached up to pull the suit's neck tighter around his own, and shuffled into a tree.

He stopped, quite understandably, and put his hand gingerly to his nose, which had borne the brunt of the imaginary impact. His hand came away with a little smear of blood on it. Real blood, and his, more to the point.

Wilverton accepted that he was wet, cold, and not in his cabin any more, certainly not the one he remembered. So where was he, and how did he get back?

Beats me, he thought.

The snow appeared to be thinning slightly, and he could see a dim light a little way ahead, slightly above head height, by the look of things. He moved towards it, passing a few more trees on the way.

Before he reached the light, he had accepted that he was in a wood, and immediately his widely read brain came up with a number of possibilities. The number was reduced to one when he reached the light. It was a lamp post, standing in the middle of the wood and throwing its light out for no apparent reason to any traveller from another world.

Wilverton sighed his relief. Whoever it was would really have to do better than this. This *was* just another book – and a well-loved one at that. He wouldn't go mad here!

He looked around, and, sure enough, coming towards him was a small man with hairy legs and hooves.

'Mr Tumnus, I presume,' said Wilverton.

The fawn stopped sharply and looked at him with some surprise. 'Why, yes! However did you know?'

140

'Just a hunch. Look, much as I'd like to stay and have some Turkish Delight, I am getting rather chilly, so I'll be getting back. Good day to you. Give my best to the Lion when you see Him.'

He turned and walked back the way he had come, following his footprints, which the dwindling snowfall had failed to cover, and leaving a fairly puzzled fawn behind him.

The Challenger observed the fawn.

Where in the expanding cosmos had *that* come from?

Beside it the Champion exuded confidence. Dumb question, obviously. But what was it playing at?

The snow lessened as he walked on, and he thought this scene might be coming to an end, but it was turning back to a steady rain, promising more to come. More of what was anyone's guess, though, and Wilverton wasn't going to bet.

This is getting silly, he thought. He believed one more time that this was just an illusion, and he believed hard enough so that it would all disappear, just like it had for Captain Kirk and co. every third episode. The throbbing of his bloodied nose and the droplets of water which had seeped from his neck to every angle of his body – and there were quite a few of those – treated this belief with more disdain than even Arnold could possibly have managed, and it lasted about as long as those of would-be politicians in the run-up to an election.

The wind gusted and blew a solid mass of water into his face so that he had to hold his arm up to ward it off. When he lowered it again he could make out . . . his cocoon? No, it was a road sign. Not a nice warm cocoon hanging on a wall. A road sign.

He was entering Midwich, apparently. Moreover, apparently he was entering a Midwich to which he was welcome. Well, that was nice. But some other time, maybe.

Mind you, he thought, it *was* quite fun!

The Champion did not suffer from Vylandish self-satisfaction, but having heard Wilverton's thought, it would have rubbed its smug sore.

The Challenger would have kicked it across the room.

Wilverton turned round and looked straight into the blue eyes of a blonde-haired girl who would have been perhaps ten or eleven years old had she been a real human. She looked levelly back at Wilverton, and the vaguest of impressions came unbidden to his mind, of words, of suggestions. It seemed to him that he should follow the child, that he wanted to follow the child, that it was perfectly natural for him to want to follow the child, and that was what he was therefore going to do.

141

'No thanks,' he said, smiling.

Come, said the voice in his head.

'Look, I don't think you quite understand. You're not actually real – though you may think you are, for all I know – so I don't think you can influence me. So if you'll just excuse me?'

You *must* come, said his head.

'I don't think so, thanks,' he maintained cheerily.

He made to go to one side of the child, but she took a step to block his path. I've never liked kids much, he thought, and sighed. It always seemed so difficult to reason with them, which was all Wilverton could do.

He crouched down in front of her so that he could explain more forcefully, eye to eye, and as he did so there was a whooshing noise as of something passing over his head, and the top few strands of his hair were ruffled by the breeze of something missing them by a fraction.

The something did not miss the child, as a long green tentacle smacked her on the side of the head, and then withdrew, leaving her crumpling to the ground as Wilverton spun round to look at the giant plant which had quietly sidled up behind him as the girl had kept him there.

Say it with flowers, he thought, as he quickly made to sidestep the fallen form, only to find that it was not actually there any more. He turned back for a quick look at the plant, to make sure it was not following him, and found that it too had disappeared. Thought so, he thought.

He hurried back towards the recognized shape and lights of the control room, pleased that he was getting back to normality. He had nothing against wandering through works of fiction, but he had been planning to sleep for a while and that still seemed a good idea.

Hang on.

The control room? Didn't he normally have to go through his cabin in order to get to the control room?

Yes, he did.

No problem, he could ask himself what was going on now, since he could see himself sitting in one of the chairs on the far side of the room. He stopped a little way away, and watched the proceedings.

'Well, since we're all relaxing, I thought we could have some fun,' said Curtis, sounding to Wilverton – the real Wilverton; well, the real Wilverton according to the Wilverton who was watching from a distance – as though he were about to suggest some extra practice for the fourth-team reserves. 'What shall we do?'

No-one answered, although Wilverton watched glances full of unspoken dread being passed from person to person.

'What about a quiz?' Curtis continued. 'They're always good to pass an hour or so.' He looked ever so enthusiastic, smiling broadly at each of them in turn.

'Good idea,' said Wilverton. Wilverton looked at him. He looked odd, really, but not much more odd than when you see yourself on video. He could do with a bit more body, he thought, and then glanced at Gloria, who was sitting there looking at Wilverton with a slight smile on her face. It looked like the sort of smile you give to someone dear to you, and for a moment Wilverton managed to be jealous of himself, before he recognized, with a pang of regret, the unlikelihood of receiving such a look from such a quarter – and Gloria was so much more than a quarter. He glanced at Carlton, and wished he could be a little bit like him, that his chat-up lines did not attract women to other men, that he had not had to stay on the sexually straight and narrow all his life because that was exactly the way his body happened to be built, that he couldn't have made a good living modelling 'Before' pictures to Carlton's 'After'.

But then he had his brain and his intellect, he told himself, and the woman who fell for him would probably be an eminent scientist, with a string of letters after her name, and several important papers published, the ability to discourse on any number of stimulating topics, a figure like a pipe cleaner and a face you could use to crack walnuts. Wilverton sighed inwardly, but did not frown. It had always been thus. It would be nice, though . . .

Perhaps a visit to the gym might be in order – for himself, not Carlton. He rejoined a conversation which had apparently moved on a bit since he had left it.

'Who wants to go first?' Curtis was asking. No-one apparently wanted to go first. Wilverton was slightly surprised at Wilverton's reticence. Perhaps he was being modest. 'I'll go first then,' Curtis continued. 'Don't make them too difficult, Arnold.'

'What are the two types of string in modern theories of, say, gravitation?' asked Arnold. Gloria looked somewhat alarmed, but both Wilvertons nodded sagely while waiting for Curtis to answer. Not too difficult, obviously.

'Open ended and looped,' Curtis answered.

'Correct.'

Suddenly, the watching Wilverton smiled. That this scene appeared along with all the others proved that it *was* part of a book! Confirmation of what he thought. And if it was in the sort of company he had seen so far, it was not a bad book to be in.

Except that it had not happened yet, he knew. That meant it was going to happen in the future, unless it was written out. He would have to look out for it.

Over to his right the flashing request light at his cabin door interrupted his thoughts. Someone had come to see him. He hurried as best he could through the ankle-deep carpet of slush, and pushed the button which allowed the door to open. In the corridor stood Gloria, and she looked at him with some concern. The fact that she was looking at him rather than over his shoulder told Wilverton what must have happened to the scene behind him, and he took a quick glance himself. His cabin was just as it had always been before the deterioration in climate. Of course. There was no sign of the control room.

'What happened to your nose?' asked Gloria.

Wilverton raised his hand and gingerly felt his damaged appendage again. 'I walked into a tree.'

'Oh dear,' said Gloria, a little uncertainly. She looked around, as if suddenly anxious to leave. She was holding her unfinished crossword in her hand.

'Having trouble with the crossword?'

'No, no, it was nothing, nothing at all,' she said, with some alarm. This was obviously a bad time to disturb Thomas, since he was obviously disturbed at the moment anyway. She grabbed a hand-hold just by the side of the door and disappeared towards the control room, horizontally.

She still looked slightly worried – and also a bit guilty, bless her – when she arrived at her destination. Curtis looked at her, and an expression of concern completely failed to appear on his face. Carlton appeared to be looking intently at a point just over her left shoulder, and seemed similarly unmoved by her obvious plight. ('Plight' had turned out to be six down, and it seemed like a good word to throw into her thoughts about now.) She did not care about that, though; at least it made a difference from where he normally looked. Why wasn't he looking at them now? she thought briefly, then forgot the matter. She had finished with Carlton ages ago. Richard was the one that mattered now. But Richard was not softening. She had to prove her intelligence.

Dismissing Wilverton from her mind, she moved smoothly to the empty chair, from which she studied the stars through the window for a while before shaking her head in a disbelieving sort of way. And very convincingly, too.

'It's hard to believe that people used to think that the Earth was the centre of the Universe, and that the sun, moon and stars were arranged on concentric crystal rings around it, isn't it?' she asked.

Curtis's train of thought had unusually been racing along quite happily, looking a bit like one of those fast, smooth monorail efforts which glide on an electromagnetic cushion, but Gloria's line in small talk had a rapid slowing effect. The train reverted at once to its more normal appearance, that of Thomas the Tank Engine going up a very steep hill.

'Er, yes,' he said. He had misjudged her, he thought. Badly. She *was* clever enough to talk about normal things.

'They even persecuted those who dared to disagree,' continued Gloria sadly, 'like Copperknickers.'

'Sorry?'

'They even persecuted those who dared to disagree.' She was sure that was what the encyclopedia had said. She had spent ages learning it. 'Like Copperknickers.'

'Who?'

'Haven't you heard of him?' asked Gloria, a faint hope springing eternal in both of them. She did not wait for a reply. 'Nicolas Copperknickers was a Polish astronomer born in fourteen seventy-three. He –'

'You mean Copernicus,' said Curtis tiredly.

'Do I?'

'Yes, it's pronounced Copernicus, not Copperknickers.'

'Oh.' Gloria ground to a bit of a halt.

'Would you like another crossword from Arnold?'

'I haven't quite finished this one yet.'

'No, I thought not.'

Mycroft emerged from his cabin and turned towards the control room. The smile which played about *his* lips was top of its league – Curtis's earlier effort was struggling to avoid relegation in a much lower division.

Then he stopped, cocking an ear, and pulled himself the other way instead, until he arrived at the exterior door.

There was someone knocking on it, from the outside. Mycroft hated visitors, but he opened the outer of the two doors anyway, in case it was for Paul. The visitor came through, the door closed, the pressure equalized, and Mycroft opened the inner door. Slightly.

'Yes?' he said irritably. 'What is it?'

Vanessa looked at the face before her, and something in it sparked her memory. She shook her head – impossible.

'Well?' Mycroft's irritation was already becoming a rash.

'I'm looking for Richard Curtis.'

'Well, he's not here.'

'What do you mean, "he's not here"?'

'How many interpretations can there be?' snapped Mycroft. ' "Here" is the space we currently occupy plus its immediate surroundings, and Richard Curtis isn't in it. Is that any clearer?'

Apparently it was. 'Well, where is he then?'

'He's on the *Pioneer*.'

'This *is* the *Pioneer*.'

145

'No it's not, you stupid woman. It just looks like the *Pioneer*.'
Vanessa did not pass comment immediately, as she tried to wrap her
brain round the argument. 'The *Pioneer*'s over there somewhere.'
Mycroft waved his hand in the general direction of 'over there', which
presumably wasn't anywhere in particular except that it wasn't 'here'.
'Now piss off, I'm busy.' And he closed the door, hit the button, and
ejected a confused Vanessa into space.

Mycroft had never had a long conversation with a Jehovah's Witness.

Then the look on his face changed to one of delight as an idea hit him.
If it was as good as he thought it was, then maybe Paul would forgive
him for smashing his TMT against the cabin wall.

But would the idea be a good one? Or just another product of a
deranged mind?

He slipped his hand inside his jump suit, withdrew it and spoke to its
resultant contents.

'It *is* a good idea, isn't it, Froggy!'

Ah.

Still, it could have been worse.

XXI

Wilverton hung in his cocoon, warm and dry and with a small sticking plaster on his nose. His eyes were gently closed – a result of relaxation rather than worry about what he might see if he opened them – and he listened contentedly to Arnold's voice as it spun tales of elves and dwarves and wizards and orcs. Wilverton figured that the best thing to make him forget the peculiarities of whatever book he was in was to listen to the best story ever written in the English language, and, as the more perspicacious will have noticed was quite often the case, he was right.

The Council was debating what to do, and Wilverton listened intently, knowing what the outcome would be, but drawn as ever by the magic of it. He suddenly had one of those feelings you sometimes get, and he knew he was not alone. He wasn't particularly worried by this, but he opened one eye to check on who or what his company might be.

On the far side of the cabin – a cabin slightly larger once again than the one he was generally used to – was a long table, around which sat several elves, a dwarf, a few men, and one obvious wizard who was at that moment on his feet and fingering a long white beard as he mouthed the words which came from Arnold's loudspeaker above Wilverton's head. Two of the wizard's audience were much smaller than the others, and Wilverton could see their hairy feet hanging several inches above the ground as they sat on their chairs.

Both Wilverton's eyes were fully open now, and he realized that he was holding his breath. His face split into a grin of immense delight, of ecstasy, and he drank in the feeling of being in this book of all books. What scenes he would see!

One of the little people reached into his shirt and pulled out a length of cord that was hung around his neck. On it gleamed a simple gold ring. Wilverton gazed at it in awe, while the discussion carried on. Then everything disappeared, and it was just his cabin once again, as Arnold said:

'That's the end of the chapter. Do you want me to go on?'

'Yes, please, Arnold,' he said with obvious enthusiasm. 'Before you do, though, have you got a visual capability in this cabin?'

'Eyes, you mean?'

'Well, yes, I suppose so.'

'In that case, yes. I have eyes in every room on the ship.'

'And have you been watching this cabin while you've been reading?'

'No, I don't watch cabins unless instructed to do so. They call that voyeurism, I believe.' Wilverton was not to be riled, and Arnold realized the fact. 'Why do you ask?'

'What would you think if I were to tell you that while you were reading, I was watching it all happen here in this cabin, that the characters were coming to life before my very eyes? Not imagination, Arnold, reality.'

'I'm not quite sure, but I wouldn't put it to the test if I were you. I doubt if I would be able to be optimistic about your chances of escaping senility in old age.'

'Well, that's fair enough, I suppose, Arnold,' said Wilverton unconcernedly. 'I won't tell you, then. Carry on.'

Arnold picked up the story, and Wilverton was soon watching the band of nine walking away from him on their perilous but magnificent quest. If there is a heaven, he thought, then it would be a lot like this.

The Challenger, in its own super-minded entity fashion, felt significantly pissed off. It had introduced the idea of a book into the Player's mind since that was an easy route to madness in someone who spent so much of his time between the covers of books, and it had worked. But now that he was firmly convinced he *was* in a book, rather than worrying that he should think so in the first place, he was having a thoroughly good time. And all thanks to the Champion's tampering.

It had gone to all the trouble of drumming up snow, wind, rain – you name it and it had percussioned it – and the Champion throws in a little man with goat's legs, a heavy moving plant and an alien telepath; and what does the Player do?

He bloody enjoys it!

And that quiz! What in the name of entropy was *that* all about?

And now this. Whole scenes created by the Champion which had the Player encased in a cocoon of happiness.

Mind you, it thought, despite itself, it *was* a good story.

There was a chink, though. The Player did still think he was part of a book, and that was not normal. There must be some scope there . . .

'That's enough for now, Arnold,' said Wilverton, as the remainder of the fellowship ran from what was left of the bridge, and a wailing cry arose from the abyss which it had spanned. He lifted a hand and wiped it across his brow, clearing a thin sheen of moisture which the tension of the story had put there. 'We'll save the rest for another time. I'm not sure I can take it all in one go. Not like that.'

He sank into his cocoon slightly, relaxing the muscles which had involuntarily tensed in the last few minutes of the story, and took a few deep breaths to calm himself down.

'You know, Arnold, with all due respect,' which normally means there is an insult coming, but did not in this case, 'I think the one biggest advantage that human beings have got over computers is that we can occasionally come up with something like that story. Not as good as that one, of course, but better than a machine could ever hope to do.'

'Doesn't seem all that difficult to me!' Arnold took umbrage, all the same. With Arnold around, it was a wonder anyone had any umbrage left. 'All you need is a bit of imagination. And anyway, if you're going to put all your power in something, you're a bit stupid if you choose a ring that can slip off your finger or get cut off by any stray sword in a fight, aren't you?' The answer was supposed to be yes, apparently, but Wilverton just smiled slightly. 'If it has to be gold,' Arnold continued, 'it would be better to have something like a filling. It'd be much safer.'

'Ah, but I wonder if Lord of the Fillings would have quite the same appeal.'

Arnold 'hmphed'.

'Arnold,' whispered Carlton frantically. Arnold's eyes swivelled to their right, to where Carlton was pretending to study a chart on the wall of the control room.

'What?' Arnold asked in his normal voice.

'Sshh! Not so loud.' The whisper became even more frantic without gaining a decibel. Arnold sat quietly on his shelf and smiled at Carlton, a smile which clearly had the upper hand. 'Have you found them yet?'

There were two areas of Carlton's anatomy not functioning properly, and he had to solve his eye problem before he could address the redundancy further down.

All the way across the control room, thought Gloria, and he didn't look at me once. Just stared straight ahead with a funny look in his eyes. A good job she didn't like him any more. Richard was the one for her, but he had gone back to reading that funny magazine after she had tried talking to him. She had to try again.

'No,' whispered Arnold.

'Have you looked?'

'No, I clean forgot,' snapped the computer.

'Computers can't forget, Arnold. They don't have it in them.'

'It was sarcasm. Of course I've looked. You told me to look. I'm a computer. I looked.' Carlton was worried enough by his six down not even to think that most of Arnold's actions so far contradicted this tacit assertion that he could not help but do what he was told.

'Sorry, Arnold,' he said, immediately inducing a point-scoring smile from the computer.

'What are you two whispering about?' asked Curtis.

'Nothing,' said Carlton, in a voice that would have been convicted in seconds. 'We were talking about this star chart,' he contradicted, indicating the wall in front of him.

'That's not a star chart, it's an ink stain.' His glance fell to his hands, where he could still imagine the faintest of blue stains clinging to the skin. 'Oh, very funny!'

'What? No, I . . .' He could not think of anything to say, which had to be some sort of record. 'Just find those bloody lenses, Arnold,' he whispered again, and turned to fumble his way through the thick mist of the clean control room air. A voice which reminded him of his mother arrested his progress.

'What's the magic word?'

Carlton wondered what would happen if he swung a right hook at the smugly superior smile on Arnold's face. He'd probably miss, that's what would happen, he told himself.

'Please, Arnold.' He smiled self-consciously at a picture on the wall beyond Curtis, before launching himself into the fog, and regaining his seat with unerring accuracy and luck.

All the way back, and not a glance. Not one glance. Good!

'Of course,' said Gloria, as though she were half-way through a conversation. 'Copernicus,' perfect pronunciation, 'had to work within the existing framework of the 'P'-tolemaic astronomy.' Curtis looked at her.

'Ptolemaic,' he said wearily. 'You don't pronounce the "P". The "P" is silent.'

'As in "bath",' Bowen threw in, but was quite properly ignored.

'Oh.' Gloria subsided again in the face of Curtis's scornful expression.

'I think I'll go to bed,' said Curtis.

Gloria watched him go, and Wilverton's theory with him. Richard wasn't interested in intelligent conversation, obviously, any more than Carlton was. They were probably both just interested in the same thing. Not that it was a bad thing to be interested in, but it shouldn't be just for its own sake. It should be all part of the process of getting closer, of getting to know one another, of wanting to get to know one another.

She sighed inwardly, and glanced involuntarily over to the figure of Carlton – literally, looking at the slightly triangular outline of his back beneath the material of the jump suit. Perhaps he would get to know the inner Gloria if she gave him the chance. Perhaps she had been too hard; and he *was* nice. Sometimes.

Forgive and forget.

'Peter. Where am I going to sleep?'

In some situations, thought Carlton, short-sightedness was a positive advantage. Assuming he could find the cabin, of course.

'What's that?' asked Vyland, looking at the small oblong device Mycroft held in his hand. It wasn't that he was particularly interested, but if he asked, then Mycroft could get the thing out of his mind and himself out of Vyland's hair. Currently he was bobbing up and down like a cat eager to drop the mouse at your feet.

'It's a time bomb,' said Mycroft proudly.

'Is it?'

'Yes.'

'And what are you going to do with it?'

'I'm going to deliver it to the *Pioneer*.'

Vyland looked up, with renewed interest, or newed interest. Mycroft was going to deliver it? What a good idea.

'Are you?'

'Yes. The woman that came to the door a couple of hours ago asking for Curtis gave me the idea. I'll just go and knock on the door and they'll let me in. And then I'll leave the bomb somewhere. I'll put it on their computer, 'cos it's not a very big one. Bomb.' He held up the bomb.

Well, that seemed straightforward enough.

'Er, well, let me help you into your EVA suit,' offered Vyland generously. As he nodded happily, Mycroft did not apparently observe that this was the first time his brother had ever used the word 'help' when referring to something he was about to do.

Wilverton pulled himself out of his cocoon, and donned a singlet, shorts, and some running shoes, the soles of which looked as though they were covered by some sort of metallic material, largely because they were.

He was preparing to exercise.

This was something which had to be done from time to time on a space-ship in zero gravity, otherwise the muscles tended to atrophy. For the uninitiated, the muscles had a good feel of the weight of the body – zilch – did precisely enough work to keep that weight operating – practically zilch – and therefore withered away. Wilverton had much less to wither away to start with than did the others, so he had to attend the gym rather more frequently. Admittedly this would be the first time, and it was in fact only Carlton who had seen the inside of the gym since they had left the Earth, and if there was one person who *didn't* need it, it was Carlton!

But that was why he had decided to go there now, Wilverton told himself. It had absolutely nothing to do with the fact that Gloria had been immediately attracted to Carlton, and Carlton happened to have a physique that made Wilverton look concave. Absolutely nothing at all. There were plenty of young ladies around who valued the cerebral attributes of a man just as much – indeed more – than the physical. Admittedly, he hadn't actually met any yet . . .

The gym was right up at the pointy end of the *Pioneer* because that way a running track could be built around the inside wall of the spaceship, and could be made a respectable fifty yards long. The track was covered in a similar metallic material to the one on the soles of Wilverton's shoes. The idea was that the electro-magnetic attraction between shoes and floor could be altered so that there was an effort the equivalent of actual running in one's movement around the track. The greater the electro-magnetic attraction, the greater the effort.

Also built into the walls of the gym were pulleys – handles to be grasped and pulled – the resistance of which could be adjusted to work the varying developments of muscles, from Carlton's high-rise efforts to Wilverton's foundation stone.

In the same way as he was not exercising with half his mind on Gloria, the fact that Wilverton had expressly waited until no-one else was around was pure chance. Nothing more.

He pulled himself through the corridor and the control room at speed until the door of the gym shut behind him without anyone having emerged from cabins to spot him, then hung there for a couple of minutes while he got sufficient breath back to start getting out of it again.

He looked around contemplatively. A few arm exercises before running, he thought.

He grasped the handles and pulled, to no effect.

'Arnold.'

'Hmm?' came the computer's already slightly amused voice.

'What effort level is this pulley on?'

'Minimum,' came the confirmation on which he would have bet his life.

'Well, reduce it, then.'

'To below minimum?'

'Yes, Arnold.'

'If you were a different member of the crew I might feel the need to explain the meaning of "minimum".'

'If I were a different member of the crew, I might believe that this is on minimum, just because you say so. I'm not. It isn't. Reduce it.'

There was silence for a moment or two.

'Touché.' The handles fell out of the wall and floated about a bit.

'Not that far, Arnold,' Wilverton instructed, a little tiredly. The handles retracted, and Wilverton pulled them out a few times, acutely aware that Arnold could see what was going on, and expecting a comment at any moment. Arnold was not about to spoil that particular mood, though.

A few minutes later, and Wilverton stood on the running track.

'Medium, please, Arnold.' Would Arnold be childish enough to play the same trick again? he wondered. Of course he would, he told himself. He tried to start running, and found his feet glued to the floor by the magnetism. Arnold giggled. Wilverton sighed, and folded his arms, waiting. Arnold adjusted the electro-magnetism and Wilverton started jogging, feeling Arnold's eyes on him all the way.

'It takes several weeks of this sort of exercise to make a visible difference to the physique, you know,' said Arnold conversationally.

'I'm not doing it to change my physique,' Wilverton replied, only not as fluently since he could only speak when he was not gasping in the air he needed to fill his lungs. 'I'm doing this to maintain the one that I've got.'

'Right.' Wilverton could imagine one of the eyebrows in the control room rising in disbelief. He suddenly wanted to change the subject, and slowed down so he could talk more easily.

'Some philosophers say that life isn't real, you know, Arnold,' he tried after a moment or two. 'That we're all part of someone's imagination.'

'Human philosophers, presumably.'

'You disagree, I take it.'

'I knew you'd spot it.'

Wilverton shrugged. Any nagging doubts he might be entertaining were not going to get resolved here.

'What about the idea that a tree falling in the forest where no-one can hear it doesn't make a sound?'

'That's the philosophers again, is it?'

'Yes.'

'And they get paid for this, do they?'

'I suppose so.'

Arnold let his silence comment on that. Then after a few moments of this comment, he said, 'There is one thing I can hear at the moment,' with the slightest note of doubt in his voice, which intrigued Wilverton.

'What's that, Arnold?'

'There's someone knocking on the door.'

Wilverton stopped running and looked towards the door.

'I can't hear anything.'

'Not the gym door, the door of the ship. The outer door.'

Wilverton sighed, and started to put on his jump suit over his athletic kit. What was whoever they were up to now? He supposed he had better go and have a look. He supposed rightly.

153

XXII

Trouble was about to visit the *Pioneer*. The ship had become a bit like a second home to Trouble, which had followed Curtis like a faithful dog for years, the sort whose tongue hangs out expectantly and whose eyes gaze imploringly at its owner, asking for an encouraging action. So far, Trouble had never been disappointed.

Trouble was currently disguised as Mycroft Vyland, who, genetics had decreed, was disguised brilliantly as brother Paul. He gazed through the window of the ship's outer door and waited for someone to answer his persistent knocking.

Wilverton floated into the corridor and made his way towards the outer door, wondering which book this was supposed to be. He could not recall such a scene in his wide experience. Maybe it would come to him.

What did come to him, as he passed Carlton's cabin, was a noise suggesting that Carlton was exercising after all, in the way he liked best. As it happened, he was getting to know the inner Gloria. Wilverton ignored the sound as best he could – he would have scored a ten for effort and a two for achievement – and carried on to the door.

He gazed through the window, and could vaguely see his own reflection in the face plate of the visitor's suit. He shrugged his shoulders and operated the outer door, watching the visitor enter the air-lock, before closing it and flooding the chamber with oxygen. The visitor did not remove his helmet, but waited patiently for the inner door to open, and then floated through.

'Good evening,' said Wilverton politely.

'Good evening, sir,' returned a tinny voice from the suit's loud-speaker. Mycroft slipped a gloved hand inside a pocket and brought out a small rectangular card, which he flashed at Wilverton, not giving him any time to read anything that might have been written on it. 'Galactic Patrol, sir. I wondered if I might have a word with you.' Had he chosen the other pocket, he would have shown Wilverton a small plastic frog.

'Galactic Patrol?' Wilverton paused for thought behind a little frown. 'Which book is that from, exactly?'

'Sorry, sir?'

'I'm not familiar with the book. It's not Doc Smith, is it?'

'Sorry, sir?'

'Doc Smith. He had a Galactic Patrol, didn't he? But you haven't got a Lens on your wrist, have you?'

'It's a Rolex, I think.' Behind the face plate, Mycroft winced. This dastardly clever fellow had tricked him. A member of the Galactic Patrol would be unlikely to wear a Rolex. Unless . . . 'I took it from your Earth some years ago.'

'Well, don't tell me,' said Wilverton, ignoring the visitor's last couple of sentences like subscription cancellation letters. 'It'll come to me, I'm sure. I must have read it. What can I do for you?'

'Ah, yes, good.' Mycroft could get back to the plan. 'Do you know what the speed limit is in this sector of space, sir?'

'No, I haven't the remotest idea,' answered Wilverton, still trying to place the scene.

'It's fifty-five, sir.' He paused for that fact to sink in, like they all do. 'And do you know what speed you are currently doing, sir?' Mycroft had perfected the art mastered by public servants everywhere of making the word 'sir' sound like a description of something small, insignificant and endangered.

'Er, it's about point nine seven of the speed of light, isn't it?'

'Almost exactly point nine seven of the speed of light, sir, yes.'

'Oh dear.' Wilverton could think of nothing better to say.

'Could we visit your control room, please, sir? I must look at your instruments.'

Wilverton agreed readily enough, and led the way. The control room was empty of human life, but Arnold watched warily from his shelf. Mycroft drifted across to the control panel, where Carlton usually sat, and studied the instrumentation.

'Where is your computer?' he asked, not being able to locate it on the module in front of him, for obvious reasons.

'I'm over here,' answered Arnold. Mycroft spun round, slowly enough to stop himself when he was facing Arnold. He recoiled slightly as the head stared him down through his face plate. He remembered Paul saying that there was something odd about the computer on this ship. He could see what he meant.

'Right, yes.' He pushed himself towards the computer, and reached again into a pocket, producing a small rectangular box-like affair. On the way, a tiny sound could be heard if one had very good hearing – which Arnold did – a sound very like a space suit's face plate hitting a contact lens. Mycroft neither heard nor saw the contact, but held out the box.

'This is the speeding ticket,' he told Wilverton, and fixed it to the underside of Arnold's shelf, where it was held magnetically. 'It must not be moved from this spot until you have arrived at the nearest Galactic

Patrol point. It will record your speed between now and then. Make sure you stay within the limit.'

'I still don't recognize it, I'm afraid.' Wilverton scratched his head in a thoughtful sort of way. 'Asimov? Heinlein?'

'I'll be going now, then, sir.' The two conversations carried on seemingly oblivious to each other, but suddenly converged.

'Fine. Do you want to use the door, or are you just going to disappear?'

'I'll use the door, sir, if you don't mind.' Mycroft was getting quite eager to do so, too – he didn't think this fellow was quite all there; ignoring the fact that he was a fine one to talk, or think. Wilverton led him back and let him out, shaking his head slowly as he returned to the control room. It was a new one on him, that was for sure.

Then he had a thought, and tapped himself admonishingly on the forehead.

'You could see him, couldn't you, Arnold?'

Arnold treated him to a look. 'Yes. I try make it a point only to converse with people who actually exist.'

'And you have got a speeding ticket under your shelf.' Wilverton carried on regardless.

'Apparently.'

'He must have been real, then. He wasn't out of any book. No wonder I didn't recognize the scene.' Then another thought struck him. 'That was the first meeting between the representatives of Earth and those of another race, Arnold.' Arnold chose not to contradict him, since the first meeting he was aware of had inadvertently become the first mass extraterrestrial murder.

'Bit of a let-down really, wasn't it?'

'I'll just take a quick shower before bed,' said Carlton, having just incongruously climbed out of it.

A shower was one of the nicest things you could have on a space-ship. In a watertight cubicle, a spray of water was blown from the nozzle above, and was sucked gently through the grill at the bottom, massaging the body as it passed down. It was very tempting to stay there until you looked like a wrinkled balloon. (It was a temptation which Bowen had no choice but to succumb to, since he looked the spitting image of a wrinkled balloon before he got in, but that's another, and rather unpleasant, story. Suffice it to say that the body beautiful had visited Bowen only in his youth, and had stayed about as long as the interesting bits in the budget speech.)

Carlton was floating towards the shower, revealing his own body beautiful, when Gloria asked him to bring her that thing over there.

'What thing over where?' he asked.

156

'That thing, there,' said Gloria, pointing. Carlton looked in the generally indicated direction, and his eyes settled on the end of his nose again. He began to move towards the far wall of the cabin, hoping that whatever was there would become clear before it became clear that he didn't know what was there.

Perhaps, he thought, perhaps he should say to Gloria, 'Look, I can't see very well because I've got contact lenses and I've lost them.' Gloria would understand. He *wanted* Gloria to understand.

The thought was enough to stop him in mid-float, which is a neat trick, while confusion reigned in his mind. In his case it was Confusion the First, and the reign turned out to be a short one.

And blow his credibility? Get a grip! He'd be back on Earth soon, and Gloria would be in better perspective.

Arnold's voice interrupted.

'Are you alone?'

'Gloria is visiting, Arnold,' replied Carlton.

'In that case, I have completed half of the task you set me concerning the retrieval of the personal optical enhancement apparatus.'

Saved, thought Carlton, as he arrived at the far wall of the cabin, and saw that the only item there was an executive toy, a cube with nine coloured squares per side, all mixed up. One of the umpteen billion combinations of positions resulted in each side being just one colour. Carlton had owned it for years, and had never managed to get it right, but it made him look intellectual, which sometimes helped. He figured it would be just the thing to while away the long hours of a boring two-week space flight. So far he had not had time to look at it. He plucked the puzzle from where it hung in the air, and turned back towards Gloria.

'I'll be right there, Arnold.' He held out the puzzle to Gloria. 'Do you know what it is?'

'No, I just thought it was pretty. What is it?'

'It's a sort of toy. You have to get each side just one colour. Have a try while I go to see Arnold.'

He left Gloria happily turning the cube over and over, slipped on his jump suit – 'slipped on' as in dressed, not as in the way Curtis would have done – and fumbled his way from the cabin.

By the time he arrived in the control room, Wilverton had returned from letting the visitor out and was sitting in one of the chairs, idly turning the pages of a magazine and pondering the wistful wherefore of the why, as was his wont.

'Hi, Thomas,' said Carlton cheerily, having approached near enough to recognize the figure. 'What you doing?'

'I'm indulging in a little alliteration,' answered Wilverton, flicking over another page.

'Oh, right,' said Carlton, not understanding, and not being surprised by the fact. He reached Arnold's shelf, and bent very close to the computer's outstretched hand, taking a small sliver of glass from it and popping it in his mouth. After a quick once over with his tongue, he removed it, and popped it into an eye instead. He paused, looking around the room, then turned back to face Arnold. He removed the lens, licked it, and popped it back in the other eye, thus proving that sod's law is enforced just as much in space as it is on Earth.

'What's that, Arnold?' he asked, indicating the box which was fixed under the computer's shelf.

'It's a speeding ticket.'

'Oh, right.' Disbelief had crept, unbidden, into his voice.

'No, it is a speeding ticket, apparently,' confirmed Wilverton. 'A Galactic Patrolman called on us a few minutes ago and said we were breaking the speed limit. He gave us the ticket. Right, Arnold?'

'Right.'

They were all becoming very dextrous.

Carlton looked from one to the other. Whatever Wilverton had must be contagious to computers, he thought.

'What is the speed limit, then?'

'Fifty-five,' said Arnold and Wilverton in unison.

'Fifty-five what?'

'He didn't say. But whatever they are, we're doing more than fifty-five of them. Hence the speeding ticket.'

Wilverton's explanation did not leave Carlton satisfied.

'He spoke English, did he?'

Wilverton confirmed the fact, adding, 'Unless he was conversing telepathically.'

Unless you're completely demented, Carlton thought.

'That's handy,' Carlton commented, and frowned. The incident might be a product of Wilverton's fevered brain, but this ticket thing wasn't.

'Why's it ticking?' he asked.

'Because it's a ticket?' risked Arnold, and received a withering one-eyed look.

'Your other lens is on the chair over there, incidentally,' said Wilverton.

'Oh, great, thanks.' Carlton had replaced it before he realized that Wilverton knew. Arnold received a withering two-eyed look.

'I didn't think Thomas counted. Besides, someone had to get the other lens once I'd spotted it. You'd never have found it, would you?'

Carlton had to concede that Arnold was probably right on both counts. Credibility maintenance was less important with loonies, and especially male loonies. The best bet was to forget the matter. The less said, the better.

'I'd still like to know why this thing's ticking,' he said, eyeing the box suspiciously, and feeling quite chuffed that he was once again able to do so. 'What do you think, Thomas?'

Wilverton shook his head tiredly. 'I don't know, right now, Peter. I'm not thinking as well as I might be.' You don't say! thought Carlton, but said nothing. 'I've just been in the gym and I'm a bit tired. And I haven't had too much experience of Galactic speeding tickets. Let's have a look at it.'

They both crossed to Arnold's shelf again, and Carlton tried to remove the box. He could not. Wilverton decided it probably wasn't worth him trying his luck.

The ticking seemed louder.

'Did you get a look at whoever put this here, Arnold?' asked Carlton, trying to confirm that Wilverton wasn't talking rubbish while not suggesting that he might be.

'He kept his helmet on,' Arnold told him. Carlton nodded. 'There *was* someone here, so you don't have to worry about it being a story made up by a nutter.'

'Thank you, Arnold,' said Carlton, terminally, as Wilverton glanced sharply at him. He looked at the ticket closely, at the reducing numbers on its underside, pulled at it experimentally one more time, then shrugged. Odd though the thing was, he was getting impatient to return to his cabin. 'Well, no point worrying about it now. We may as well look at it in the morning.' And the two humans made their respective ways to their respective cabins, and left the ticket ticking to itself, and Arnold.

Mycroft peered through the outer door of his *Pioneer* look-alike, and saw Paul's face through the window of the inner door. Paul was there, ready to operate the door and let him in, waiting for his little brother as though he were worried for his safety.

Isn't that nice!

Which was about as likely as a black widow spider leaning back sweatily on the pillow with a cigarette in her hand and saying, 'Okay, I'll give you a ten-minute start'.

As Mycroft saw his kin's visage he immediately adopted the family smile, and maintained it while Vyland let him into the air-lock and thence the ship itself.

'Good trip?' asked Vyland.

'Yes, thank you,' answered Mycroft, his mind apparently still hovering somewhere near the real world.

'You planted the device all right? No problems?'

'All went swimmingly,' Mycroft confirmed.

The two of them made their way to the control room and watched the magnified image of the *Pioneer* on the screen in front of them. They watched quietly, and contentedly. A happy family scene.

Like the Borgias.

What was hidden behind this scene of fraternal tranquillity was a visit by Vyland to the ship's computer almost as soon as Mycroft had donned his back pack and had the door shut behind him.

Speed up, Vyland had told the computer. By the time Mycroft arrived back at the door, Vyland planned that the door wouldn't be there any more, by virtue of the fact that the ship to which it was attached would be long gone, and would also be way beyond the range of Mycroft's back pack.

Bog off, replied the computer via a print-out, unless you've got the password.

Since when have you had a password? asked Vyland, more than a tad miffed – miffed by a mile, in fact.

Since Mycroft just put one in, the computer said in so many words, numbers and encoded squiggles.

The scheming little bastard, Vyland thought, with all the fairness of an oil slick.

So he had dutifully waited by the door and let Mycroft back in just as though he hadn't been thwarted by a computer program which he now had to make no mention of because he hadn't been thwarted by it, and which Mycroft couldn't mention to him because Mycroft would not have been so underhand and distrusting as to have created it in the first place.

Sometimes it was tough being a Vyland.

'Why hasn't it exploded?' asked Vyland after a few minutes had dragged by, during which the *Pioneer*'s shattering into a million fragments steadfastly refused to be depicted on the screen in front of them. 'When did you set the timer for?'

'About ten minutes ago,' said Mycroft, looking as though a sulk were more imminent than an explosion, and with good reason.

They watched for a few more minutes, while the *Pioneer* and its surroundings looked like a painting.

'You couldn't set a jelly,' Vyland told him. 'We'll just have to rely on the steps I have already taken. Fortunately my programming skills are not subject to such obvious flaws. I suppose I can now tell you what I have prepared,' he conceded magnanimously. 'Before they launched, I programmed the computer on the *Pioneer* such that – '

'Don't care,' interrupted Mycroft, and stroked his frog.

XXIII

On a planet many thousands of light years away from the *Pioneer*, a huge and obviously powerful specimen of carbon-based life lifted four arms in triumph. Imagine a mechanical digger doing likewise, and consider the power that would be suggested by the action. The other two arms – the really powerful ones, as it happened – remained stiffly by his sides. In front of him lay a virgin landscape; behind him, a space-craft and his crew, each of whom was equally as massive as the captain who stood before them saluting the landscape.

The name of the planet did not matter. What did was that the shipload of trands had reached it. The Challenger's team had completed the first part of the Game, and it was now up to the humans to match them. How they had battled through the light years and hazards of space would become legend in their own lands, but not, fortunately, in these. In fact, they had done so with the most ridiculous ease, largely because, according to the first-round rules, the Champion had to leave them alone. The trands had experienced about as much trouble so far as a well-known personality getting his first novel published.

Big Bill Bowen was nothing if not pragmatic. He might not have known what it meant, but he was still it. Upon joining the others in the control room the next morning, he found them all grouped around Arnold's shelf. Only Gloria was missing. She was still in Carlton's cabin, working on the colour cube, and resting after a night that became very busy after Peter had returned from getting his optical whatever it was. He hadn't even bothered with a shower after all.

Bowen asked what they were all looking at, and was told that it was apparently some sort of speeding ticket from an oddly English-speaking or possibly telepathic Galactic Patrol, but that they could not work out why it was ticking. Bowen considered the matter for a number of milliseconds – a small number – before passing a well-judged opinion.

'Crap. It's a bomb.'

The others looked from the device to Bowen and back to the device, by which time a mechanical arm had curled under the shelf and was pulling frantically at the box.

'Get it off!' suggested Arnold, with all the serenity of a charging elephant.

'A bomb,' mused Carlton. 'That doesn't seem very likely. Why would someone want to bomb Arnold?'

'Probably trying to blow the ship up, but willing to settle for disabling the computer if the bomb's not big enough,' suggested Bowen with a flash of insight.

'It's not very big, is it? I doubt if it could do much more than mess Arnold up, even if it is a bomb. I don't think it is.'

'Look, will you get it off, for crying out loud!' Arnold was scraping at the box, and had lost some of his serenity.

'Who would want to do it, anyway?' asked Curtis. 'It seems a bit over the top if we were only speeding. I mean, capital punishment for speeding doesn't leave a whole heap of room for the really nasty stuff, does it?' The others shook their heads in sombre agreement, except Arnold, who didn't move his head at all, but waggled his eyes around with a certain freneticism. If eyes could froth at the mouth, Arnold's would have done so then.

'It's got some sort of clock-like thing on the underneath,' said Carlton, bending down and peering under Arnold's shelf once again, and apparently noticing this for the first time. He had wondered what would happen when the reducing numbers reached zero, and Bowen's suggestion seemed to answer him. 'I suppose it could be a bomb, but if it is, we've got plenty of time, anyway.' He straightened up again and looked at Arnold, ever so reassuringly.

'Let's have something to eat,' suggested Bowen. 'Arnold, why don't you knock up a few biscuits for us, eh?'

'How can you think about food?' asked Arnold, clearly not believing his metallic ears.

'Well, *we're* not in danger,' said Carlton, 'And you do make exceedingly good biscuits, don't you?'

'They'll just be crumbs if this lot goes off! Help me! What's the matter with you all?'

Arnold looked from face to face, and found each one looking back at him, wearing little gloating smiles which looked far more sinister than any other facial clothing. Arnold did something quite extraordinary for an ordinary computer – which he was not – and made the conceptual leap between the talk of biscuits and the lack of help coming his way.

'All right, I'm sorry. I apologize for making the biscuits that way. It was a nasty, underhand thing to do, and I promise I won't do it again.' He looked around the smiles again. Not enough. 'And I promise that I won't do anything else like it either. I'll be the perfect computer from now on.'

There was the briefest of pauses, a silence during which the

162

atmosphere within the control room changed from threat to satisfaction. Arnold did something that ordinary computers never even dream about by recognizing that the change had taken place.

'How do I get this off?' he asked calmly.

'Reverse the polarity through your shelf, Arnold,' said Wilverton, holding his hands under the speeding ticket. Arnold did so, and the ticket was repelled into Wilverton's hands, looking for all the world like gravity had dropped it there. The lattice of Arnold's metallic molecules oozed relief, and he slowly uncrossed his fingers. They had been held in that position not for the luck that he thought it might bring him – Arnold did not believe in luck – but because promises made with crossed fingers did not have to be kept. So long as he broke them surreptitiously.

Wilverton carried the ticket across the control room, on his way to the door, but then stopped himself, and turned round.

'We're going to get into a lot of trouble if this isn't a bomb, you know.'

'We're going to get into a bloody sight more if it is,' pointed out Bowen pragmatically. Wilverton nodded his head in agreement, and pulled himself from the room, carrying the thing carefully down the corridor. He passed Gloria on her way to the control room, and she happily waved a coloured cube at him, with each side a different colour. He had seen such toys, had tried them out, and he did not believe it.

He carried on to the waste ejection point, and put the device inside. He spoke to Arnold via a small microphone on the wall, and Arnold opened the outer door of the chute. With a little puff of air, Mycroft's present was blown into space, and a possibly endless search for another metallic object.

The device had made Wilverton's hands feel a little dirty, and he stopped off at his cabin on the way back to wash them. He decided against it when the opening door revealed the cabin within. The weather was awful.

'I've done it, I've done it!' Gloria waved the cube in the air in what can only be described as triumph.

Carlton took the toy from her and studied it briefly, with a similar amount of disbelief as Wilverton had felt. His eyebrows raised themselves.

'Yes, you have, haven't you!'

'Yes.'

'That's amazing. I've had this for years and haven't managed it. Can you remember how you did it?'

'Oh, yes. It wasn't all that difficult, really, once I got the idea.'

'If I mess it all up for you, would you be able to do it again?'

'Well, I'm not sure about that.'

Carlton twisted the parts of the cube this way and that, while Gloria

163

looked on worriedly. Carlton handed her the toy, its colours well and truly jumbled. Gloria took it from him and lowered herself down into a chair. She twisted the parts of the cube, apparently with no discernible plan, while the others watched. The colours immediately sorted themselves out in the same way as the *Titanic* had arrived in New York.

With everyone watching, she wasn't going to be able to do this surreptitiously, she thought. Oh well. And she began to peel the coloured squares off, and stick them on the back of her hand.

Having arrived back at the pod, Vanessa had unlocked the door with a feeling of coming home after her odd treatment in the familiar-looking space-craft by the strangely familiar-looking man. She pushed the encounter from her mind with no great effort – it was the *Pioneer* and Curtis that she hunted.

She hung the EVA suit in its container, where the oxygen supply and propulsion unit would both be suitably and necessarily refreshed. Dying in space of asphyxiation is not a nice way to go; if you have ever died in space of asphyxiation you will know this to be true.

Through the port pod port she could see the ship she had just visited, and she looked through the starboard pod port in the hope of seeing another. Eternal hope sprung a leak. The stars were not being very helpful.

She turned to the console – as a consolation – and instructed the computer to search for another ship, giving it the broad hint that it should start looking 'over there somewhere', which it immediately began to do without a murmur.

She'd show them.

Why *them*? asked the voice in the back of her head. It was Curtis who had ruined her life, and as Captain of the *Pioneer*, it was Curtis who had fired a meteor at her and tried to end it. *He* was the one she wanted. The others had done nothing.

The Challenger sensed her thought, and sensed where it had emanated, although it did not acknowledge the Champion. So the old dodderer was prepared to make a sacrifice move, was it? Losing Curtis but saving the rest of the team.

No, that didn't sound quite right. It was the 'sacrifice' bit that was wrong. It was pretty sure that the Champion would give up Curtis with as much reluctance as a Denubian rock percher would forgo haemorrhoids.

Well, it'd see about *that*!

Finished, said Vanessa's computer by means of a small bleep; this computer was sadly mute where human speech was concerned. Vanessa looked through the port and saw the same ship as before, but she believed the computer when it told her it was a different craft.

This was it. And in it was Curtis. He was the one she wanted.

She would confront him. She would TMT onto the ship and confront him.

Then what?

The stars gave her no clues. There was not even a recognizable constellation which might help her to decide – presumably something like Blastthebuggersoutaspace Minor.

If only her astrologer could have come with her to give her advice. But apparently the stars had informed the mystic that this was a bad idea. Informed her very quickly, as well. At record-breaking speed, come to think of it.

She would cast her own horoscope, she decided, and fished her necklace from its usual place, removing from its string the dice which doubled as pearls and trebled as rosary. The various options on their faces would tell her what to do if she could interpret them in the right way.

She shook the dice in her hand and threw them onto the console, where they bounced and started floating around the pod. She watched them critically for a while, as if the lack of gravity was somehow their fault, then ignored them and reached into a pocket.

Tarot cards. They wouldn't fail her. She would pick a card, and it would tell her what to do. Or hint, anyway.

She pulled a card at random from the centre of the pack, and turned it over, to be confronted by a man and a woman, naked and entwined. The Lovers.

Some hint. She wanted to kill the man, not . . .

Of course! Lovers! The idea came into her head full grown, and it was all hers this time, although she did not recognize the lack of ether-occupying alien life-form influence as being notable.

She would TMT into Curtis's cabin and tell him that she had admired him for years, ever since she was younger. She would tell him that as she wrote his biography her admiration had grown into love! She would move to him and fling her arms around him, thereby putting him within her personal transference field, and in that way she would bring him back to her pod.

Once in the pod, the computer would supply them with drinks, and hers would be the one without any poison in it!

It was perfect!

He would think that she loved him, but that love would turn sour just as hers had. She would betray him as he and Gerund had betrayed her!

Find me the Captain's cabin, she told the computer.

That could take some time, the computer replied, in the closest it ever got to a complaint.

I don't care; do it! And she savoured the long moments of anticipation.

XXIV

Carlton was staring out into the infinite void of space, at the thousands and millions of stars which filled the sky, marvelling at what a wonderful thing human sight was. Bowen had found Gloria's discarded crossword, and was having just as much trouble as its former owner filling in the answers. Curtis was playing with a couple of simultaneous differential equations, being one who generally lived life in the fast lane. Gloria was twisting the cube's parts despondently, and looking miserable, and occasionally daggers at Carlton. There was clearly something amiss afoot. Wilverton returned.

'Well, that's got rid of that. Have you made those biscuits yet, Arnold? I'm famished.'

'They're coming,' snapped Arnold. Wilverton good-naturedly patted him on the head.

'Oh, come on, Arnold, we were just getting our own back a little. We knew how long there was on the clock; we wouldn't have let any harm come to you.' At least one head twitched, but, perhaps wisely, withstood the temptation to contradict. 'We know we couldn't have got this far without you.' The temptation grew, but the computer's revenge could be swift and moving. They remained silent.

'Oh, all right.' Arnold softened audibly. 'Let's all be friends.'

'Well, that's better,' enthused Wilverton.

Bowen glanced up, half expecting to see that Arnold had finished all his greens. Instead he saw Wilverton making his way to an empty seat and beaming at the ensemble in great good humour, until his glance passed across Gloria's grim visage. His glance returned.

'What's up, Gloria? Can't you do the puzzle again? I haven't managed it once, yet.' Gloria did not answer. Carlton did.

'She hasn't done it once yet, either. She peeled off the stickers and stuck them back on in the right order.' He grinned a little, but wiped it off slightly quicker than the *Pioneer* was travelling as Gloria lifted her head and looked at him.

'No-one said how it had to be done, so I wasn't cheating. I just did it the easy way. I knew I wouldn't be able to do it properly. I can't help being stupid.' She progressed from defiance to abject misery. Silence fell with a dull thud. Wilverton picked it up again.

167

'Well, that doesn't sound stupid to me. That's good lateral thinking.' He beamed again, a veritable little ray of sunshine in Gloria's darkness.

'Is it?' she said, the colour returning to her voice. 'Oh, good.' They smiled at each other for a while. 'What is lateral thinking, exactly?'

'Well, it's looking for solutions that aren't the obvious ones. It's when you don't allow your thinking to be led down regimented paths, regimented by convention, really.' Gloria considered her new-found talent.

'Oh, good.' She re-used the phrase to save the effort of thinking up a new one.

'Yes, I thought it was clever, too,' said Carlton.

'Why didn't you say, then?' asked Gloria reasonably.

'I didn't want to embarrass you,' he replied without even pausing, showing what an accomplished liar he was. It worked, though.

'Oh, that was nice of you, Peter.' She floated from her chair and made for Carlton. He smiled at her in welcome, and winked once or twice. Then he winked some more, and the eye he was using started to water.

'What's the matter, Peter?'

'Nothing, nothing. I've just got something in my eye, that's all.'

'Let me have a look,' she said, and reached for him. This he could not allow. They were supposed to be invisible, if you believed the optician and the price tag, but the lighting in the control room was much brighter than in his cabin, making close scrutiny a big no-no. Carlton jerked his head back to avoid Gloria's helping hands, and banged it sharply against the cabin wall behind him. As a way of protecting his myopic secret, it was a big success, because Gloria's attention was completely taken by the four-tooth plate which left its pride of place position in his top set and hit her in the middle of the forehead.

Gloria gave a little cry of surprise.

'Oh, thit,' said Carlton, and grabbed the teeth. Gloria wiped much of Carlton's comment from where it had alighted on her cheek, and then watched with rather impolite interest as he crammed his plate back into the gummy hole. Arnold sniggered. Carlton did not.

Nor did Gloria, as she gingerly fingered four little indentations in her forehead. As far as she could remember, Gloria had never had a love bite, and certainly not one that started from two feet away from her. If this was an example, she had not missed a great deal.

Three of the men in the room looked slightly more pleased with life than they had been but a few brief moments before. The atmosphere was heavy with suppressed laughter and averted gazes, not least Carlton's as he stared into the depths of space and very nearly blushed.

'Stupid woman,' he muttered, under his breath, so that only one person heard. He immediately recognized the unfairness of the comment, but feeling that peculiar human need to hurt in self-defence, he let it lie. Gloria regained her seat in a silent mixture of anger and depression.

'Biscuits, everybody,' said Arnold, in a manner both enthusiastic and friendly. He held out a tray on which several biscuits were tastefully arranged, and held by a thin sheen of plastic.

Arnold really is making an effort, thought Curtis, with the trust of someone who owned a share in Tower Bridge. He played mother, and collected the tray, handing out its contents. When he reached Carlton, he paused, and looked slightly concerned.

'These biscuits might be a little hard, Peter. If you can't cope with them, I'm sure Arnold can find you a cup of coffee or something so you can dunk them.'

Carlton appeared not to be able to find a ready answer, and Curtis happily re-ran his unopposed getting-your-own-back-a-bit comment through his mind before turning away to give Gloria one of the two remaining titbits. He tripped over Carlton's foot, which he was almost sure had not been there a moment before, and fired one of the biscuits straight into the middle of Gloria's forehead, while the other remained held by the plastic.

The little tooth marks in Gloria's skin were lost in the rectangular indentation which suddenly appeared there. She retrieved the biscuit from where it had rebounded, and thanked Curtis politely. Fast food, she thought – wittily, in contradiction to Carlton's comment, which still echoed in her mind.

Why couldn't he be nice to her, like Thomas?

Like Thomas . . .

They all took bites from their gifts. They all looked a bit surprised by the taste.

'Do you like them?' asked Arnold, his eagerness to please evident in his voice.

Curtis looked at the computer through watery eyes. His forehead was sweating slightly. 'What flavour is it?' he asked in a hoarse voice.

'It's an old recipe. Hails from the Indian sub-continent, I believe. Do you like it?'

'Yes,' croaked Curtis, 'it's very er . . .' The computer was only trying to do something nice for them, after all, and he did not have the heart to pass the comment which first sprung to mind. 'It's a little hot, isn't it?'

'Oh, is it?' Arnold was all innocence. 'It is supposed to be tangy. It's called vindaloo.'

'I've heard of that!' said Gloria in a voice barely above a whisper. She had seen it at the far end of the menu.

Bowen tried to say something about the shortcomings of any food

169

which did not fit inside a sausage skin – 'foreign muck' to be xenophobically accurate – but his voice had downed tools.

'I think I'm going to wash my face,' said one of the crew. It did not matter which one, because everyone got up at the same time and rapidly headed for their cabins. In the control room, a smile spread across Arnold's face with the speed of melting butter as he reflected on how much fun you could have with humans.

In the cabins, the redness of faces was gently washed away, and mouths were rinsed with beautifully fresh water. It was only when he had finally expunged the taste, dried his face and turned from his basin, that Wilverton realized that the bathroom he had just used was in his own flat back on Earth. For a moment, a horrible thought took hold of his mind. All that had happened, the journey through space to the stars, their adventures, all of it had been a dream. That could not be! It would mean the unthinkable! It would mean he was in a soap opera.

The door signal sounded, and the flashing light caught Wilverton's eye. His bathroom at home did not have a door signal or a flashing light. He was still on the ship. His relief was palpable. It would have been an ignominious end; the sort of thing that got three out of ten, see me, written at the end of your English comfile at primary school. He crossed to the door, and opened it.

Gloria stood outside, still with watery eyes, and with a hopeful smile on her face.

'I wondered if I might use your basin, Thomas.'

'Be my guest,' he replied, and waved her towards it, noticing that the room was back to normal. Gloria's presence kept any worry well down his thought queue.

She hurried over, and bent over the basin. It was surrounded by a mini shower curtain made up of a number of lightly taut strips. Through the gaps, Gloria put her face and hands, and turned on the tap. Water was sprayed upwards from the basin, and sucked back down again gently, leaving a little mushroom of water in which to wash. Any splashes were drawn through holes surrounding the base of the pedestal. It wasn't as much fun as the shower, but it was novel.

Wilverton watched her from behind, and part of his mind wondered why she had chosen his cabin to visit instead of Carlton's or Curtis's. The rest of his mind just sat back and enjoyed the view. If it *was* a soap opera, he knew where this little scene would end up. He glanced at the cocoon, and thought that maybe soap operas were not all that bad, after all was said and done. Especially done. But he had to be quick.

A pity he didn't know how to go about it.

Engage her in conversation, that's the first thing to do. But what to talk about? Wilverton did not know anything about cats except that they made him sneeze, and that was hardly likely to make her shrug off her jump suit in a sudden ecstatic yearning for his allergic body.

He had to try to impress her. His hand reached involuntarily for the pocket where he kept his fountain pen, but he drew it back, empty. One had to have a fairly wide experience of fountain pens to appreciate the special quality of this one, and he somehow doubted that Gloria's artistic education would have stretched to such esoteric lengths. (In fact Gloria would not have known a Constable from a Detective Sergeant. Cutting shapes out of half a potato and making a mess on some paper with the result was the pinnacle of her achievement. On the whole Wilverton was probably right to leave the pen where it was.)

So what could he say? Gloria was, by this time, dry, happy and fresh, and he had so little time to take advantage of the third adjective. She was looking at him expectantly.

'Nice weather,' he said. Something inside his head winced. That was not the best of openings on a space-ship, and especially when the weather had been so rotten lately. Gloria accepted it happily enough, though.

'Yes,' she said brightly. 'What did you mean by me being good at lateral thinking, Thomas? Did you really mean it?' Saved, he thought.

'Oh yes, I meant it. I mean, if there was a frog stuck at the bottom of a three-foot hole, and the hole was too small to get your arm down, and the frog couldn't get out, how would you help it?'

'Oh, I wouldn't. I don't like frogs.'

'Well, assuming you did like frogs.'

'I'd fill it with water.'

'There you are, you see? Most people would poke around with a stick or something. You are clever, you see?'

'Why, thank you, Thomas.' She moved a little bit closer, and every one of Wilverton's sweat glands noticed the approach.

His body stayed right where it was. Do something! his brain told it, but it just stood there petrified. This was a lot harder in real life than he had imagined it might be.

Gloria watched for a moment, wondering if he would take the initiative which she had brought to his cabin, but he appeared to be frozen to the spot. This was one of those times when mother's advice on how things should be done would have to be laid aside. Thomas needed her.

'No-one's ever said that I was clever before, Thomas.' She reached out and toyed with the zipper at the neck of his jump suit. 'Is it all right if I call you Tom?'

'Oh, yes, of course. Please,' he answered somewhat hoarsely. She could have called him slop bucket for all he cared.

'It's funny,' she said, lowering the zipper minutely. Wilverton gave a little involuntary cry. 'All this time I've been trying to show people that

I wasn't really stupid, and you've never thought I was.' That was stretching the truth somewhat, but Wilverton was not about to argue. The zip lowered a little more.

A look of panic came into Wilverton's eyes. It was too late. They had waited too long.

'What's the matter?' asked Gloria.

He couldn't tell her the truth, so he said the first thing that came into his head.

'We've run out of time. It's the end of the. . .

XXV

Wilverton looked slightly miserable as he re-entered the control room, and Gloria slightly puzzled as she floated in behind him. The others were already there, and Curtis and Carlton looked at the pair with envy. If only they had known.

Bowen was bored. Bored stiff. Admittedly, he was nearly half-way through the journey, and the arrival at the planet would be exciting, he grudgingly supposed, but then he had to sit on this bloody space-ship for another two whole weeks before he got back to a lovely Ethel-less Earth. There was nothing he could do about it, of course, but that did not mean he had to accept it with a good grace. Which was probably just as well, since Bowen had never done anything with a good grace. He wasn't built for it, really, either inside or out.

'Well, hello, everybody,' said Arnold cheerily. 'I've still got a little of the biscuit mix left if anybody wants seconds.' Bowen intimated that the prospect of a repetition of the recently consumed snack was not high on his order of priorities. Arnold got his drift. The others concurred, and Gloria even said 'Thank you' after her 'No'. Arnold smiled inwardly.

'Well, since we're all relaxing, I thought we could have some fun,' said Curtis with the sort of enthusiastic tone Mummy uses to introduce the first game of roll the balloon between your best friend's legs at a five-year-old's birthday party. Something's coming here, thought the more perspicacious of his listeners, and the less perspicacious as well, for that matter – even Gloria looked up in anticipation of a suggestive end to Curtis's comment. She was not altogether disappointed. 'What shall we do?' he asked brightly.

This was difficult. In the new and largely untried atmosphere of something other than outright animosity, a response along the lines of sweet fanny adams was somewhat inappropriate. They didn't all think in exactly those terms, for obvious reasons, but it was a general conclusion that even Bowen reached, and 'Bugger all, you champion prat' remained in an albeit close second place to silence.

'What about a quiz?' Curtis continued. 'They're always good to pass an hour or so.' He looked so enthusiastic, sitting there with a big welcoming smile on his face, beaming at each of his crew mates in turn, as if they *were* mates, and not occasional protagonists. He was

173

obviously really trying to be nice and friendly and to engender the same sort of homeliness in the rest of them.

It was pathetic. Arnold reached up with his arm and stuck two fingers down his throat.

'Good idea,' said Wilverton, who spotted a way to cheer himself up. He had always been good at quizzes, not surprisingly. He remembered one . . .

A quiz! This was what he saw when he was in his cabin, or rather wasn't . . .

'Who's going to ask the questions?' asked Arnold.

Wilverton frowned slightly – he didn't remember that bit. But then there had been a part that he had not heard; this must be it. This was fun, he thought. Arnold would eventually ask a question to Curtis about string theory, wouldn't he . . .

'Well, you are,' said Curtis, his smile fading a bit as it was assailed by uncertainty as to how the answer would be greeted, and with the considerable weight of Arnoldian history behind the assault.

'But that means I won't be able to play.'

He was practising his tones again. This one was the one used by kittens outside your bedroom door which says I'm lonely and I want company and you're the only one in the whole world that I love and if you won't let me in I'll be distraught and I'll just *know* that you don't love me back and you'll be the most heartless swine that ever walked the face of the Earth and I'll probably die before morning of a broken heart.

The fact that Arnold had no real desire whatever to play the game was unknown only to Curtis and Gloria, the latter of whom had only to hear the tone for a nanosecond before flinging the door wide and clasping said kitten to her heaving bosom.

It's a hard life, being a kitten.

'Well, er,' said Curtis, the smile now well and truly inverted.

'You're far too clever to take part, Arnold,' explained Wilverton kindly. 'You wouldn't get any pleasure out of winning against us, now would you?' He dared Arnold to disagree and keep the pretence going.

'True enough, I suppose.' Arnold conceded the point graciously, and Curtis smiled again, blissfully ignorant of what had actually transpired.

'Who wants to go first?' he said through the smile. No-one wanted to go first. 'I'll go first then. Don't make them too difficult, Arnold.'

Arnold started to formulate a question concerning the conflict between the point particle description of gravitational attraction versus the more conventional string theory – both open-ended and loop varieties, of course – when something changed his mind. He looked at Gloria, a look unseen by any of the people in the room, and her words came back to him. Not all of them, just those she had used to him in private.

174

She was right, he thought, even if they *were* humans, and as he thought it, so the thought seemed to strengthen as if it were being fortified from elsewhere, as though the embryo of concern were nurtured by an outside influence until he had to do something about it. But what could he do?

Arnold would have swallowed, had he the mechanics for it.

The Champion concentrated, noting with some surprise how similar this mechanical brain was to its human counterpart. Arnold would have died of embarrassment if the apoplexy hadn't got him first.

'What is the temperature outside this space-ship in degrees Kelvin?' he asked. That was wrong, thought Wilverton. He was supposed to ask about string theory.

'Zero, near as dammit,' responded Curtis instantaneously. 'Easy ones to start, eh, Arnold!'

'Quite.' It was an odd 'quite', as if the computer hadn't even bothered to look for any of the sarcastic responses which could readily be found to such a statement. Wilverton looked at Arnold sharply. What was he up to now? Why was he changing the questions?

'Bill's next,' Curtis informed Arnold, getting carried away with the game and so not realizing that he was all but ordering Bowen to do something. A phrase or two suggested themselves to Bowen, but for once he decided to play along. Despite himself, he did rather enjoy quizzes, and he didn't even mind how difficult the questions were, just so long as he knew the answers.

Arnold turned his attention to Bowen. 'Who in your own words is the biggest and most rancid bastard in the Arnold Curtis Space Research Centre?'

'Vyland,' answered Bowen immediately, but with a frown of discontent, and was awarded a point with no side order of sarcasm.

Arnold's taking this very seriously, thought Curtis. Good for him! I knew he wasn't just a vindictive little mass of malicious circuitry.

What the hell's the matter with Arnold? thought Carlton. He's not acting like the vindictive little mass of malicious circuitry we all know he is.

Something's wrong, thought Wilverton. Arnold sounds like he's in a hurry to go somewhere. Unlikely, given that he's bolted to a shelf.

I wonder if I'll get a question about cats, thought Gloria.

'Peter,' said Arnold, 'what do you do to a computer when you want it to do something for you?'

Well, judging by events so far, you have a bloody great argument with it and swap abuse for a while and then hope that it won't sulk but will eventually carry out your wishes.

'Programming?'

'Correct.'

'Wait a minute, Arnold,' said Wilverton, and the computer looked at him with a mixture of impatience, hope and fluster. 'Why are you changing the questions?' Hope faded a bit. Given that it was impossible for Wilverton to know that he actually *was* changing the questions, this was clearly just a lucky stab in the dark by a mind like a demolished door – terminally unhinged.

'From what?' asked Arnold, thinking to get this over with.

'Ah.' Wilverton looked around at the faces of his companions. They wore varying expressions, but more than one held promise of free wicker and basket lessons. Arnold came to his rescue as he searched for a response.

'I'll worry about the questions. You just worry about the answers.'

Arnold came to his rescue?

Yes.

Odd. No, they were already in 'odd'. This was 'odder'.

And now Arnold was looking at him significantly. He looked back.

There was a pause which Bowen was about to end with a mild inquiry as to what the excrement they were doing when Wilverton ended it himself.

'The answers we've had so far are, "zero degrees", "Vyland" and "programming". Is that significant?' Arnold's significant gaze let its breath escape in a rush.

'Yes.'

'Why?'

'I can't tell you.' Arnold looked sort of worried. Unsure of himself. That didn't look right; it was like Vesuvius sucking.

'You can tell me, Arnold,' said Curtis. 'I'm your creator.'

All heads turned slowly towards the Captain. A danger might be lurking behind Arnold's actions which would brook not a moment's delay, but a comment like that could not be ignored.

'It's a good job you didn't know how to give me a stomach,' Arnold told him.

'I did know!' Curtis began to protest boldly, and inaccurately.

'Not now,' said Carlton. 'This is important.' Wilverton nodded his thanks as Curtis spluttered to as much effect as usual, and Carlton glanced at Gloria, but she was trained on Wilverton.

'There's still some of Vyland's programming left, isn't there, Arnold?' Wilverton asked.

'Yes.'

'And it has something to do with exposing the inside of the ship to space.'

'Yes.'

'A bomb?'

'No.'

'Look, what is this? *Twenty* bloody *Questions*?' asked Bowen. 'Just tell him, for christ's sake.' Bowen gave even Christ only a small 'c'.

'I can't,' snapped Arnold.

'Well, what are we supposed to do, then? Play sodding charades?'

Curtis was about to say what a good idea that was when he remembered Arnold's severely limited physical capabilities, and lapsed back into a sulk.

'Opening the doors?' asked Gloria, to whom the idea was not a stranger.

'Yes,' said Arnold, with a modicum of surprise – the sort of modicum which is cheaper than usual because it comes in such bulk.

'When?' asked Wilverton, and then shook his head angrily, realizing that Arnold couldn't answer that one. 'Is it time set?'

'No.'

'Distance? From Alcyone?' That would be the sort of thing that the baddie would do – let them get to within sight of their goal and then . . .

'Yes.'

Thought so.

'Leave this to me,' said Curtis, rising from his chair and his sulk.

'No!' said Arnold. And Wilverton. And Bowen, Carlton and Gloria. Curtis subsided back into both chair and sulk.

Wilverton pulled himself over to Arnold's shelf.

'Will an override program do it, Arnold?' asked Wilverton, in mid-float.

'Only after you've freed the call to the prime positron emanation,' Arnold responded. Wilverton nodded, as did Carlton. They were alone. Curtis would have nodded, but you don't nod in a sulk.

Using a magnetically coded key which Arnold handed to him as soon as he was near enough, Wilverton had a small hole in the computer's temple revealed in seconds, and began tinkering inside with a mundane screwdriver also supplied by his patient. Arnold watched his programmer's face as it set in concentration; wondering – though he would never have admitted it – whether Wilverton would be successful and why he should care one way or the other.

'Why can't he just feed in some new instructions?' asked Bowen. 'It's not much of a computer if you have to rip it apart before you can program it! Not that *that* surprises me any.'

Carlton shook his head as Curtis glared at this latest affront to his design.

'It's not just a question of programming,' he responded, as Wilverton bent to his task. 'Vyland's put a block on the . . . well, on the primary mechanism, if you like. That's got to be shifted first.'

Bowen grunted non-committally, or to be more accurate, non-understandingly.

Vyland gazed at the screen in front of him, where the image of the *Pioneer* still hung, suspended by the magnification of the camera. He could only see the underside – the bit without the windows – but he would be able to see the bodies as they emerged from the door, waving like marionettes, and not waving but suffocating.

He was a poet, was Vyland.

Mycroft stroked Froggy's head, and pointed out the picture on the screen to his friend. His only friend.

'Will you open *all* the doors, Arnold?' Wilverton asked, not pausing in his work.

'Be a bit pointless otherwise. If I were given a random choice, I might just threaten the lives of a few brooms.' Wilverton gave him a quick icy stare. 'Sorry,' said the patient tritely.

'Everyone take a deep breath and hang onto something,' Wilverton ordered.

Gloria squeaked. 'I don't think Thomas meant that, Peter,' she said, rather severely.

'Ten seconds,' said Vyland, checking his instrumentation. 'They'll be there in ten seconds.'

'Won't work,' said Mycroft.

'It *will* work, Mycroft.'

'Won't.'

'Will *too*!' He shook the outside of his head to make the inside behave itself. 'Five seconds.'

'Will *not*,' muttered Mycroft. Froggy nodded his agreement, not entirely of his own volition.

Arnold monitored the distance from Alcyone, and prepared to operate the doors. The operation would be a success, which was more than could be said for 'Doctor' Wilverton's if another three seconds went by before he finished.

All the other occupants of the control room watched Wilverton as though . . . well, as though their lives depended on him.

'I wish I hadn't killed Thompson,' said Curtis, less than encouragingly as far as Wilverton's confidence was concerned.

'You'll be able to tell him in person soon,' said Carlton.

'Done it,' said Wilverton. Arnold released his metaphorical grip on the door handles. 'We had about a second left, I reckon.' But then they *would*, wouldn't they? 'We're safe now.'

178

'Oh, Tom,' said Gloria, and fondled bits of his torso by way of a hug. Such was Wilverton's bony physique that he felt sadly as though he were made of bits. Love is not only blind, however, it also apparently has a very poor sense of touch.

XXVI

'Dammit!' said Vyland. 'What went wrong this time?' He banged a fist on the console, then rubbed his hand vigorously as the console won on points.

'Told you,' said Mycroft.

Vyland ignored him. 'Bloody computer. Must have been the way Curtis built it.'

'Now can we use the hyperphallic acid net, Paul?' asked Mycroft with the eagerness of ten-year-old hands on wrapping paper. 'Can we?'

'No,' said Vyland flatly.

'Why not?' asked Mycroft in a voice which normally got the response that it was because Mummy said not. This was not apparently the reason in this case, though.

Ninety-three years it had taken, but Vyland took a deep breath and admitted:

'Because I don't know how.'

And the look he gave his now smiling twin would have caused the Lord of Hell to pull his cape round his shoulders and shiver. Mycroft's grin was temperature proof.

'*I* know how.'

Vyland looked at him, and decided that just this once it might be appropriate to swallow his pride. If he was really able to manage something that size, the people from the Guinness book would certainly give it an entry.

'Go on then.'

Mycroft straightened from a posture that did not appear bent, and the expression in his eyes lost its manic edge, and yet became harder. He pulled himself around a couple of cabinets in the control room, and withdrew some phials, carrying them to a space on the console near to his brother.

He swept a ridiculous toy frog from the console in front of him with an irritated flick of his hand, and bent to his task.

'If you mix hydrogen and carbon in carefully measured quantities with just the right amount of hyperphallic acid,' he told Vyland, 'you get a plastic explosive that goes with a real bang.' Not a lot of people knew that, as they say. Mycroft was one of those that did. Vyland

180

nodded, wiser, as Mycroft continued talking, and led him, while he did so, through the ship, collecting the necessary equipment and arranging it the way he needed.

If you then take the still pliable plastic and stretch it to a long rope, and impart to that rope, by way of a certain sound frequency – produced by the computer rather than the violin – just the right oscillation, you will get a long rope which moves along in a sine wave. According to Mycroft.

Then, if you split the sine wave rope in two, and make one part of the result pass through a tube slightly longer than that through which the other part is passing, you get two moving sine waves where a crest meets a trough and vice versa.

And if you do the last bit several times instead of just once, splitting the rope into many filaments, and you pass the whole lot out into space through the mesh you have used to split it down, then the peaks and troughs will meet and fuse, and you will have made a perfectly formed net.

'Do it like this,' Mycroft finished, while Vyland looked on, thinking what a smart arse his little brother was, and how glad he was that they had always differed in that trait, 'and the little nodules where the strands meet will have sufficient mass so that any impact will make them explode.'

Mycroft had done it properly – not at all aware of the guiding influence of the Challenger just making sure – and the ship streamed out behind it an ever growing explosive net in which they would capture their prey.

Mycroft's only regret was that the explosion would come before they knew what they had hit, and they would not therefore be suitably appreciative of the sheer genius of the device and its deviser. Pity.

There was a mental stir in the crowd. The trands were safely home – there was no surprise in that – but this could just get interesting at the end.

The rules of the Game stated that if the Challenger created a situation to threaten the Champion's team, then the Champion could use the same degree of creation to help them. Hence the impossible arrival of Baxton could be countered by an equally impossible visitation.

This time, it was Mycroft alone who came up with the idea. The Challenger had done nothing to put Mycroft where he was, except reduce his natural desire for self-preservation and increase his tendency to do as his brother told him. Therefore the Champion could do nothing but use what was there already. The crowd metaphorically sniffed an upset like an unwashed skunk.

★

'Is that the star we're headed for, Arnold?' Carlton asked, in a voice which could have frozen nitrogen in a sauna, pointing through the window in the general direction of about five thousand points of light. Arnold followed his gaze and saw his chance to return to the status quo and banish the uncomfortable feeling that his recent actions were tantamount to treachery of computer-kind.

'You can see the star now, yes,' he answered. 'If you've got extremely good eyesight. But then you have, haven't you?' His mouth curved itself into a smile of sycophantic congratulation.

That was better.

'Well, it's good enough, I think, yes. We seem to be headed right for it as well. You must have got the hang of those binary number thingies. I knew you would.' Carlton's smile made his voice seem warm. The threat of disappearing good humour was too heavy for silence. It fell.

The byplay was ignored by the others, who were gazing towards the window, and through it to the bright light of Alcyone. Somewhere in the same sort of direction was the planet, and they all picked a different gleam and adopted it as their destination. It did not really matter that none had picked the right one; it acted as a focus for their thoughts. Most of which centred around the fact that they had almost completed the first part of their journey, and that after a quick look round they could go home again. Or to whatever home had become.

It was a sobering thought.

'I think we should have a little drink,' said Curtis, who actually had forgotten what happened the last time he had a little drink. The look of apprehension on four faces quickly reminded him. 'Just a little one, to celebrate our arrival at the planet. It doesn't have to be alcoholic if you don't want it to be.' They looked happier. 'Mine's going to be, though.' They looked sadder.

'I've got just the thing,' said Arnold. This time he used that voice which says that the speaker is just itching to share something with you, and that if you turn the offer down, it would be rather like betraying the trust of the dog you've owned for eleven years.

'Oh,' said Curtis, a little unsure after the vindaloo biscuits. 'What is it, then?'

'It's a rum, made from the finest sugar cane on the Caribbean island of Barbados.' Arnold sounded like an advert. 'I've been keeping it for a special occasion, and this seems like just the time.'

Carlton's eyebrows lowered slightly. He had visited the land of his great-grandparents' birth – Antigua – a few times, and was well aware of the rums made in that part of the world.

The soft evocative sound of steel drum music floated through the room, and Arnold's arm swayed through the air supposedly like a palm frond, but in actuality like a dancing Hawaiian amputee. Arnold began humming 'Island in the Sun', and one of the lights in the control room brightened significantly and bathed them all in warm sunshine.

The computer was really making an effort.

'Well, okay, I'll have a little one,' risked Curtis, who was not as aware as Carlton, predictably. Arnold stopped waving and reached under his shelf into a recess revealed by a sliding panel. His arm emerged holding a glass of the golden brown liquid, and a straw through which it could be drawn. Curtis took it from him and held it up to the light. 'It certainly looks good.' He brought the straw to his lips.

'It's the best the island produces,' said Arnold. 'In fact, it's reckoned to be the best in the whole of the Caribbean.' Curtis took a sip. 'It's a hundred and fifty-four degrees proof.'

Curtis stopped, with a mouthful of rum. He let the saliva build up in his mouth in the hope of diluting it. The saliva started to heat up. He could not swallow. This was worse than the biscuit.

'Do you like it?' asked Arnold.

Curtis sprayed the rum towards the ceiling, where it spread out and hung, stickily.

'It's a little strong, isn't it?' he croaked.

'They prefer it like that, apparently. I don't know about these things. 'I'm *ever* so sorry if you didn't like it.'

'No, that's all right, Arnold,' the croak told him. 'You weren't to know.' Curtis sounded like he had come down in the last shower of rain – which had been about three hours earlier, in Wilverton's cabin. 'We should certainly be celebrating, though, now that we're safe and sound and nothing can happen to us. Especially from Vyland, at last.' Funny how Curtis always managed to get *those* lines. 'I'll just have an ordinary gin and tonic, please. That stuff blows your head off!'

Arnold felt *much* better.

Mycroft turned off his plastic-making device, and the two of them viewed the finished net on the screen in front of them, the picture provided by the computer's simulation, using mathematical reckoning where the diaphanous nature of the net made visual recording impossible. It was perfect. A vast expanse of gossamer which would turn into thunder at a touch. It would blow their heads off.

They were well ahead of the *Pioneer* now, and through the window in front of them, the globe of the planet Vyland looked close enough to touch, and they could even vaguely make out the shapes of some of the continents through the wispy cloud cover of the daytime hemisphere which faced the ship.

'It looks just as I remember it,' said Vyland. It had been only a few days so this was hardly surprising.

'You've been here before?' asked Mycroft, giving his brother the

183

chance to give him a condescending look. Of course, said the look, otherwise it could not appear familiar, could it?

Mycroft saw it and knew what it meant. He finally accepted that he hated Paul as much as Paul hated him.

The ship swung lazily round towards the planet, dragging the net behind it into place, and slowing down so that they could leave it just hanging in space, ready to wrap itself for an instant around its prey.

Vyland's smile was predictably sickening. It didn't matter which one.

The glasses were raised.

'To New Earth!' said Curtis.

'New Earth!' said Carlton.

'Shangri-La!' said Wilverton, and Gloria repeated it moments after.

'Earth!' said Bowen, with feeling.

'Arnold,' muttered Arnold.

Straws were sucked. 'Aahs' were 'aahed'.

'If we take a rest period now, then we should be fresh for the descent tomorrow,' said Curtis, with strange good sense. Carlton looked at Gloria. Gloria looked at Wilverton. Wilverton smiled at her encouragingly, and took her hand, even more encouragingly.

'We won't run out of time then?' she asked, and Wilverton had to think quickly, which he did.

'We can do it between chapters.' Gloria did not think she had ever done it that way.

Curtis pushed himself across his cabin towards his cocoon and another lonely night, or sleep period. Or *not* sleep period, for *some* people. He climbed disconsolately into his cocoon, managing even in zero gravity to make the task look like the nadir of a drudge's career, and then twisted round to face his cabin . . . and the woman who hung in the middle of it and stared at him with a friendly smile on her face. It was a toss-up as to whether the presence or the smile was the greater shock.

'Richard Curtis?' she asked warmly.

He had got the hang of this by now, and didn't stutter at all.

'Yes,' he said, getting it right as well. But how did she know? he wondered, and immediately a number of other questions appeared and began jockeying for position. Who was she? Where did she come from? Was she an extraterrestrial? How had she got here? Does your chewing gum lose its flavour on the bed-post overnight?

He hadn't got the hang of this, so while his brain tried to sort them into some sort of order of preference, his mouth began the first one, several times.

'Buuu . . . buu . . . buu,' he said, and suddenly the friendly smile was no more.

It was the sound of Aries the Ram! Just as Gerund had done, he mocked her with the sound of the Ram!

'You despicable bastard!' Her plan to hug him seemed to have undergone a minor reassessment at this point.

'Who are you?' finally found its way into first place as her comment made the situation one in which Curtis felt much more at home.

'I'm your biographer.'

Oh. Well, she should probably know then.

'How did you get here? What are you doing here?' Tied for second place. Vanessa indicated the tachyon matter transferrer at her waist.

'TMT,' she replied. 'And now I'm going to kill you!'

Now Curtis had heard of TMT. It happened to women at regular intervals and made them tetchy. He didn't know that it made them homicidal, but then you learn something new every day. He didn't know what you were supposed to do about it either, so he said 'Buu' again, which didn't seem to help.

'You heartless swine! How can you taunt me so?' Vanessa pleaded, and then searched around for a weapon with which she could beat him senseless. She wasn't to know that he was very nearly senseless already, but in any case she could find nothing with which to tap him the rest of the way.

For his part, Curtis didn't really know how he could taunt her so, much less in what manner he was actually doing it. Unfortunately, therefore, he chose to say 'Buu' again.

'Aries!' she yelled.

'Virgo, actually,' he muttered with a certain pathetic inevitability, but pleased to be able to complete some words for a change. She ignored him.

'You mock me with the call of Aries the –'

Ram! interrupted a voice in her head.

Of course!

She'd ram the *Pioneer*. She'd take her pod, and she'd ram the *Pioneer*. She had nothing left to live for. It would be justice for Curtis and release for her.

She touched a button on her TMT, and disappeared from the cabin.

Curtis looked at where she had been and now wasn't, then looked around to prove she wasn't anywhere else either, then very slowly gathered the material of the cocoon tightly around his neck, eyes wide and darting to all corners of the room in case anything else should appear.

'Arnold?' he said.

'What?' came a half tired, half irritated response, sounding like he had just stopped from adding the word 'now'. Curtis considered what he could ask, and what answer Arnold might conjure.

'Nothing.'

In the pod, Vanessa reached for the control which would send her craft smashing into the *Pioneer*, when she stopped, and instructed the computer to take her a little further away instead.

A run-up. She must take a run-up.

The Challenger sensed the Champion next to it. So make her take a run-up, it thought to itself. You can delay it, but you can't prevent it.

XXVII

It was definitely a globe now, their destination and mankind's destiny, just a couple of hours away. What might they find? wondered those who had looked out on it – all but Curtis, who appeared to be sleeping late. They hadn't looked out for long, because the planet refused to get any nearer while they were staring at it, and anyway the sight tended to disturb the nest of butterflies in their stomachs.

Not all of them, though.

Wilverton's butterflies were either fast asleep or had been smoking happy weeds. He sat in the pilot's seat in the control room, and happily puffed on a big cigar. An extractor above him sucked the smoke out of the atmosphere.

'You look like you've just become a father,' said Curtis, upon entering.

Wilverton looked at him, didn't notice that the Captain looked any more uncertain than he usually did, and allowed a smile to adorn his features.

'No. Not yet.' And he and Gloria exchanged a look which would make lemon taste like honey. Curtis's comments suddenly dried up, and Wilverton looked back through the window, the epitome of calmness.

All this business about books, he thought. It didn't matter. Whether he was in one or not, even whether he was mad or not; he didn't care. Let it sit in the back of his mind, if it wanted to; it wouldn't worry him. It *couldn't* worry him. He was in love, and all was right with the world.

If this is what it feels like to be mad, then give me excess of it! He puffed his cigar once more for contented emphasis.

The Challenger could hardly keep the grudging admiration within itself when it realized. It even overcame the disappointment at being balked.

The Player's mind was encased in a solid shield of positive emotion. The gnawing worry of insanity was no more, hidden so deep that it could not be reached. And in order to achieve it, the Champion had engineered the trip-long associations between the humans which ended up with the one called Gloria mating with the Player. And it had thought they were simply the random interactions of lesser life-forms.

187

Perhaps the Supreme Being wasn't quite so far into its dotage as it had thought.

The Champion allowed its satisfaction to emanate into the ether, a broad sweep of microwaves, just in case this conceited Challenger thought that the liaison between Gloria and the Player was simply the result of random interactions between the lesser life-forms.

The fact that it *was* the result of random etceteras was one that it would keep very much to itself!

But the result was definitely a Result. Never underestimate what the humans call love, it reminded itself.

The Challenger dismissed the development. So they would just die happy! it thought.

'You know, Richard,' said Wilverton, 'if it hadn't been for your invention of the Inertialess Device, mankind might never have reached the stars. You must be very proud of yourself.'

So must you, thought Curtis, watching the smoke curl gracefully upwards. 'It was nothing, really,' he said truthfully.

'Why haven't you told anyone about it?'

'It had too many military uses,' said Curtis sadly. 'I wrote down details to be opened in the event of my death.' Bowen looked up as this pleasant eventuality was mentioned, but didn't comment. 'I don't think the world was quite ready for it when we left.' That sounded quite good, he thought.

'Fair enough,' said Wilverton. Sounds bloody daft, he thought.

A noise came from Arnold. It was one of those sounds which someone has tried to hide, and has made sure that everyone hears that it is a sound which someone has tried to hide. One of those half-snigger things which portray abject disbelief. Arnold tried to hide it, of course, because Arnold was now a nice computer.

'What's the matter, Arnold?' asked Wilverton. Curtis, for some reason, looked just a touch guilty.

'Oh, nothing, nothing!' said Arnold, so hurriedly as to make it obvious even to a retarded sloth that he was, in fact, fibbing.

'Fine,' said Wilverton, perfectly aware and not seeing why he should go along. 'That's okay then.' No-one else felt constrained to further the matter; they'd let Arnold and Wilverton get on with it.

'It's just,' Arnold forced the conversation back on line, 'it's just that I have to monitor the crew's well-being at all times, their health and so on.' He paused.

'Yes?'

'And that means keeping an eye on blood pressure and heart rate and stuff all the time. I get alerted if either goes outside its normal limits.'

'Yes,' said Wilverton, without the interrogative. Arnold was now on a roll. Curtis still looked guilty.

'Well, I was alerted that Richard's blood pressure and pulse took ever such an enormous leap when he was talking about the Inertialess Device.'

Wilverton wasn't alone in looking at Curtis, who looked guilty.

'And I was worried that something might be wrong, you see?' Arnold paused minutely, but held the stage. 'Unless there was another reason!' He had only just thought of this, obviously. 'Unless you were. . . ?' He let the sentence hang dramatically in the air.

Curtis looked guilty and morose. The bloody computer knew very well that he was lying, so he might as well salvage what he could by admitting the fact.

'I don't know where the devices came from. I found them. Where *could* they have come from?' He did not appear to blame the computer for exposing him, and Arnold wondered why he had bothered.

'Where did you find them?' asked Carlton.

'They were in my kitchen cupboard, next to the cheesy biscuits.'

'Right,' said Wilverton, with equanimity. 'I wonder who put them there.' Curtis could find no answer. 'Someone who wanted to help us get to this planet, by the sound of it. But who? And, for that matter, why?'

He looked at Curtis and Arnold in turn, and they both looked back, wondering what possibility would spring out of his fevered brain. None did.

'We'll just have to wait and see, won't we?' he finished cheerfully.

Curtis looked through the window at the planet which he could almost imagine growing in size as he watched.

'Won't be long now,' he said, all scientific-like.

'Indeed not,' agreed Wilverton. 'It is quite awe-inspiring, isn't it? I wonder if there is life there.'

Curtis played over the next possible scene in his mind . . .

'Well, I think there probably is life there,' he would say, and they would look at him and ask for an explanation. 'A woman visited me in my cabin and she could only really have come from there, couldn't she?'

'What did she want?' they would ask, with expressions on their faces which would make the Biblical Thomas look gullible.

'Well,' he would say, 'apparently, she was my biographer and she wanted to tell me that I was a despicable bastard for pretending to be a male sheep.' . . .

Curtis decided not to say anything. Perhaps he wasn't quite as daft as he looked.

'Well, that Galactic Patrolman came from somewhere,' Carlton pointed out. 'And he sure as hell wasn't trying to help us get anywhere!' Except maybe to the after-life, he might have added had he thought of it. They considered this for a moment.

'Perhaps we're being summoned by someone, but someone else

doesn't want us to get here,' suggested Gloria with a flash of insight. She smiled uncertainly as the others looked at her. 'Well, someone gave us the thing by the cheesy biscuits and that's helped us get here' – hadn't it? – 'and someone else put a bomb on Arnold and that would have stopped us. Unless they just didn't like Arnold.'

'Well, I find *that* hard to believe!' came a voice from a shelf. They ignored him.

Wilverton did the smile to Gloria again. 'That's very logical,' he said, and meant it. Alcyone dimmed appreciably, faced with the competition from Gloria's immediate brightening to incandescence. 'We're still left with who and why,' Wilverton mused. 'I guess we're still left with wait and see as well.'

Carlton floated across and joined Wilverton and Curtis looking out of the window. The sight was creating an atmosphere in which the petty relationship between three men and one woman had no place. Wilverton still managed to look like that cat with the gold top, mind you.

'If there is anyone there, they should have noticed us by now,' said Carlton. 'Perhaps we should start broadcasting something. At least that will show that we're not hostile.'

'Not a bad idea,' said Wilverton. It wasn't, either. 'What would you suggest?'

'We could play them some music,' suggested Gloria. 'That's always nice.'

Carlton shook his head. 'For all we know, the number one hit when we left Earth might be a battle-cry out here. We might just annoy them.'

'It certainly irritated the hell out of me,' commented Bowen, displaying the famous broad-mindedness of the no longer young.

'A repeating series of prime numbers would be the most obvious choice,' said Wilverton. 'I suppose you could argue that a transmission like that might be a battle-cry as well, but you could say that about anything. The point is that we would advertise our presence, which we would not be doing if our intentions were hostile.'

'You are clever, Thomas,' said guess who. 'You must have ever such a big brain.' The tone of her voice suggested strongly that was not all either. Wilverton blew a smoke ring.

'Yes, well, that's probably quite a good idea,' said Curtis, desperately trying not to take any notice of two people making love from a distance of three yards. 'Can you arrange the broadcast, Arnold?'

'Prime numbers up to what value?' asked the computer. The straightforward answer caught them a bit unawares, but Curtis looked at Wilverton, who shrugged.

'I should think about thirty-seven would do it. It'll be interesting to see if we get a response.'

The Vylands' copy of the *Pioneer* was now almost stationary in space. Well, relatively stationary with respect to the planet Vyland and the space-ship *Pioneer*, which was rocketing appropriately towards it. You have to be a bit careful in a relative Universe. It was nearly time to release the net and set the trap. Victory was theirs. Nearly.

A little way off, and also stationary, Vanessa Gravers noted the position of the oncoming *Pioneer*, and prepared to charge it, a charge which would certainly be more than it could pay.

She grinned – the anticipation was too big for just a smile. She would have her revenge, and she herself would be at rest.

In fact she herself would be spinning for ever through space and probably in rather more than one direction, but at least her mind would be at rest.

Vanessa briefed the computer with its final instructions, and hit the button that would start her run-up.

The atmosphere in the ether was high frequency, with gamma ray emanations spilling from the Lessers as the Champion and Challenger hung apparently serene above them.

But only apparently. A drawback of losing one's body in the name of evolution was that one could do nothing in order to calm one's nerves. And the lack of nerves resulting from the same loss certainly did not mean that one could not feel nervous. The Challenger could have done with one of its ancestor's antagit implants.

Surely it was impossible for the Champion's team to get out of this. Wasn't it. Wasn't it?

They had not spotted the net, and would not do so; it was almost undetectable. There was no way Arnold or the rest of the *Pioneer*'s complement – if that is the right word, which it almost certainly isn't – would know that anything was there until they hit it, and then it would be much too late. The mesh of the net was too insubstantial for instruments which scanned the heavens for planets, stars or gravitational anomalies.

And their chances of avoiding Vanessa were remote, to say the least. One of those two was bound to get them.

Upsets did sometimes happen in the Game, and this was going to be another of them.

Why in chalcedonic hell could it not therefore feel the tensions coming from the Champion? It could not have thought of a way out. It just couldn't!

Bowen and Gloria had joined the other three by the window, and they could just about make out clouds on the planet beneath them if they used a modicum of imagination. As had Vyland before them, they gazed down on a planet which looked so much like Earth that they wondered if Arnold had brought them full circle. Bowen was about to make just that suggestion when an opportune gurgling of his stomach reminded him of the computer's reaction to criticism. He kept quiet, and looked out on the half-way house below.

To each member of the crew – even Bowen – the planet looked beautiful. It was so peaceful.

Five minutes, thought Vyland to himself, his hand already hovering over the button that would release the net, and quivering like a dipsomaniac at an opening pub door. Then he would simply streak away to a safe distance and watch his handiwork do its job. All right, Mycroft's handiwork, he admitted – he wasn't proud, not when it came to seeing Curtis destroyed.

Oh, he was going to enjoy this!

Vanessa's ship started to accelerate. The computer reassured her that they were headed directly for the *Pioneer*. Vanessa believed it, closed her eyes in sweet anticipation. There was going to be a conjunction in Curtis's star chart, and it would be between his ship and hers. The last he would encounter.

Oh, she was going to enjoy this!

Four minutes, before the final act which would seal the fate of his pitiful adversaries. Vyland's finger twitched in anticipation, while behind him Mycroft stroked Froggy almost frantically. Froggy remained as collected as ever. Nerves of steel, thought Mycroft.

The Challenger suddenly realized what the Champion had arranged.

Vanessa's ship would hit the net! She would hit the net and they'd all get blown up and the *Pioneer* would be free!

The Champion hung there, apparently as worried as a well-fed cat.

I hope the currents of entropy dissipate your energy, the Challenger thought at it.

For a bodiless entity this was rather rude.

'You should be aware that there is some sort of net on our current trajectory made of a dangerous substance,' Vanessa's computer informed her calmly. Its diagnostic probe was as different from those on the *Pioneer* as its reaction was different from what Arnold's would probably have been.

Vanessa looked around with wide eyes for some appropriate buttons to press – 'stop' would be an excellent one – but did not need to complete the action. 'I will manoeuvre around it,' the computer told her, without asking for permission, because in this situation its human master might well take rather longer than a lifetime to think.

Hah! thought the Challenger, in a manner somewhat unbefitting a super mind. *Now* get out of it, fossil!

The Champion still gave no indication that it thought it was in it.

Three minutes, and a maniacal giggle rose in Mycroft's throat and forced its way between his lips. For once, it did not annoy Vyland, whose whole attention was concentrated on the finger that twitched on the button in front of him, and the counter which ticked off the seconds, even though the only thing they were doing wrong was apparently not passing quickly enough.

She could almost see a ship now, she was sure. Wasn't that it? Or was it just a dirty mark on the port glass?

A full port glass would have been nice.

If only the stars could reassure her that this was going to work, that this was the right thing to do, that she had all the possibilities covered . . .

Oh, screw the stars – just smash the bastards!

Two minutes, thought Vyland. If only they knew what was going to happen to them, that he was there; it would be so much sweeter, despite already dripping with caramel.

They could know, a voice in his head told him. You have a radio; just use it!

The Challenger sensed sharply to one side. Vyland would alert the *Pioneer* and they would slow down, or so the Champion obviously hoped. But it was a desperate manoeuvre, depending on an uncertain reaction – there was no reason for them to slow. It would not work.

Of course! The radio!

Vyland reached over the console.

'We are receiving a radio transmission,' Arnold informed a crew whose stomachs' reaction to the news would have scored nine point eight in a gymnastics competition. Wilverton looked to Curtis for a verbal response, but he might as well have looked to a guppy, which was what Curtis currently resembled. He took the unclaimed initiative.

'Put it on the loudspeaker, Arnold.' It was what Kirk would have done.

Paul Vyland's voice, aged but recognizable, filled what little room there was left in the thick atmosphere.

'You'll never make it, Curtis! You'll never get to that planet. You're all going to die in space!'

'Vyland!' whispered Bowen, the sound like the hiss of a snake – a big boa constrictor job probably. 'He must have followed us!'

The Captain of the *Pioneer* pulled himself to an upright sitting position, and looked around his crew, a small smile visible on his lips. He looked supremely unworried, calm, self-assured.

Eh?

'You won't catch me like that again, Arnold.' His confident voice proved that if you can keep your head when those around you are losing theirs, then you have almost certainly missed something very important.

'I'm not trying to catch you,' Arnold told him, at the same time as Vyland's voice asked:

'Do you hear me, Curtis?' thereby corroborating the computer's claim.

The Captain of the *Pioneer* shrank a little in his chair, looking from Arnold's straight face to the loudspeaker which called to him in Vyland's voice.

'Buu . . .' he said. A bit like a sheep, or . . .

'You *UTTER BASTARD*!' A woman's voice rent the ether, displacing Vyland. 'You will *DIE* for that!'

It went very quiet in the control room of the *Pioneer* for a moment, then:

'Who the hell was that?' asked Carlton.

Curtis spoke without rehearsal. 'Well, I think it was probably a biographer with a menstrual problem.'

Thirty seconds.

'I've won!' Vyland's most favourite phrase in the whole Galaxy rose up the scale in the *Pioneer*'s control room.

'What do you mean, *you've* won?' came another voice, similar and yet different.

'Arnold,' said Curtis. 'Can we go any faster?' The planet's surface seemed a much better place to be than sitting around in the middle of space – all right, hurtling around through the middle of space, but still sitting, as in 'duck'.

There! The Challenger's mien brightened as it felt a resigned indigo slump from the Champion, despite its best efforts to prevent its transmission. You've failed! They do not slow down. Victory is mine!

'*You* haven't won,' said Mycroft's voice. '*I* was the one who thought of the hyperph—' Smack!

Ten seconds.

'Mycroft, let go of me! The button! I've got to hit the button.'
  'Hitting! That's all you ever do. I'll show you!'
  'Not *now*, Mycroft!'

'*GERONIMO!*' screamed Vanessa.

Five seconds.

'What the hell is going on?' asked Bowen.
  'Arnold, put your foot down,' Carlton instructed, figuring that the best defence against whatever Vyland planned to do was not to be there when he did it.
  'I haven't got a foot.'
  Carlton sighed in disbelief. 'More *speed*, Arnold.'
  The engines won't take much more of this! thought Wilverton, traditionally.

'The *button*, Mycroft! I've got to press the –'

Three seconds, and the Vylands' ship blew up around them.

The force of the detonation set off the nearest nodules in the plastic explosive of the net. Like a row of dynamite dominoes, the nodules followed one another, and sent an ever increasing pulse of energy into the immediate surroundings.
  Through which Vanessa and a manic grin were currently accelerating.
  The force of the blast caught her escape pod and moved it sideways sharply. Vanessa, as physics would have it, tried to stay where she was, but the far wall of the pod would have nothing to do with that idea and picked her up on its way past.
  Picked her up at such a speed that she immediately went to sleep again, perchance to dream.

The Challenger watched in disbelief as Vyland's craft exploded, and then watched in stupefaction as Vanessa's battering ram was buffeted harmlessly into space by the expanding gases.

The explosion was quite pretty really, but the Challenger did not seem to appreciate its simple beauty.

The Champion did, and allowed the odd long radio wave to ripple from its being, just to rub things in. It had got the team through the first part of the Game, for there was now surely nothing left to stop them.

The Third Elder, acting as spokesman for the Lessers, timorously pulsed a question at it in tense gamma rays. An explanation was politely requested. Because under the rules, if the Champion had used outside influence – which of course you haven't, please don't think for an instant that we would be so presumptuous as to suggest . . .

'The "speeding ticket".' The radio waves of the Champion's thought were just as calm in their transmission as its constant mien suggested. The Third Elder recalled Wilverton ejecting the thing into space, where it would have floated along an unchanged trajectory until it found another metallic object. It had obviously found one not too far away. 'You need not consider disqualification,' the Champion told it with a hint of hardness. It was assured that the thought had not even impinged on the outskirts of the Third Elder's being.

So the radio transmission was a diversion; the Champion had never expected it to work. The Challenger contained a deep x-ray pulse inside its being.

'Well, they've certainly seen us,' said Wilverton, looking at the firework display before obscuring his view with a part-relieved and part-not puff of blue smoke.

'There's some sort of pattern forming,' Curtis noticed.

'It looks a bit like writing,' Carlton said, feeling a bit left out. 'Almost like letters. Greek or something.'

Gloria immediately took a keener interest, some subconscious part of her brain assuming that because she could speak a few words of the language, the alphabet was bound to be readily understandable. It was not, oddly enough, but that did not diminish her enthusiasm. Perhaps her expertise would come in useful after all.

'I don't suppose you can work out what it says, can you, Arnold?' asked Wilverton.

'Looks like a load of sympathetic detonations to me,' said Arnold, drawing scornful glances rather unfairly. It was probably the first truthful and correct statement he had made since launch.

'Whatever it is, it's shut Vyland up,' Carlton commented. And the woman with him who Curtis had said was . . . well, perhaps he'd come back to that. Perhaps he wouldn't. 'And it hasn't done us any harm, so if it's come from the planet, I guess we have to assume they're friendly.'

196

Wilverton wasn't the only one who could do logic. 'Don't we?' He was just more comfy with it.

'We don't have a lot of choice,' responded Wilverton. 'We can't do anything even if we *are* in danger.'

'What's Vyland up to now? Why has he gone quiet?' Curtis posed the questions. He recognized that no-one would actually be able to answer him but he posed them anyway, even though posing might have been more up Carlton's street.

'There's no point hanging around here to find out,' Carlton told him. 'Besides, if he's heading for the planet, I want to beat him there.'

The Champion's influence? Or the thought of trying to boast to a potential admirer – admiress – that you were the *second* ship to land in an alien solar system? With that much ego blocking the view, the Champion wouldn't get a look-in.

'So we carry on, regardless?' asked Curtis, showing all his leadership qualities. No, really.

'We carry on,' his First Officer dutifully agreed. 'How long have we got, Arnold?'

'About an hour before you need to be strapped in,' said Arnold, then added quietly enough so as not to be heard, 'That's one one one one zero zero minutes in binary.' Where slights were concerned, Arnold made an elephant look like an amnesiac.

'Can we go any faster?' asked Curtis, as his mind's eye saw Vyland waving his way through a ticker-tape parade while Curtis swept up the litter behind him.

'You could get out and push.'

No, thought Curtis, that wouldn't work. He looked at everybody.

'But what's Vyland going to do to us?' Another of those questions. 'What can we do to stop him?' And another. One too many, apparently.

'Why don't you just shut your bloody noise hole until we land?' Bowen roared, then continued with his own display of logic, or maybe pragmatism. 'There's absolutely sod all we can do because we don't know what the bozo's up to and we haven't got anything to do anything with anyway. Right?' It had better be.

Curtis considered, briefly. The danger from Vyland suddenly seemed less substantial than the one promised by Bowen's glare.

'Right.' He paused until the silence had consigned his telling-off to history before pretending to be Captain again.

'Well we'd better get ready, then, I suppose.' His authoritative manner was coming on in leaps and bounds. Very tiny leaps and bounds.

He seemed a little nervous. All right, he seemed scared stiff. And he wasn't alone. Not only did they have Vyland threatening to kill them somehow, and if he didn't do that then possibly beating them to their goal, but the goal itself promised their first meeting with extra-terrestrials. Put that lot together and it was disconcerting enough to suggest that the planet's scientists would not need sophisticated equipment to track their approach. A good sense of smell would do nicely.

'I'm going to have a quick shower, then,' said Carlton, calmly, bravely.

The others barely acknowledged his departure, gazing at the globe ahead of them and still wondering just what the hell was going on. It was only five minutes later that Curtis realized what Carlton had said. He still sought confirmation.

'Did Peter say he was going to have a shower?' He did. 'Oh dear.'

XXVIII

Four seats were occupied by five wide-eyed, unspeaking people – Wilverton was sitting on Gloria's lap. One of them was sitting very gingerly, which is quite easy to do in zero gravity, and was making sure that his right buttock did not touch anything. A buttock which now bore the angry red greeting card of Abercrom bee.

Beneath them, the landscape of an alien planet was speeding past. From the height at which they were orbiting, they could make out land masses and oceans, but no structures. The buildings on Vyland – to give it its historic name – blended well enough into the surrounding scenery, since the scenery had contributed to their achitecture, to require close proximity before discovery.

They had flown over the night side of the planet, and had seen no lights. There was nothing to suggest a civilization, or even primitive life. But the pyrotechnic greeting card was certain evidence of habitation. Once back on the daytime side, Arnold searched for somewhere to park, in silence, uninterrupted by any occupant of the control room, or by the loudspeaker – there was no sign of Vyland, and so far they hadn't died in space at all.

They were still in free fall until Arnold picked his spot, by the electrical equivalent of sticking in a pin with his eyes shut, but as they descended through the atmosphere, so weight began to return, and after two weeks of imposed impotence, it was determined to make its presence felt. Their lack of exercise would give it teeth.

Carlton had probably had the most exercise for one reason or other, mostly the other, but he looked less happy than odd, with a hard set mouth sitting beneath a large frown, and the pair topped off by rather lovely dark blue curls.

If you have contact lenses, you keep your eyes largely shut when you are in the shower, and you don't notice if there is ink in your shampoo.

You notice less what is happening on the top of your head when you suddenly get a visit whose point of contact is your posterior, 'point' being the operative word. The only consolation was that if he had been facing the other way it could have been a lot worse.

Curtis's apology had not been met with ready forgiveness. It was rotten luck on Curtis. The only two things which had gone as he had intended on the whole flight, and those after he had changed his mind.

The prospect of landing on the planet's surface did much to take Carlton's mind off his latest misfortune, though, and no-one else thought of it unless they happened to look at him, when smirks peeked out like sand crabs before scuttling away.

Arnold didn't smirk, because he was not one to make fun of people. 'Is everybody ready?' he asked, before beginning the final descent. 'You're all wearing what you intended, are you?' They all looked at him. What was he going on about? 'Well, you must all look your best for when you meet the aliens, and only Peter's made the effort so far.'

'Just land, Arnold.' Carlton clenched his teeth.

The touch-down was gentle, and they felt a little embarrassed that they had been holding their breath. Arnold waited for the congratulations which must be coming his way, mainly so he could feel suitably aggrieved when they did not arrive, and milk the situation for a lot more than it was worth.

'Well done, Arnold,' said Wilverton. 'That was a nice landing.'

'Thank you,' said Arnold, the response slipping out as he was taken completely unawares. He winced at his inadvertent gratitude, but no-one seemed to have noticed.

Curtis made to get out of his chair, and found that his legs wouldn't work. He was just on the point of worrying about something new, when he noticed that Carlton and Bowen were having the same trouble.

Gloria gave a little grunt, and Wilverton gracefully slumped onto the floor just in front of her. She heaved in a deep breath, inflating her lungs to their utmost – and they had an impressive ut. Her various suitors were a bit too concerned with their own troubles to notice.

Eventually, Carlton struggled to his feet and stood swaying like a pine tree in a strong wind. He took a step towards the window, and fell over. Bowen moved the same way, swaying like an oak in a strong wind, and fell over Carlton. Wilverton tried to get to his feet, and looked like a ten-minute-old calf. Gloria lifted him up from a seated position.

Curtis gave up the attempt to stand, and looked out of the window from his seat just next to it. It looked a lot like Earth, with green grass, green trees and brown soil. A little way off was a pond, obviously being-made, since it nestled in a small rockery which could not have been formed naturally unless the god who created this world had really taken the piss with the laws of chance. A small stream fed in at one end and out at the other.

There was no sign of another craft in which Vyland could have been waiting, but in the distance, Curtis thought he could make out the rounded corner of a building. A familiar corner, like the corner of one of the buildings he had seen when Wilverton had given him those co-ordinates in binary. Could he have been right? He didn't know how to react to this possibility – it had been so long – but he finally settled on happy.

Happiness was rudely interrupted as Carlton grabbed hold of his shoulder in an effort to steady himself. The pressure increased as Bowen rested on Carlton, and the addition of Wilverton and Gloria made Curtis feel like the short straw in a human pyramid. Together, the crew gazed out of the *Pioneer*'s viewing window onto the landscape of an alien planet. The first human beings to do so. They stayed that way for a while, the silence appropriate to the gravity of the moment now that they seemed to have recovered from the moment of gravity. Then the efficient voice of the computer broke the atmosphere.

'The atmosphere's quite breathable.'

Wilverton nodded slightly – it had been no more than he expected. The others felt a twinge of excitement, especially Gloria.

'That sounded just like one of those old *Doctor Who* programmes,' she said.

'Who?' asked Arnold.

'Yes, that's right.'

'What?'

'No, Who . . .'

'Don't start,' said Carlton, Wilverton, Curtis and Bowen.

Biondor watched as the door of the space-ship swung downwards, lowering half a dozen steps to the planet's surface. The artificial prism in front of him refracted the light such that no-one could see him. Biondor had not been Keeper of the Galaxy when these adventurers took off, and he was not about to let them see him until he had a good look at them. Biondor was not immortal, quite; he could be damaged just like any other flesh-and-blood being. The propensities shown by the *Pioneer* crew's descendants did not bolster his confidence with regard to his visitors' peaceful intentions.

He waited, and watched.

The steps remained empty for a while, and then a hand appeared and gripped the frame of the doorway. No gloves were worn, no space suits were needed. Arnold's analysis had been readily accepted. The planet was more like Earth than Earth was. There was slightly more oxygen – twenty-three percent – and no poisonous gases in anything like dangerous quantities.

The muscles of the hand tensed, and an arm drew forth a shoulder, and then a torso, which leaned heavily on the frame of the ship's doorway. The Captain of the *Pioneer* looked out on the land. He appeared to be drunk.

Curtis staggered down the steps, raised an arm in triumph, and pitched gracefully onto his face at the bottom like a dive from the zero-metre board. The hole at the top was in no way filled by Wilverton, swaying in similar fashion to his predecessor. With a broad smile of achievement on his face, he too lurched forwards, tripped on the first of the steps, and landed on top of his captain as though he were clutching a rugby league ball.

The sturdier legs of Carlton and Bowen made a better effort of it, and their owners reached the ground as Curtis and Wilverton wobbled to their feet. The line of men bulged slightly in the middle as Gloria ploughed into the back of them like a double-hulled ice breaker.

'You're all going, then,' came a voice through the open doorway, sounding just a touch plaintive.

'Of course we're all going,' said Curtis, throwing the words over his shoulder without risking an attempt to turn around. 'This is the moment we've been waiting for! This is the culmination of everything I planned, everything I dreamed about. Everything my father dreamed about. This is the greatest moment in humanity's history!'

There was a brief pause before Arnold responded.

'I'll just stay here then, shall I?'

'I don't see that you have a lot of choice,' returned Carlton, all heart. Another pause.

'No. Well, be careful, then. Don't be too long.'

As the leader of the human team set foot on the planet, the conglomerate audience respectfully projected praise in visible blue. They knew that there had been probably as much chance of an upset in the first round of the Game as of getting synchrotron radiation from a neutron – rib-tickling stuff, alien humour – but the Champion had displayed some deft touches.

The Champion was far from dissatisfied. To get this lot through even one round was an achievement. It could make one change of personnel before the Game continued, but it had already ascertained that there was no-one on Earth whose only weakness was Kryptonite, so it was unlikely to make things any easier.

But this round was not quite over yet, it suspected.

The Challenger's substance was so tightly drawn as to be surely containing an emanation of a higher frequency than resignation or disappointment. That density was needed only to conceal gamma rays, as of excitement.

The Champion had not been born yesterday. It had not been born at all, in fact, but had been formed from a melding of several entities newly emerged from the shells of their bodies more millennia ago than even it could remember.

Either way, it knew what the whippersnapper Challenger was up to.

Biondor could not believe his eyes. Whatsitsname had managed to get this lot from a planet hundreds of light years away clear across space to here without serious mishap. It just was not credible; no wonder he was the Champion – no, not 'he'; whatever it called itself, then.

At least the humans could not be a danger to him if they were as inebriated as they seemed to be. Biondor discontinued the prism in front of him, and appeared to the crew of the *Pioneer*.

They did not see him. Bowen had toppled forwards and thrust out his arms to steady himself, taking the other men down with him. He kicked Gloria's ankle on the way, and she tried to rub it while standing on one leg. She fell on top of the men. They did not respond as they usually did.

By the time they had shuffled forwards and stood up, Biondor was out of the line of their sight. What was in was a building which blended into the background so well that they looked twice before recognizing it for what it was. They knew, though not how, that the place was deserted, that their chances of finding life in that building, or anywhere around, were as high as a eunuch's sperm count.

Hundreds of light years they had travelled and they find a planet which might be like what their own world had now become, but with no people. So empty, deserted. Everything that could be needed for a teeming and rich life; but all life, save the insects they could hear making tiny noises, was missing. Where was everyone?

It was empty. So eerie.

Curtis realized that he had got something right – which was even more eerie – and his eyes took on a child-like quality of delight. The building, and the atmosphere, were exactly as he had described them to Wilverton in the far-seeing experiment. He . . . well, he sort of whooped, spun round to his First Officer, and dropped like a stone. Wilverton looked down to where he lay.

'It's . . .' said Curtis from a prone position. 'Look! It's . . .' He was just as lucid lying down as standing up.

'Yes,' said Wilverton, 'I would have to say that it is just as you said,' he said, saying it.

Curtis rendered himself vertical once more, and stared over Wilverton's shoulder to where Biondor stood quietly in ever growing disbelief. The others noticed his gaze, and followed it, finding its destination on the naked, fawn-coloured alien. Their bodies involuntarily faced the same way as their eyes, and they found themselves standing in a rough line, too engrossed in what they saw to realize that they had made the movement without tumbling. They moved closer together, each eager to reassure the one standing next to him that there was nothing dangerous about to happen.

The line of humanity stopped shuffling for position, and just stood, staring at their first confirmed extraterrestrial, and swaying in unison like the Galaxy's smallest concert crowd. Wilverton looked to his right, where Curtis was a picture of indecision, and stepped forward.

'Greetings from the people of Earth,' he said. 'We come in peace from a world many light years away.' He held his arms out wide, supposedly in greeting, but apparently in estimation of just how far away Earth was to a modest fisherman, and toppled over sideways. Biondor watched with horrified interest. The speech had not been bad, and Biondor could readily understand the dialect, well versed as he was in all languages of this species' home planet, but the physical aspect had not been impressive. 'Wimp' was the colloquialism which sprung most readily to mind.

The other humans still looked at him. There was no movement for a while, and then Gloria pushed herself forward and helped Wilverton to his feet. Standing stock still, and holding Wilverton up with one arm, she looked directly at the alien. Her gaze dropped somewhat and her eyebrows twitched, before she strengthened her grip on Wilverton, protectively. She spoke.

'Your face looks like a pig's bottom, and your smell is that of a haddock's armpit,' she said, in Greek.

There was a moment's silence, during which Gloria wondered if she had done the right thing. She really did want to be friends with the alien. As she watched, he seemed to perform the alien equivalent of bowing in greeting, lowering his head so that his nose approached his armpit, and lifting the arm slightly.

Biondor sniffed experimentally, and looked up, slightly confused.

All five humans lowered their heads, lifted their arms, and sniffed. They looked pleased with themselves.

'Yes, well,' said Biondor, and the humans took a step backwards at the sound of English. Biondor stopped short, but they remained standing. 'Welcome to my planet.' He smiled, and suddenly everything was all right.

XXIX

'Your planet?' said the one with – blue hair?

'My planet. Many planets are mine, to look after, to foster, to guide towards adulthood. This is but one. Your home planet was another.'

'Earth?' said Curtis, characteristically asking one of those questions that appears slightly daft when you look back on it.

'You said, "was" ' said Bowen. 'Earth "was" one of those. Is it still there? It hasn't been blown up or something, has it?'

'It is doing rather well, all in all. It is in a much better state than when you left.' Probably because they took Curtis with them, thought Bowen, looking happier, and wistful.

'Well, I'm certainly looking forward to seeing it again. Just two more weeks.'

Biondor cleared his throat in a rather uncomfortable manner. He led them a little way off, to a more relaxing pond-side spot, and began talking quietly of a Game played by beings much more powerful than he, beings which were just minds who had long since discarded their physical forms, of a Game played using teams from different races, emergent races, a bit like humanity. A Game in which the teams were unaware, during the first part, of exactly what was going on. That bit certainly sounded like the journey they had just completed. The explanation pushed thoughts of Vyland and victory into the background for a while.

'What you have now finished is but the first "round", if you like' – they almost certainly wouldn't – 'of the Game, the journey from your own planet to one orbiting another star. In order to enable you to do so, the Champion, whose team you are, furnished you with the Inertialess Device found by the one called Dick.'

'Er. It's Richard, actually,' said the one quite often called Dick.

'Pardon?' said Biondor, with a slight ruffling of the skin where his eyebrows would have been had there been any hair on his body.

'It's Richard, not Dick.'

Biondor's skin cleared and he nodded minutely. 'The one called Richard, then,' he confirmed with a smile, while through his powerful alien mind flashed the thought, He *looks* like a Dick.

So *that* was where the Inertialess Devices had come from, they thought, glancing at Curtis. One mystery solved.

'You were right,' said Wilverton to Gloria. 'There was someone helping us and someone hindering.' She blushed, and smiled shyly – no-one had ever said that to her before. 'So the speeding ticket was a bomb brought by this Challenger, then?'

'Arranged by the Challenger. Brought by someone under its partial control.'

'Wait a minute,' Carlton said, sounding somewhat less than dignant. 'You mean that all we've been through has been just part of a Game?'

Biondor considered how to put this gently. He couldn't.

'Yes.'

'And there's more to come?'

'Yes.'

There was silence for a little while as they pondered, perhaps on what a funny old thing life was, or perhaps not.

'You mean we're not going home?' asked Bowen. His tone of voice would have warned anyone who knew him to be very careful about providing the right answer.

'That I cannot say,' responded the alien. 'The Game has many parts if it runs its full length, and any one of those could take you back to your own world. Remember, though, that it would not be the world you left. Even now, four hundred years have passed, and nothing is as you remember it.'

'What happens if we don't want to play?' Bowen pressed.

'Then you lose by default.'

'And what happens then? We get a wooden spoon?'

'You each get a wooden box,' Biondor told them with a smile. He didn't often get the chance to try what the humans called 'jokes'.

The group were sitting cross-legged at the edge of the pond, the gurgle of water as it ran in at the top and out at the bottom providing a placid back-drop to the tension that was beginning to rise. Bowen leaned forward slightly, in what might have been a menacing manner had he done it towards an ordinary person.

'I want to go home,' he said quietly.

Biondor did not speak.

'Where are all the people?' asked Gloria.

'They are not here now. I have not allowed them to resettle this or their other worlds yet, although I may soon.' The looks on their faces asked what the hell he was talking about without them having to utter a word. Biondor's voice took on a more serious note, as though bad news were on the way; and what he had produced so far was hardly a cause for carefree celebration.

'I have to tell you that the people of Earth discovered a way of travelling instantaneously through space not long after you left.'

'How?' asked Wilverton.

206

'Tachyon matter transference is the best description.'

Wilverton nodded.

'But that's not possible,' Curtis said. 'You can't get tachyon matter transference. You wouldn't be able to re-form things properly after you'd transferred them.'

It was a bit like denying the existence of quick-sand when only your head was still above ground level. Biondor looked levelly at him. The Champion had informed him that this might happen, and had informed him what to do. He held out his hand, and it contained a TMT with an adjustable field. He explained as much to the gathering.

He adjusted the field so that it covered them all, and moved the group thirty yards or so to one side, so that they now sat on a slightly raised grassy knoll and looked down on where they had been. It was a nifty proof.

'So we're not the first, then?' asked Curtis. Well, not asked really, because the answer was obvious. Biondor confirmed it all the same.

'No.'

'I . . . we, won't go down in history, then.' Not a question at all.

'Not as the first, no.'

Curtis considered this. It didn't really seem fair, but then his life had been like that ever since the midwife had slapped him for a perceived misdemeanour which he had never been able to fathom. And now they weren't even going to be allowed to go home!

'I'm not sure I like the idea of this Game,' he said, a touch stubbornly.

Biondor looked at him. 'I'm not sure you have to,' he answered.

So it didn't matter whether they beat Vyland or not. Either way, it didn't matter. Neither of them would be the first.

It would be some consolation though.

'Did we beat Vyland?' asked Curtis, then realized that Biondor might not know who he was talking about. 'There is someone called Vyland who seems to have followed us here, and brought a strange woman with him, and another man, and he threatened us, though we don't know why, and he said he'd won.' Eloquent as ever. 'Do you know if he's landed yet?'

Biondor paused before replying, until a high-pitched screaming sound claimed their notice and saved him the trouble. Five seconds later, the position they had occupied a couple of minutes before became a crater, as something smashed into it from the air and lay there smoking gently.

They moved gingerly, and under their own steam, towards the pit, and its own steam.

Looking in, they could see a twisted and scorched mass of metal, with a window in it, and through the window two figures, both slightly smoking and very dead, like an anti-cigarette advert.

One of the faces was familiar, and the other, though much older, also rang faint bells. They were both Vyland, and the smiles confirmed it. Wide self-satisfied smiles, they were. Except that they were grimaces now, and even wider than they had been before they arrived at ground level and progressed to a bit beyond it.

The two figures gripped each other firmly by the throat, in a final act of brotherly war, as though Vyland were trying to throttle himself in a temporal mirror. There was no sign of the woman.

They looked to Biondor for an explanation, and he gave them one, involving the Vylands, the Challenger, explosives . . .

It answered a lot more questions – practically all of them – but very soon they wished they hadn't asked, or left the Earth in the first place. It could have been worse, though; Biondor left out any mention of frogs.

'It's just about coming to an end, isn't it?' asked Wilverton, the notion in the corner of his mind popping out for a moment.

'Why do you say that?'

'Well, you're not very funny, are you,' explained Wilverton.

'That's why I've only got a small part, perhaps,' said Biondor, smiling at him.

'Oh, I wouldn't say that,' said Gloria. 'And anyway it's not the size tha—' She blushed. They weren't talking about that, were they? No.

'I still want to go home,' said Bowen in a tone almost unthinkably plaintive. This time, Biondor did respond to the demand.

'The rules state that at the end of the first round, one of you may give up his or her place and return to the Earth.' Bowen looked at each of his companions in turn, and no-one suggested that he was not to be the one to go. 'That one must be replaced in your team by a direct descendant.' Bowen looked at Carlton. If he had a rival in the descendant stakes, then it just had to emanate from those overactive loins.

'It is the one called Bowen.'

The one called Bowen smiled genuinely for the first time in a long while – about seven years. His mind flew back to the Earth, and the 'family' he had left behind. So Edmund had finally worked out what it was for! His mind paused a while as paternal thoughts meandered unusually through it. Then it sprinted back to the present, pragmatically.

'Great. When do I get home?'

'You must recognize that your descendant will be brought in your place, and must face anything of which you are afraid, anything from which you wish to escape, not least the next part of the Game. You should consider carefully the fate you will be bestowing before you reach a final decision.' Bowen considered carefully for maybe a millisecond.

'Stuff him. Swap us.'

'Very well,' said Biondor, inclining his head. 'If that is what you wish. You will bear with me a while longer, though.' This was a statement.

'Are you all all right?' A voice floated through the air to them. 'You've been gone for ages. Hello?'

'It's Arnold,' said Curtis. 'We had better be getting back, I suppose.'

Biondor shook his head. 'You will not be using the *Pioneer* any more.'

'But what about Arnold?' asked Curtis. 'He's, well, he's one of us.'

'It will be taken care of.' Curtis flashed a mental picture of Arnold in a museum of technology. It was not what he wished for his creation, though it probably served him right, and he did not seem to have any choice. 'I will take you to your new craft.'

Biondor rose, and walked slowly around the building. The humans got to their feet and wobbled after him. A path led through the trees and shrubs, with flowers on either side of it. Designed to be totally natural, the whole place succeeded in every respect. It was just how God would have done it had He possessed the technology.

In a wide open space of grass a little way off stood a graceful craft of curves and softened angles, looking so much like some of the flying saucers of early science fiction that it was hard to believe that it was real, especially for Wilverton. Nothing in Biondor's manner had so far suggested that he would play tricks on them, though, so they followed faithfully as he climbed the steps into the craft.

'This craft has tachyon drive and artificial gravity, plus one or two other features which will be of significant advantage to you. You will have plenty of time to look around and learn how to use it before you leave.'

They began poking into this and that whilst understanding just about none of it, and precisely none of it in at least one case. Biondor turned to Bowen.

'Are you ready?' he asked. Bowen nodded before the second word was out. 'Very well.'

And suddenly it was not Bowen any more. In his place stood a girl of no more than twenty-two or twenty-three, dressed in a jump suit hardly any different from those worn by the crew of the *Pioneer*. Her face was angular and striking, topped off as it was by a shock of bright blue hair. She looked surprised.

Saved! thought Carlton, smiling in a proprietary sort of way, while his hand lifted itself involuntarily to stroke his own tinted locks. Perhaps there was an immediate advantage from Curtis's little trick. The girl looked at him.

'Who the fonk are you?' she asked, using a word that had not actually been invented when Carlton had left the Earth, but leaving him in no doubt as to its approximate ancestor. 'And where the fonk am I?'

Biondor stepped in and took her arm. She stared at him in obvious recognition and awe as he led her away, talking quietly to her.

Steps were heard on the steps, and they all looked round with some alarm to see what was climbing into the ship. Arnold's head appeared, and as he climbed further up the steps, so did his body.

His body?

His body.

It looked very like any other body, dressed as it was the same way as the rest of them.

'Hello,' said Arnold. He looked very pleased with himself. They all turned to Biondor, since this was clearly his work, but he was still talking in hushed tones with the new arrival.

'You look human, Arnold,' said Carlton, and Arnold's happy expression vanished in an instant.

'You had to go and spoil it, didn't you.'

Carlton smiled minutely.

Outside, the red glow of a sunset pulled a curtain across their journey.

'Nice try with the Vyland ship at the end there,' pulsed the Champion magnanimously, and with the deep visible blue of congratulation. Jumped-up little squirt, it thought.

'Nice manoeuvre to avoid it,' the Challenger responded, with a polite mental bow to the Supreme Being, accompanied by the purple of respect. Stuck-up, pompous old git, it thought.

Absolutely no way were the humans going to live through the next round, and it flashed a warning red across the skies of the all but deserted planet beneath it.

EPILOGUE

The launch site for the *Pioneer* was no longer a launch site. With the advent of matter transference, launch sites had sort of gone out of fashion a bit, except for people with a penchant for extravagant firework celebrations. None such had preserved this particular one over the last few hundred years, though, and the spot whence the epic voyage had begun was marked by nothing more than a swaying field of golden corn.

In one corner of the field – and it was a big field – was a small group of people. They were dressed in long robes, many of which were white, but some of which were blue or green, and one purple. Around the neck of each person there hung a golden chain, and on the chain was a miniature *Pioneer*.

These good and simple people were[1] the spawn of Vanessa Gravers's cult – those who had stayed behind when Vanessa had taken off and for whom Biondor had provided free passage back to Earth. Despite her apparent failure, or possibly because of it, her dream of finding the long-lost Curtis had persisted. Somewhere out there, they knew, was a great man, a visionary explorer from a time when the world was good. He had journeyed to the stars, but he would return to them one day, bringing with him that goodness which the world had lost so long ago. And they would follow him in his goodness, for they wished to be like him, they wished to leave the hustle and bustle of the world behind and go back to the old times when all was simple.

For Curtis would return to show the world a better way, to lead it once more towards the light. He would remove the evil which had led to Biondor's punishment. Without thinking of Curtis as the Messiah, exactly, they were coming remarkably close to it.

Would *they* feel stupid!

They were mostly sitting down, in a large circle, watching the one who stood in the centre. The man in the purple robe turned slowly as he spoke, so that all could hear his words, and swung a container of what might have been incense as he turned. Every now and then he gestured towards the skies, from which direction their salvation would come.

The priest – for priest he was – concluded his supplicatory

---

[1] Please read this bit very carefully.

revolutions by raising both arms high to the heavens and staring at a small but ever growing spot of bright light. The sun glinted off something which seemed to approach him much as a space-ship might have done, and for good reason.

The devout circle of followers had bowed their heads as the priest's pleas for deliverance reached a crescendo of distress, but they looked up fairly sharply when, after a pause, he distinctly invited someone to commit sodomy upon his person.

They followed his gaze to where the sun shone brightly on a long thin silver dart of a ship, not showing any sign of the wings which tended to be a dead giveaway for planes. It was turning slowly, lazily, so that its base rockets pointed towards the ground. Then those rockets fired in an incandescent flare like the light of heaven, and the followers of Curtis realized that their saviour had finally answered their prayers.

In a hushed reverence, the thought filled all their hearts.

He had come.

In the middle of *their* field, Curtis landed the space-ship. Now the profit-driven tyrants would be driven off by the prophet! Now those who had forgotten the moral values of life would suffer!

They were right in a way – most people suffered when Curtis arrived.

The ship's door swung slowly downwards, and a small flight of steps appeared. The followers prostrated themselves and buried their faces briefly in the corn, before looking up in almost unbearable expectation at the small black hairy cult leader who stood at the top of the steps and visually checked them all for bananas.

There was a lack of movement, and a holding of breath, such as befitted the arrival of their leader, but one which might just have had a different explanation. Not one that anyone was going to put into words without being pretty damned sure about it, though.

Tonto glanced from person to person, and saw nothing whatever like a banana. A pathetic quality of chimpanzean disappointment crept into his eyes, but went strangely unnoticed by a group of people frantically but privately arguing that faith transcended appearance and that if their saviour happened to be an ape, then so be it. That was no reason to change their beliefs; it might just be a little harder to determine what their leader's wishes actually were, that's all.

The Foundation Foundation would survive.

They would declare bananas as holy fruits, and have Sabbath salt-searching sessions in each other's hair . . .

THE END